SOUTHERN PERIL

SOUTHERN PERIL

A Jersey Barnes Mystery

T. LYNN OCEAN

MINOTAUR BOOKS ≈ NEW YORK

A THOMAS DUNNE BOOK FOR MINOTAUR BOOKS.
An imprint of St. Martin's Publishing Group.

SOUTHERN PERIL. Copyright © 2009 by T. Lynn Ocean. All rights reserved. Printed in the United States of America. For information, address St. Martin's Press, 175 Fifth Avenue, New York, N.Y. 10010.

www.thomasdunnebooks.com
www.minotaurbooks.com

ISBN-13: 978-0-312-38347-3
ISBN-10: 0-312-38347-9

First Edition: July 2009

10 9 8 7 6 5 4 3 2 1

SOUTHERN PERIL

PROLOGUE

March, twenty-one years ago
Near the campus of Duke University
Durham, North Carolina

Will was unanimously designated as the driver since he had drunk only Dr Pepper, and he tried to remain a good sport about it despite John's and Mike's obnoxious behavior. After all, every med student had to cut loose once in a while, especially after grueling midterm exams. He and his frat brothers were invited to another party tomorrow night, where he'd be the designated drinker. Somebody else could drive.

"Guys, cut it out already, would you?" His friends playfully slapped each other on the backs of their heads, and John, the front-seat passenger, rolled into Will's lap each time he reached over the headrest to retaliate. "I'm trying to drive here."

They were only about ten miles from the apartment the trio shared, but Will had taken an unfamiliar shortcut through the wooded back roads. It neared two o'clock in the morning, and the only other cars on the main roads at this time of day would likely be cops. Even though he hadn't been drinking, Will knew it was best to avoid a confrontation with the law. They loved to give college kids a rough time, especially frat boys, and especially in the middle of the night. He couldn't wait to get home and crawl into bed. He was tired.

Overhead, low-hanging clouds began spitting mist, and on the ground, a set of blinding high-beam headlights flew at the boys from the oncoming lane. The other driver either didn't care or didn't notice when Will flashed his lights in protest. He depressed the windshield washer button, hoping that clean glass would cut the glare, but the fluid container was empty. Moving wipers smeared a fine layer of mist and bird droppings across the windshield. Squinting, Will slowed and concentrated on the serpentine road, trying not to look into the other car's headlights.

"Heeeeeere's Johnny!" Mike leaned in from the backseat, trying to get a clean shot at John's face. Will was about to yell at them to stop when somebody fell across his right arm and the steering wheel jerked to the right. The front tire wrenched off the pavement and spun in loose gravel as the inside of the tread scraped the road's edge.

Will yanked the wheel hard to the left. "Dammit!"

The boys' car overcorrected and fishtailed across the center line. The oncoming vehicle swerved to avoid a head-on crash with them and went airborne over a water-filled ditch. It clipped something and flipped onto its roof, spun in a 360 as it continued toward a clump of trees, and rotated back upright before slamming to a stop against the trunk of a thick oak with an earthshaking boom.

Panicked, his heart revving, Will stomped the brake pedal and they squealed to a stop. If the other car hadn't reacted so quickly, he realized, he and John would have gone through the windshield. Maybe even Mike, too, from the backseat. They all could have been killed.

Forcing a deep breath into his lungs, Will made a U-turn and drove the hundred yards back to the wreck, his mind recalling emergency response procedures for accident victims. All three boys ran to the damaged car—one of its wheels jutted out, still spinning—and Will yanked open the driver's door to see two men. The one in the passenger's seat moaned. The driver, his face bloodied, pointed a gun at them. "You tell Denny he can go to hell," the man snarled.

Stunned, Will froze, but only for a split second. He grabbed the driver's wrist and fought to get the weapon pointed in any direction other than at him and his friends. The pistol went off with a sharp pop that sent a jab of pain through his eardrums. A spray of blood and pulp coated the crumpled car's interior as the bullet punched a hole through the passenger's skull. Will felt some stray bits sting his face.

"You made me shoot him, you bastard," the driver growled. Will stopped grappling with the stranger when he realized the gun's muzzle was now pressed directly into his stomach. It felt hot. "You still ain't getting the money."

The driver spat out a mouthful of blood and teeth. Illuminated by the car's yellowish dome light, his face looked like one of those gory rubber Halloween masks that cover the entire head. But this man was not a ghoulish prankster. The coppery smell of blood was real, and the metal of the gun pressing into his skin was real. Will's body went numb. He would probably die. It all happened so *fast*. One minute, he's driving his friends home from a frat party. And a minute later—not even a full sixty seconds later—he witnesses a shooting. And it looked as if he could very well be next.

He struggled to remember the prayer he'd learned during Sunday school classes at church. Growing up, he hated getting up early for church. His mother always made him, up until he reached sixteen and told her he believed in science—not God. The prayer was something about darkness. Or was it light? He wondered if he'd go to heaven, even though he hadn't seen the inside of a church in years. He wondered if he'd feel pain as the bullet ripped through his midsection. He didn't want to die. He wanted to finish school.

He'd wanted to be a doctor ever since the third grade, when he went to the emergency room with his parents after his sister jumped on top of a glass coffee table. He couldn't recall the prayer. Sweat beads popped through the skin all over his body. A wall-mounted epidermis chart flashed through his mind. That had been a test question at some point in his life, the one about the skin being the largest organ. Most people didn't think of their skin as an organ, just like the heart or the liver, but it was. Will couldn't remember the prayer. He wondered if the man was truly going to shoot him. He debated as to whether he'd die instantly or lie in the grass slowly bleeding to death, like in the old westerns. He wondered if he'd ever be able to watch a movie again. He loved movies.

"We don't know anybody named Denny, I swear," Will heard himself say. The man's fingers were now curled around his shirt collar. "Me and my friends don't even know you. We only stopped to help."

The driver gurgled out a laugh and pulled the trigger. The revolver misfired. When he hesitated for a split second to look at the malfunctioning gun, Will slammed his forehead into the other man's. A shot violated Will's eardrums for the second time, and pain exploded in the center of his head. He sucked in a breath and opened his eyes to find the shooter slumped over the steering wheel.

Will had been next to corpses only in a sparkling clean and brightly lit laboratory, and then they'd been laid out on stainless-steel tables. But he knew without checking for a pulse that the driver was dead. The man had mistakenly shot himself in the head, just like he'd accidentally shot his passenger. The driver was a really bad shot. The scene might somehow be funny, Will thought, if he were watching it at the movies. Or maybe not. It might just be gruesome.

"Crap, crap, crap," one of his buddies screamed behind him. "Who *are* these guys?"

Will disentangled himself from the dead man's grip and backed away from the car. He moved his arms and legs and felt his stomach to make sure he wasn't wounded and then took inventory of his friends. Both were standing, unharmed. John bent over to heave up some of the vodka punch he'd drunk at the party.

"I don't know who they are." Will's ears hurt, and his voice sounded like it was echoing in the distance. "He tried to shoot me. He thought somebody named Denny sent us. He thought we were after their money."

John wiped vomit from his chin with a shirtsleeve. "What money?"

"Who cares what money?" Mike said. "We've got to go get help."

Will's entire body was shaking. He spread his stance to balance jerky legs. Adrenaline, he thought. Just like the textbooks said. "They don't need help now. They're both dead."

The three boys stared at the lifeless strangers. Noticing something wedged behind the driver's seat back, Mike cocked his head. It was a large canvas duffel bag with thick leather straps.

"See what's in it," Mike said.

John giggled. "*You* see what's in it."

"Shut up!" Will screamed. "Shut up! Shut up, both of you! Two men are dead. This is serious."

"We didn't kill them," John said. "Did we?"

Will told his friends to shut up again. He needed to think. Using his shirttail to open the back car door, he worked the duffel bag loose. It was heavy, like a laundry bag of folded clothes, but much more dense. He slung the leather straps over a shoulder and moved to the rear of the car. The trunk lid was half-open, ripped off at one hinge, and displayed an empty cargo area, except for a pair of boots and a small ditty bag. If the men had more luggage, it must have flown out during the wreck. A warped New Jersey license plate hung by a single screw from one corner. He was debating whether or not to search the men's pockets for driver's licenses when fat drops of rain started to pelt his face. He looked around and saw faint pinpoints of distant headlights filtering through the darkness. Somebody was coming. Self-preservation instincts overrode his need to learn more about the man who'd just tried to kill him. "Let's get out of here."

He herded his subdued friends back to their car just as the drizzle escalated to a downpour. Good, Will thought, driving to their apartment. The rain will wash away any signs that we were ever there. The approaching vehicle never caught up with them, and Will figured its driver must have spotted the accident and stopped to help. The police would be summoned. Would they think the bizarre scene to be an accident? With gunshot wounds, probably not. Maybe it would be ruled a murder-suicide. Or maybe a double murder. But then, the car had swerved off the road and crashed. Would police think the passenger shot the driver, causing the car to flip? A flood of possible scenarios rushed through Will's head. None seemed fully plausible.

When they were safely ensconced inside their small rental apartment, Will locked himself and the duffel bag in the bathroom. He stripped and showered, scrubbing the specks of dried matter from his face until the water went cold. When he toweled off and unzipped the heavy duffel, he saw more money than he'd ever seen at once. Even in the movies. Bundles of twenty-, fifty-, and hundred-dollar bills, held together with rubber bands.

He instantly remembered the forgotten prayer. *Yea, though I walk through the valley of the shadow of death . . .*

ONE

It might never happen. My early retirement that keeps evading me like a crisp dollar bill in a windy parking lot.

I retired from SWEET after I lost my feeling of invincibility and realized the next bullet speeding my way at five hundred meters per second might manage to hit its intended target. SWEET is the government agency that plucked me from MP duty when I was a young marine, eager to help further their mission of thwarting terrorism. That's not the real name, of course. Just an acronym the field agents like to use, which stands for Special Worldwide Unit for Entertaining and Exterminating Terrorists. It might sound strange, but part of my job as an undercover agent was to entertain the bad guys—even though the bosses called it infiltration. That's why my handler signed Uncle Sam's name to pay the tab for a few cosmetic enhancements, including a breast enlargement. Of course, I got to keep my round size D's when I left the government, and I've grown quite fond of them. Unfortunately, I haven't yet had a chance to show them off in retirement, even though I bought fabulous new clothes without concern about concealing my .45-caliber handgun or my cleavage. Especially the cleavage.

I have been having something near panic attacks at the concept of leaving home without a weapon strapped to my body. Other retirees downsize homes. I could always downsize handguns, from the .45 to my new 9mm. A Ruger SR9, it's slim and sexy and has a mag capacity of seventeen rounds. A lot of people, especially men, think they have to go for the largest-caliber weapon they can accurately handle. But Hydra-Shok ammo has stopping power at any caliber. Staring at the judge who'd come to meet me for lunch, I decided that the Ruger would be perfect for conceal carry in retirement. That mental hurdle crossed, I wondered exactly what it was that my judge friend wanted me to do. She knew I'd quit working. Or was trying to, anyway.

My most recent exodus was from my personal security business, the Barnes Agency, many of whose jobs are contracted by the government. Fortunately, my partners, Rita and JJ, have proved quite capable of handling things without me. I'd done okay with the government, and the small security agency is my retirement nest egg. Best of all, I am alive and have all my body parts—plus a few. I deserved to call it quits. Play on my boat. Take up golf or tennis. Do some traveling without carrying a dossier on a bad guy. Get a tan and slurp frozen banana drinks with a blissfully blank and worry-free mind-set.

The judge and I were perched on bar stools at the Block, staring at the Cape Fear River through a wide-open industrial-size garage door. At first, I thought she simply wanted to enjoy lunch with me. Laugh about old times and catch up on current news. Boy, was I wrong. She wanted a favor.

I tilted my head back and drank a third of my beer with two swallows. "You do know that I'm retired, right, Judge? There was a party with a cake and everything. Champagne toasts. Lots of witnesses. I'm pretty sure you got an invitation." The Block is a restaurant and pub situated smack dab in the middle of downtown Wilmington, right on the bank of the river. I bought the historic building when I first moved to North Carolina, and the upstairs apartment is where I live. My best friend, Ox, is co-owner and manager of the bar, but like the Barnes Agency, it pretty much runs itself. Every once in a while, it even surprises us by showing a small profit.

The judge laughed, deep and throaty. "The day Jersey Barnes retires will be the day hell freezes over."

Hauling building supplies, a flatbed barge glided by on the glistening strip of water outside. "Why does everybody keep saying that?"

A streak of sunlight moved across her cheek, casting a golden glow on cocoa-colored skin. She smiled. "Sometimes the truth is obvious to everybody except the one closest to it."

I took another swig of beer, reminding myself to sip instead of chug. I'm trying to cut down. "What's so wrong with wanting to relax and enjoy life?"

"You're too young and too good at what you do to retire." She bit a hush puppy in half and spread butter on the remaining piece. "Besides, you owe me a favor."

"I thought *you* owed *me* a favor, after I broke into your private chambers to give you a wake-up call."

She nodded, brown black eyes blinking in slow motion. "You'll be happy to know the monster who was after me is back behind bars, where he'll stay for life."

"That's good to hear." Cracker ambled up to nuzzle my ankles. A solid white and very spoiled Labrador retriever, he wanted a dry-roasted peanut. I shelled one and gave him the two encapsulated morsels one at a time. He took them softly by sticking out the tip of his tongue.

"That favor made us even, to keep the record straight," the judge said.

"Great, then I don't owe you. My retirement is intact." I shot her my government-learned bimbette look and stuck out my chest. "I can go hit an all-inclusive club in Cancún and see what transpires when I stuff these babies into a coconut-shell bikini top." One of my weaknesses is designer lingerie. I'm hooked on the stuff and like to wear it beneath everything—even frayed blue jeans and T-shirts. But I've never owned a coconut-shell bikini top. It could be fun.

The judge smiled, but her tone was serious. "This is my *family*, Jersey. I don't know who else to turn to. Besides, you help me out with this, I'll owe you a favor. Never know when you might need a state supreme court judge on the other end of that speed dial."

Even though she lives in South Carolina and I live in North Carolina, she was right. State supreme court judges have a lot of clout, regardless of where they oversee justice. I finished my Amstel Light, deciding it's impossible to sip beer. Stupid idea. I've never mastered the art of sipping anything. "Okay, Judge. I'll do what I can. Lay it on me."

She petted Cracker's snout, and he instantly angled his wide head so the judge's hand was rubbing his neck. "Morgan is seven years younger than me. My only brother."

I motioned the bartender with my empty bottle and she replaced it with a fresh, frost-covered one. "Any sisters?"

The judge shook her head. "Just me and Morgan. We used to be really tight, when he lived in Columbia. We were twenty minutes apart and got together every week for dinner. When he moved to Dallas, Texas, for a better job, we stayed in touch by e-mail and Christmas cards."

"And now?"

"My father recently passed away. In the will, he left Argo's to

Morgan. I thought Morgan would sell the business, but instead he moved here, to Wilmington, to run it."

I studied the judge. "The restaurant Argo's?"

She nodded.

"The legendary Chef Garland was your father? If I had known that, I would have stopped by once in a while to say hello. And score a free appetizer or two." Argo's patron list is notorious. It's where all the beautiful people go to mingle with visiting celebs and Wilmington's elite. The last time Ox and I ate there was two years ago, to celebrate our lieutenant friend Dirk's promotion with the Wilmington Police Department. I enjoy rubbing elbows with the town's glitterati just as much as the next person, but a fifty-dollar plate of seafood and eight-dollar bottled beers make my wallet cringe, even if they are served on square china plates with red cloth napkins.

"I thought it was common knowledge that Dad owned Argo's. Of course, he had a head chef, so mostly he schmoozed the customers." The judge ate another hush puppy. "Anyway, he and Morgan never did have a traditional father-son relationship. Dad always expected Morgan to do better, and Morgan thought he could never do anything right in Dad's eyes. They used to fight all the time, and eventually they quit talking."

I never had a traditional relationship with my father, either. He walked out of my life when I was still wearing pigtails and didn't reenter it until six years ago, when he appeared on my doorstep like a stray cat. Spud now occupies the efficiency apartment next to my place above the Block. Our kitchens are connected by French doors that always remain open. I think we put up with each other out of curiosity. Someday I might ask why he disappeared, way back then. For now, it's not so important.

"What did Morgan do in Dallas?"

"Corporate accounting. Which is why it seems crazy to me that he's going to keep the restaurant. He has zero food service experience.

Although it's been two months since Dad died, and so far, Argo's still has a wait list every night. I guess that's something."

"The head chef stayed on?"

"Yes."

"That's a good thing, then. Sounds like Morgan wanted a career change and maybe the opportunity to do right by your father, so to speak," I reasoned. "What's the problem?"

She frowned. "I flew in a few days ago to surprise Morgan. He's not himself. He's lost weight and he's constantly fidgeting, like he's worried about something. You ride in a car with him and he keeps looking in the rearview, like he's checking to see if he's being followed. And somebody broke into his place last week."

"What was stolen?"

"He said they took cash and a few things from the dresser. His town house was trashed. I saw it. Busted furniture, bathroom mirror shattered, TV screen smashed in."

"Sounds like somebody wanted to scare him. Or else they were searching for something. Maybe both."

"That's what I said. But Morgan swears it was common burglars who got mad when they didn't find valuables."

"Hmmmn." Run-of-the-mill thieves looking to steal collectibles or jewelry or money wouldn't risk the noise. They'd simply get out and move on to their next target. "Anything else unusual happen with your brother lately?"

The judge frowned. "I'm not sure, Jersey. I just know that something bad is going on. Before Morgan moved to Wilmington, he was fine. He's always been extremely shy. Introverted. But he's never been like this. He won't admit it, but he's scared of something. Really scared. I'm wondering if it has something to do with Argo's."

"Why do you say that?"

She frowned. "He was fine in Texas. Calm, stable, his normal self.

The problems started after he moved here. And Argo's is his only tie to Wilmington."

I felt bad for the judge and her predicament but didn't see where my happily retired self fit into the equation. "What is it you want me to do?"

Her eyes locked on mine. "Fish around until you find out what's going on."

I thought about telling her to hire a private investigator. I know a few good ones.

Something powerful and discerning wrapped around me as the judge awaited the answer she wanted to hear. I'd hate to be the person on the other end of that same gaze in a courtroom.

"It will require a background check on your brother," I told her. "A magnified look into his personal life, hobbies, finances, relationships. If he's involved with something illegal, I'll find out about it." Which would present a dilemma. The judge had taken an oath to uphold the law, and her family members weren't exempt.

"Morgan is a good person."

"Good people often make bad choices."

She gave my hand an impromptu squeeze, and again, I felt the commanding energy that radiated from her. "You find out what's going on. I'll figure out a way to play the hand that's dealt, regardless of the cards you turn up."

I hoped, for the judge's sake, that there would be a simple explanation for Morgan's odd behavior, even though logic told me otherwise. The judge is a very intuitive woman.

TWO

Morgan had the unique skin color that results from a bi-racial union, and he reminded me of a male version of Halle Berry. His eyes were the same brownish black as his sister's and, coupled with an angular face, gave him an alluring look. Were it not for the underlying distress and the too-thin build, he'd have been a real stunner. Definitely somebody I'd sneak a second look at, were I not completely enamored of Ox. We'd finally slept together, and it was hands-on, mind-blowing sex with the added benefit of friendship. But lovemaking with my best friend had altered the status quo. A few magical hours in bed had changed everything, and the jury was still out on whether or not it would be for the better. I mentally reprimanded myself for daydreaming. But then, getting Ox out of my head would be impossible. Not to mention that we co-owned the Block. And that I've always relied on his help with assignments.

The skin between Morgan's eyebrows folded into three vertical rows. "So you're friends with my sister. I get that. But what do you want from me?"

"The judge is worried about you, Morgan. She senses you're having a problem with something and thought that I might be able to help."

"Help how?"

I drank some iced tea and looked around Argo's. The tea was freshly brewed and perfectly sweetened. The restaurant was closed and quiet. I imagined that it filled up very quickly each evening, as soon as the doors opened at five. The building overlooked Bradley Creek on Wilmington's north side and had a spectacular view through a wall of ten-foot-tall windows. To those who aren't familiar, the word *creek* might be misleading. Large vessels can navigate Bradley Creek. Just beyond the restaurant, a marina docked rows of private yachts, some in the neighborhood of seventy feet long.

Morgan's eyes darted to a corner table that was surrounded by glass on two sides. Sitting up two steps higher than the rest of the restaurant, it had its own level. A solid wall on the third side held a display of framed artwork and created a private sort of alcove for the occupants. "Well, anyway, I don't have a problem. I'm sure my sister intends well, but she's being paranoid. Even growing up, she was overly protective." He smiled for my benefit and forced out a laugh. "Typical big sister."

"No problems with the takeover of the restaurant, then?"

His eyes went back to the elevated corner table, and he seemed to be staring at the bright day outside. "As I said, no."

I pointed to the corner. "I'll bet that's the most popular table in the place."

His head jerked my way. "What about the table?"

I drank more tea, imagining that it would go well with the cashew-ginger fresh greens salad and a loaf of hot bread. And the broiled wild-caught Alaskan salmon served on a bed of dill mashed potatoes, garnished with white truffle slices. I'd seen both on the evening specials board when I'd first walked into the restaurant. Taste buds watering, I pointed to the far corner. "That table over there. I imagine that everybody wants that table when they make reservations. It has the best view and its own little room, sort of."

He forced another chuckle. "You're right. We call that the Green Table. Jonathan Green was a friend of my father's and his all-time favorite artist. Those two paintings you see are original oils. Worth a chunk of change, I'm told. The other three in the matching frames are signed lithographs."

"Bold and colorful." An art critic I'm not, but the portraits of women in big hats and children dancing emanated a delightful, genuine feel. Something a person could gaze at, on and off, for hours.

"Green is known for creating cross-cultural fine art." Morgan smiled and for an instant looked like an ordinary business owner with no worries. "Between the ornate kidney-shaped table, the artwork, and the view of the boats, it does make for a unique dining experience. Everybody asks for the Green Table, but we keep it on reserve for our more well-known patrons."

I tried to read the thoughts behind his near black irises. "Well, you certainly sound like a seasoned restaurateur, even though your past career was corporate accounting."

"Luckily, all the staff stayed on after Garland passed away. Even the servers. And I'm a quick learner. Basically, I keep the books and pay the invoices, which *is* accounting. And of course, I get out and greet arriving customers. Like Garland and Mom used to do. Piece of cake."

While the judge referred to their father as "Dad," Morgan preferred to use the elder man's first name, Garland, as though the two were acquaintances instead of family. Interesting. Although the judge had said that father and son were estranged before Garland died.

Somebody in the kitchen had begun prep work, and the smell of onion and spices made my stomach growl. "Do you get along well with your sister?"

"Of course. Always have."

"Why do you think she's worried about you?"

He shrugged. "Probably because I look worn out, I guess. I've been working long hours to learn the business. And of course moving and getting settled into a new place has been a chore."

"What about the break-in at your apartment?"

"What about it?"

"Do you know who did it?"

He gave me an are-you-stupid-or-what look. "If I knew who did it, don't you think I would have reported it to the police?"

"You didn't file a report?"

"Nothing was taken. And I hadn't yet bought renter's insurance, so replacing what they broke is out of my pocket anyway. Why bother with the police?"

Morgan politely answered my questions until I ran out of things to ask. I learned that he'd worked long enough at his prior job to accrue a nice chunk of change in a 401(k) plan and that he was vested in a pension plan. He'd never been married and didn't have kids. He did have a girlfriend, who had moved to Wilmington with him. He'd purchased a ring and was planning a marriage proposal when she'd suddenly broken it off, claiming the relationship had become stagnant. That was just after they'd moved, and she hadn't bothered to unpack her boxes of clothes. She'd simply showed up with a local moving truck and two men, who carried her stuff out of their rental. Morgan professed to be over the breakup. He had met plenty of new friends, he said. It was a declaration he couldn't quite pull off.

Overall, I didn't learn much, except that the judge was right. Her brother was soft-spoken and introverted to the point of being shy. And he was hiding something.

I went to the restroom before leaving and, on the way, took a bound journal from the host stand. The women's bathroom was elegant and clean and fresh-smelling. On the way out, I returned the journal, minus the past two weeks' worth of reservations and patron phone numbers. I had no idea how I'd use the information, but maybe a name on the list would connect with something else. Then I'd have an actual clue.

THREE

Smelling savory cinnamon rolls, I awakened from a dream that I was standing in line at a bakery. I sniffed the air to make sure it wasn't a lingering olfactory trick and surmised that my father's girlfriend had delivered breakfast. Either that, or Fran had spent the night and was now baking cinnamon rolls. Even though our kitchens are connected and Spud usually comes and goes through my place, his apartment has its own stairwell entrance that leads directly to the Barter's Block parking area. The building used to be a trading post in the early 1800s and at one point in history after the Civil War had served as a brothel. I imagined Fran sneaking in through Spud's private stairwell, much the way satisfied men used to exit by the same wooden stairs.

I pulled a cushy chenille robe over a La Perla chemise and followed my nose. Spud sat in my kitchen, reading the newspaper and slurping a chocolate Yoo-hoo. He'd never bothered to put a table in his own kitchen, and we'd settled into a routine of sharing our mornings on my side of the French doors. He sported a brand-new mustache that looked like it had ambitions of growing handlebars someday. Undoubtedly one of Fran's suggestions, it grew out solid white. Surprisingly thick. And currently covered with a thin layer of chocolate drink. Imagine Wolfgang Puck, shrink him down, age him twenty years, throw on the mustache, and you've got a pretty good mental image of Spud.

"Morning, sweetie!" Fran said to me, fluffing short, curly hair that was currently tinted orange. "You want some coffee?"

"Caffeine would be great, thanks."

She served a plate of hot cinnamon rolls. Steam rose from their gooey icing tops. Since she wore a robe, too, I guessed that she'd spent the night and arisen early to fix breakfast. Fran is approaching eighty, and Spud recently surpassed the milestone. Ox thinks they make a cute couple. All I know is that Fran makes incredible pies. By the smell of things, her cinnamon rolls would be just as good.

Spud peeped over the top of the sports section. "Today's paper is nugatory, for crying out loud."

"Nuga-what?"

He eyed me above his reading glasses. "Nugatory. It means worthless or of no value."

"Oh." I wondered when my father had begun exploring the English language. He's a retired cop, and his vocabulary is usually more direct and to the point. "Then why didn't you just say 'worthless'?"

Fran put a mug of coffee in my waiting hands. "I gave him a Word-A-Day calendar," she said. "You know, the little square kind, where you rip off each day? It's actually three new words a day."

"Yeah," Spud grunted. "I've got to keep my mind cuspidated."

"Huh?"

"It means sharp, for crying out loud. Like a razor's edge."

I bit into a cinnamon roll, and the dough melted in my mouth.

Maybe having Fran around wouldn't be such a bad thing after all. She could park her shoes under Spud's bed every night for all I cared, as long as she kept fixing breakfast in the mornings. "I don't think that word applies to your cerebrum," I said.

"My what?"

"Your brain," Fran told him. "Everybody knows that word."

"Whatever. Learning new words is like exercise for your head. Use it or lose it, as Frannie says. And I've got to keep my head in shape."

"Both of them," Fran said matter-of-factly.

"Thanks for the visual." I might have done a gross-out shiver.

We heard somebody jogging up the stairs from the Block, and Trish beeped her way into the kitchen after knocking once. "Hello? . . . Jersey, you here?" Trish is a local private investigator.

"Does everybody know my security code?" I asked.

"Probably doesn't help that somebody wrote it on the wood handrail," she said.

I shot a look at my father. The scolding kind.

"Wanted to make sure I didn't get locked out after you changed it last time, for crying out loud. Besides, it's in pencil. I can erase it once I memorize it."

"What is that heavenly smell?" Trish asked before I could scold Spud. "I'm about to start drooling."

Fran brought her a plate and Trish devoured a cinnamon roll standing up. She sat down for the second one. "Fran, you could open a shop and sell these things," she said, and went for a third.

When she quit eating, I asked Trish to do a detailed background check on Morgan and tail him for a few days.

Spud pulled off his readers and squinted at me. "Who's Morgan?"

"You want Trish to follow somebody around all day, sneaky-like?" Fran asked.

"And why do you want to know this Morgan person's business?" Spud's mustache moved from side to side. "I thought you're done with the dangerous work stuff."

"Does this Morgan fellow know that you're going to tail him?" Fran wanted to know.

I held up a hand to stop further ping-ponging. "It's a favor for my judge friend, Spud. And you know I don't discuss work details at home." Meaning not in front of Fran. My father nosed into my business all the time, but I barely knew her.

He caught my drift. "I tell Frannie everything anyways, for crying out loud."

"Yeah." Her head bobbed. "Ever since he almost killed me, we've been tight."

Spud and his poker buddies had been hauling a bunch of thrift store purchases down the road when a life-size anatomically correct mannequin flew off the roof of Bobby's van. Fran ran it over and damaged her scooter, at which point Spud asked her out on a date. He figured a dinner tab would be cheaper than the repair bill.

I updated the bumbling lovebirds on the judge, her brother, and Argo's.

"Huh," Fran said. "I wouldn't mind going to Argo's sometime."

"Those fancy eatin' houses cost too much," Spud said. "They're real proud of their food."

Fran fluffed her hair. "We can go, my treat."

" 'Long as you don't get involved with my work," I cautioned.

"No worries there. This Argo's thing of yours is kind of vapit." Spud turned his attention to the sports section.

"You mean vapid," Fran said. "That was one of last Tuesday's words."

"Whatever," Spud said. "It ain't one of Jersey's more interesting assignments."

The house phone rang, and Fran got to it before anyone else had a chance. Apparently, she'd made herself at home. "It's Ox," she mouthed to us before launching into a detailed conversation about life in the Jersey and Spud household. "Okay, sweetie, hold a sec. She's right here."

Fran smashed the handset into her stomach in lieu of pressing the mute button. "It's Ox," she yelled, as though I were in the next apartment instead of five feet away. "That man is pining away for you, don't you know. And you're not in such great shape yourself. Anybody who bothered to take a look-see couldn't miss the sparks flying between the two of you before he left." Fran stopped to throw back a swallow of coffee. "I'll tell you this much. If I was younger and more limber, I'd be all over him myself!"

"Not if you had a taste of me first, back when I was younger and more limber," Spud says.

"Good grief. Just give me the phone." I pulled the handset from Fran's grip and headed outside to the privacy of a balcony off the kitchen. Fran and Trish didn't bother to hide the fact that they planned to watch me through the glass doors. At least they couldn't hear.

"Hello?"

"I see things are just as entertaining around there as usual." The sound of Ox's voice was a shot of warm brandy to my insides.

"You heard all that?"

He chuckled, and the sound seemed to come from mere feet away instead of Bristol, Connecticut. "I miss you, Barnes."

"I miss you, too." The understatement of the month. "A lot."

"Five more weeks." The sentence conjured up all sorts of reunion images, and most of them didn't involve clothes. Now that we'd finally slept together, I couldn't quit thinking about him.

"How's everything been going?" he asked.

The Block was plugging along as usual, with only a few minor glitches, and I told him everything, right down to the contents of the latest mail delivery and the repair of three fluorescent over-heads, broken by a couple of drunk sports fans who were tossing a football. I brought him up-to-date on the situation with the judge and Argo's and Morgan. Listening, Ox was so quiet, I thought we'd lost the connection. When I finished, he filled me in on Lindsey's classes, face time with the camera, and Chuck's Steakhouse, Lindsey's newest favorite restaurant that was built inside an old barn.

Last year, Ox's daughter, Lindsey, got her mother's okay to move from California to live with Ox in Wilmington. I'm five eight, and the girl is taller than me, even after I've strapped on my most salacious high heels. Her features are her father's: mesmerizing cinnamon eye color, smooth olive golden skin, thick hair, and a wide smile. She has earned a nice chunk of college money by modeling, but her plan is to be a television sports announcer. She entered a contest to earn a six-week work-study program sponsored by ESPN and managed to win an all-expense-paid experience of a lifetime. There were only two stipulations. Her high school had to allow her to attend classes virtually, with the use of a tutor, and submit assignments via e-mail. The principal of New Hanover High quickly agreed, since Lindsey is one of his star students. The second stipulation of Lindsey's participation mandated that a parent or guardian accompany the teen. Ox didn't hesitate. Six weeks of concentrated time with his daughter was irresistible. Selfishly, I almost wished that Lindsey's mother were the parent to take her to ESPN's headquarters. Ox and I had just begun to explore our relationship on a level other than best friends and business partners. And then he was gone. Handling his normal duties running the Block was the easy part. Not having him in the same physical vicinity was proving much more difficult.

Through the glass, I watched the activity in my kitchen. Picking at yet another cinnamon roll, Trish read the paper. Fran was feeding Spud. Cracker paced among the humans, drool hanging from one side of his mouth. Fran finally gave the dog a morsel of banana and winked at me through the glass separating us. She pantomimed something that was supposed to mean my heart beating fast. Spud slapped her on the butt, lost his balance, and nearly fell off his chair from the effort. I rolled my eyes and looked out over the river, away from the romantic doddering in my kitchen.

"Lindsey just walked in," Ox said. "She wants to talk to you."

"Hiya, Jerz! How's everything hangin'? Bristol is totally rad— it's amazing here." Her words rushed together. "All the stuff I'm learning is incredible. And get this—they're going to let me do a real live segment on *SportsCenter* at the end of the academy program! I'm totally stoked."

Before I could respond, the girl's attention had been snagged by something else. "Later, Jerz. Gotta run. Love you!"

Ox came back on the line. "If that girl were in charge of a board meeting, it would be over before the coffee was served and everyone would know exactly what their plan of action was."

He and I had been apart for only a week and there wasn't much more to say, but I wasn't ready to hang up.

"It's not the same around here without you," I said. It was almost more intimate talking with Ox when there were several hundred miles separating us. Sort of easier, anyway.

His voice came out throaty, deep. "We need to talk when I get back, Jersey. You know that my life revolves around two women and one of them is you. Question is, how far are we willing to go with this thing?"

Was he talking marriage? Living together? Or something else? I thought about pushing the issue to get an idea of what was on his mind.

"I've got to go," was what emerged from my mouth. "Talk soon?"

"Sure."

I hung up, my emotions a braid of anticipation and uncertainty, and went inside just in time to see Fran—brandishing a rolled-up dish towel—chase Spud into his bedroom. And the word *chase* didn't equate with moving fast. You figure it out.

FOUR

Morgan knew his sister just wanted to help, but he couldn't believe that she'd gone so far as to employ an investigator. He wasn't exactly sure what Jersey Barnes did for a living, but regardless, his problems were none of the woman's business. For starters, he didn't know what he'd gotten involved in. How could he possibly ask for help when he wasn't sure what he needed help with? On top of that, he'd begun to question his late father's business ethics. Did Morgan really want his sister to learn that their father had been a pervert? A voyeur who apparently got his kicks by eavesdropping on unsuspecting diners?

Morgan wasn't sure if the tiny office in the back of Argo's kitchen was warm or not, but the cotton shirt he'd carefully ironed was now plastered to his skin. Corner-mounted on the wall in front of him, a security monitor could display six squares of simultaneous action. The discreet cameras were installed not only for the safety of the patrons, the chef had explained to Morgan, but also to ensure top-notch service. Of course, things were quiet right now since Argo's was closed. During operating hours, though, he could see when a celebrity entered with entourage in tow, allowing him to greet the party and seat them personally. He could monitor activity in the kitchen—or the back of the house, as food service lingo dictated—and at the same time, he had an overhead view of the dining room. Another camera was trained on Argo's cozy bar, and an outdoor camera enabled him to survey the parking lot. Upon discovering the system, Morgan had thought it odd for a restaurant. A department store or liquor store, maybe, but not a fine dining establishment. He had voiced his observation to Deanna, the head server, who'd assured her new boss that video surveillance was commonplace everywhere from car dealerships to coffee shops.

Morgan humored Deanna's enthusiastic explanation, even though he found many practices at Argo's to be peculiar. Especially the fact that nobody other than his father was allowed in the small office where he now sat. When first touring his newly inherited business, Morgan had learned that his father had possessed the only key to the room. He'd found it on his father's key chain, along with house and car keys. That was more than a month ago, and the eight-foot-square office— tucked into a corner off the kitchen like a storage closet—remained unchanged: computer, telephone, two filing cabinets, spin-dial safe, and loads of clutter. The walls were bare, except for the flat-screen monitor and a single framed photograph. In eight-by-ten, his mother and father laughed about something—genuine expressions that couldn't have been posed. His father's dark skin stood in stark contrast with his mother's cream-colored complexion, their cheeks touching, their eyes focused directly on the camera lens. The picture had been taken recently at his parents' house. Probably just before his mother died. He was reminded again of the fact that he was alone in a confusing world. He'd had big plans for a wife and family, but Maria dumped him. Now he had no one. No fiancée. And no parents.

The space behind his eyes flashed hot, and Morgan ignored the pressure of forming tears. He still couldn't comprehend the fact that his mother was gone, just like that, in an instant. The heart attack happened a year ago, but her death seemed like yesterday, when Morgan allowed himself to think about it. She'd been too young to have a heart attack. Too vibrant. Too healthy. Yet her heart muscle had suddenly stopped beating just the same. The experience must have desensitized him, Morgan knew, because when he'd learned of his father's death, he'd felt nothing. A little sad that the overbearing man never came to love and accept Morgan for who he was. But that was it. A hint of sadness was all he felt. Until he'd found the strange earpiece plugged into a small blue box next to the computer.

The other side of the box held a thin cable that climbed the corner of the wall and disappeared into the ceiling. Morgan had bought an all-purpose ladder and, working early the following morning, moved a string of black ceiling tiles to trace the cable. It stopped above a single table—the Green Table—where it plugged into a battery-operated wireless receiver. The receiver had obviously been installed to acquire an incoming signal from somewhere. Morgan had scoured the famous table, the chairs, the plants, and the artwork on the walls, to find nothing. Perplexed, he'd let himself into Argo's at six the next morning and searched every single table, chair, and booth in the place. He'd examined the hostess stand, restrooms, bar, and foyer. No listening devices. The third morning, he'd returned to the Green Table, sat down with a cup of coffee, and found it.

The ornate table's center held a metal sculpture of a wine goblet and grape clusters encircled by five tea candle holders woven through copper-fashioned grapevines. One of the busboy's duties was to replace the burnt candles with fresh ones after each group finished their meal. The server would light the tea candles upon greeting the next customers. The sculpture was about ten inches high and a foot in diameter, perfect for the table's centerpiece. Morgan had picked up the hunk of metal out of simple curiosity, to see if it contained an artist's signature mark on the bottom. He hadn't been able to determine if the piece was an original sculpture or a cheap trinket, but he had found a hole drilled beneath a grape cluster. The black microphone blended right in.

Morgan had reassembled the centerpiece, replaced the candles, and decided to test the apparatus the next day. Once again, he'd awakened early and headed to the restaurant, this time clutching his bedside alarm clock radio. He had put it on the Green Table and tuned it to the first radio station he'd found. Back in his tiny office, he'd inserted the earbud and fiddled with dials on the blue box until a DJ's voice filled his ear. The words were distinct and clear. Morgan had listened to a string of commercials, two country songs, and the traffic report before he'd retrieved his alarm clock radio. So his father—the big, successful, charismatic Garland whom everyone loved—had been into eavesdropping. The deviant.

As early as grade school, teachers had reported to Morgan's parents that their son didn't interact with the other kids. A few suggested a class for "special children." He had remained in regular classes and, surprising the teachers, hadn't been teased or bullied as he'd worked his way through the grades. Other students simply ignored him. The older Morgan grew, the more agitated Garland became with his son's demeanor, which the elder man perceived as a lack of ambition. Luckily, Morgan's withdrawn behavior was more acceptable in a college environment, and he'd managed to make a few friends in his dorm.

Now, as a forty-four-year-old adult, Morgan had to force himself to smile and nod at customers in the restaurant. Mingling wasn't his thing. He never knew what to say. But at least he didn't get off on listening to private conversations, like his father must have been doing. After all, the Green Table was where everyone who was anyone sat. A nationally read food critic declared the table to be the absolute best table in the Carolinas. Not the food, but *the table*.

Had his father listened to kinky foreplay suggestions between seemingly dignified socialites or taken notes on confidential business dealings among high-powered stockbrokers? And how long had the table been bugged? Had his mother been aware of it before she died? She used to work at Argo's, helping to greet and seat customers. Surely she'd been allowed to enter Garland's private office.

Morgan had planned to dismantle the listening device right away, before anybody else had a chance to learn what Garland had been up to. His first order of business, though, was to finish poring through all the file folders loaded with suppliers, invoices, recipes, employee information, and miscellaneous correspondence. And find a safecracker. Morgan had already tried the usual birthdays and anniversary dates. He'd searched the desk drawers and computer's contacts database for the combination. He and his sister had gone through all the personal documents and belongings in the house and found nothing that resembled a numerical combination. Argo's had another safe—one where money and deposits were kept—but at least three people had the combination to that one. At worst, Morgan thought, the second safe might hold his father's porn collection. At best, it would contain answers.

A delivery truck appeared on the monitor, snapping Morgan out of his fog. He'd come in early to get rid of the Green Table's microphone apparatus. But now, it was already noon. Had he really been sitting at his desk like a zombie for three hours? Apparently so. Deliveries were arriving. Prep chefs would appear next. Soon, the phone would start ringing. He'd wasted so much time that now he couldn't chance removing the microphone and receiver. Tomorrow would bring another chance. Morgan decided to go home as soon as the head chef arrived. He was exhausted. Dealing with his father's estate, taking over the restaurant, and being ruthlessly dumped by his fiancée had messed with his head so much that he'd turned into an insomniac. Not to mention that strange happenings were pricking him like metal shavings flying at a giant magnet. He knew his apartment had been searched, even though he'd played dumb with the Jersey Barnes woman. His car had, too. He didn't bother to lock his car doors because he never left valuables inside. And who would want to steal a run-down Ford sedan? Twice, though, Morgan had sensed that somebody had been in his car. Once he'd caught the distinct smell of cigar smoke. A few days later, he'd found a packet of tissues on the floorboard. They'd obviously fallen from the glove compartment, but Morgan hadn't opened the compartment for days.

He stood on shaky legs that were numb from sitting too long and went to accept the produce delivery. As he checked off a box of artichokes against the invoice while a route driver waited, it occurred to him that in addition to eavesdropping, his father might have recorded conversations. Was Garland into blackmail? If so, did one of his father's targets think that Morgan now possessed the dirt on them? The theory didn't make sense, Morgan told himself as he felt avocados to make sure they weren't overly ripe. He'd searched the office and found no tapes or recording equipment. And why would his father try to blackmail somebody? The man had been wealthy.

Morgan finished checking in the delivery and thanked the driver. Turning around, he almost lost his balance when a wave of vertigo caused his brain to think he was falling. That happened when he got stressed out. The vertigo. College exams used to bring it on. First dates. And family gatherings. His inner ears were wreaking havoc with him lately, and he'd felt off-kilter since moving to the East Coast. Morgan wanted to get drunk. Then he'd have to sleep. Or at least get some rest while he was passed out.

Ten minutes later, two employees arrived. Morgan told them he'd be out for the day and headed home. He bought a bottle of vodka and a pint of orange juice on the way and, on impulse, stopped at a convenience store for a cup of ice. He downed an entire drink sitting in the parking space and poured a second to summon up courage. Before putting the car in gear, he dialed his ex's phone number. Maria was still in town, as far as he knew. Maybe she'd come to her senses. Maybe she would move back in with him.

"Why are you calling, Morgan?" she answered.

"I just want to talk," he lied. He wanted to see Maria. To be with her and run his fingers through her hair and inhale the floral scent of her perfume.

"I'm busy."

She didn't sound busy to him. "Doing what?"

"Shopping for a dress, if you must know. Anyway, it's none of your business."

When had she suddenly turned into such a bitch? He poured another splash of vodka into his cup and gulped. He rarely drank anything more than a glass of wine in a single sitting, and the strong taste made his eyes burn. A cash register sounded through the telephone. So she really was shopping. "You're my fiancée, Maria. I love you. I need to understand what happened to us."

"I am not your fiancée anymore, Morgan. If you want the ring back, fine. Although I was going to have it made into a nice drop, to remember you by."

If he'd wanted her to wear the six-thousand-dollar diamond around her throat instead of on a finger, he'd have bought her a necklace. "If you hate me so much, why do you want to remember me?"

Maria thanked a clerk, and when she returned her attention to Morgan, her voice warmed a notch. "I don't hate you. We had fun together, you know? I really thought I was ready to do the marriage thing. But moving halfway across the country made me realize that I'm not ready to settle down."

It wasn't the answer Morgan wanted to hear, but at least she was talking to him. "Then let's go back to dating, Maria." He hoped that his voice didn't sound as desperate as he felt. "I need you in my life right now. You're my only friend in Wilmington."

She hesitated, just long enough to give him hope, before crushing his world. "I'm moving back to Texas. I mean, why would I stay here? I don't know anybody. I've already shipped my stuff. I'm driving back in a few days."

Vertigo kicked in, and the dashboard moved. Morgan had planned to go home to Maria every day, forever. To share thoughts and dreams and laughs with her. Travel. Make kids and grandkids and guide them into responsible adulthood. Take each other to doctor's appointments when they grew old. Now, she was driving halfway back across the country, out of his life. "So that's it, then?"

"Take care of yourself, you hear?" The tone of her voice was so *final*.

It was over, just like that. Morgan disconnected and pulled into traffic, vertigo causing the road to sway beneath him. Driving home, he focused every ounce of attention on keeping his car between the lines. Once there, he stumbled inside and fell onto the sofa, too dizzy to do anything else. He couldn't even finish drinking the vodka he'd bought. All he could do was lie there, curled on his side, and think. Maria's actions were out of his control, and he knew there was nothing he could do, short of tracking her down and pleading his case. Which would look like stalking from her point of view. He could only hope that she would come to miss him and realize how great they were together. There was always a chance she'd come back to him. But probably not.

Either way, Morgan thought, he was stuck in Wilmington. His old job had already been taken by an associate. He'd moved all his possessions. Transferred bank accounts. Changed his driver's license. Forwarded his mail. There was nothing to do but throw himself into his new position as a North Carolina restaurateur. He'd already been spending a lot of hours at Argo's, but now he planned to give it everything he had. He felt overly dramatic just thinking it—but in reality, the restaurant was all he had left. His mother was gone. His father was gone. His sister lived hundreds of miles away. The few friends he had were in Dallas. And now, Maria had officially dumped him.

Despite the odd blue box, the bugged table, and the strange happenings since he'd taken over Argo's, the upscale eatery just might be his salvation. Running it would help keep his mind off the fact that he was completely alone.

FIVE

I drive a tricked-out jet black hearse. It's a long story, but I can sum it up in one word: cheap. I obtained it with help from my friend Floyd, who handles automobile auctions for SWEET. The main problem with the corpse caddy—aside from being conspicuous, of course—is that dead bodies creep me out. Ugly, mean, and danger-ous? No problem. Bloody and beat-up? No problem. But take away the pulse and I freak out. My government file has the condition offi-cially identified as necrophobia, but way back then, a shrink assured my bosses that it wouldn't interfere with my job. I dealt with a lot of bad guys, but they were all alive. At first, anyway.

Even though Floyd swore the hearse had been used to carry drugs and weapons—not lifeless bodies—I still can't quite shake the willies when scooting behind the wheel. But, hey. It has a leather interior with bun warmers, bucket seats in the rear where the casket should go, and a sound system worth more than I paid for the vehicle. Speak-ers blaring and tinted windows down, I pulled into the Barnes

Agency driveway. A nondescript building with no signage, it looked more like a personal residence than a security business. Trish's Honda was already there.

"Nice wheels, Jersey," she said, sitting on a desk, popping bubble gum. "But aren't retirees supposed to drive Lincoln Town Cars? It's in the manual."

Trish has waist-length blond hair that she usually wears pulled into a ponytail high at the back of her skull. She looks more like a college student than a licensed P.I., which is probably one of the reasons she's so good at her job. She has a knack for sniffing out unfaithful rich husbands, and the agency's old Chevy van has earned her a very nice living thanks to suspicious wives in the greater Wilmington area. I'd asked her to keep an eye on Morgan for a few days.

"She must've skipped class that night." Rita came out of the blue room with JJ and Andy. "You know, during her Retirement 101 course."

Rita and JJ are partners in the agency. Andy is a masseur by trade, but Rita had hired him part-time to fill in for our secretary, who was out on maternity leave. The blue room holds lots of nifty gadgets, and not all of them are legal for a civilian to possess. A temp shouldn't be in there.

"Suzie decided to become a permanent stay-at-home mom, so we've just hired Andy as our full-time secretary," JJ explained.

"I think the correct term is 'office assistant,'" Rita said. "Or is it 'administrative assistant'?"

Eye candy would be more like it, I thought. Although he did give a great massage. I'd had one on the portable table he'd erected in our office. Rita claimed the extra money we paid him per hour was well worth the stress reduction, and I had to agree with that.

"Hey, call me whatever works, girls. I kind of feel like that dude on *Charlie's Angels*, you know? Not Bosley, but the other one. What was his name?"

I raised my eyebrows at Rita, high up as they'd go, which isn't easy. I'd had a government-ordered brow lift to go with my boob job.

"He's much more intelligent than he appears," Rita said. "Degree from East Carolina University, karate and judo instructor, licensed real estate agent, private pilot's license, and he's got the massage therapist thing going on, too."

I aimed my raised eyebrows at Andy.

He smiled. "I dig it here."

"Welcome aboard," I said, feeling out of touch. The downside of turning over control of my agency to Rita is that I no longer make the day-to-day decisions. The upside is that I no longer make the day-to-day decisions. Retirement is strange.

Flipping pages on a clipboard, Trish scanned her notes and gave me the rundown on Morgan's whereabouts. "Overall, nothing out of the ordinary, except that he goes into the restaurant ridiculously early. It's interfered with my beauty sleep. Anyway, that's all he does. Grocery store, dry cleaner's, and Argo's."

"And I thought my life was dull," JJ said. She used to be an army sharpshooter and is the first to volunteer for the Barnes Agency's more unconventional assignments.

"Your life can't be dull," I said. "You're one of Charlie's Angels, remember?"

"Bosley!" Andy said, making a big deal of slapping his forehead. "Of course it was Bosley, because the other dude was Charlie. The girls were all *Charlie's* angels, right? So Bosley is the one I meant."

I eyed him. "You get that East Carolina diploma with a mail-in coupon from the back of *Rolling Stone* magazine?"

"Nope, did it the old-fashioned way. Attended classes."

"But here's the interesting part," Trish continued. "I think I spotted somebody else tailing Morgan." She rattled off an out-of-state license plate number. "Problem is, that tag expired years ago. The individual it was registered to sold that vehicle and turned the tag in to their local DMV."

"Which means it could have ended up in a dump bin any-where." Such license plates are discarded, recycled, or given to any number of municipalities for use in their undercover departments. Even unmarked cop cars and the highway patrol sometimes bolt a bogus, out-of-state tag on their bumper to fool speeders. The vehicle Trish had spotted was a dark blue Nissan Murano with a "swim-mingly handsome" male driver.

"Try a loose tail on Morgan, see if you can pick up the Murano again. If you do, maybe we can find out who he is."

"Will do."

My phone rang. Caller ID said that Spud's girlfriend was on the other end.

"Jersey, it's Fran. Can you come and get your father at the emer-gency room? They say he's fine, but he's a little out of sorts, and I don't think I should haul him on the back of my scooter." Fran shouldn't be hauling anyone—not even herself—on Wilmington's roads. She'd presented a plagiarized eye exam to renew her driver's li-cense. Which incensed Spud no end, since he hadn't thought of doing the same thing when the state revoked his license owing to deterio-rating eyesight.

"What happened?"

"He came to my yoga class and got his leg stuck behind his head. Stupid man, trying to prove something. That wasn't even one of the stretches! He was just trying to show off. Anyhoo, the instructor got Spud untangled from himself, but when he stood up, he fell over and hit his head on the floor. Kaplunk! They called an ambulance to make sure he didn't damage anything inside that thick skull of his."

"When was this?" I asked.

"Few hours ago. But don't worry, sweetie. They took a picture of his head and said it's perfectly fine. They gave him pain pills, though, since he pulled a muscle in his leg."

"Good grief." I told Fran I'd be right there and disconnected. First, Spud is spouting big words as though he were practicing for a Scrabble tournament. And now he was doing yoga? I wasn't so sure that hanging out with a peppy girlfriend was a good idea after all. Trying to keep up might kill him.

Nobody was overly surprised when I gave them the Spud update.

"Want me to come over and give him a massage once you get him home?"

"You might break something. He's eighty," I said. People seeing us together always thought me to be Spud's granddaughter. They didn't factor in the fact that my mother was barely half his age when I was born. "He's fragile."

The office erupted in laughter. Apparently, they all disagreed.

I angled the hearse lengthwise along the curb directly in front of the hospital's patient pickup area. I'd been there before and was quite familiar with the process. A nurse at the information booth told me they'd bring my father right out.

Ten minutes later, automatic sliding doors swooshed open and a nurse wheeled Spud through. He wore a pair of running shorts and a sleeveless muscle shirt with spurts of wiry gray chest hairs sticking out in all directions. Dressed in a skintight pink bodysuit, Fran strutted behind them, clutching a striped gym bag and Spud's walking cane.

Seeing the hearse, the nurse cocked her head. "You're here for Mr. Barnes?"

I opened a rear door of the corpse caddy. "That I am."

"He's not dead yet, dear," she said.

SIX

Since absorbing the reality that he and Maria didn't have a future together, Morgan had existed in an off-balance fog. He'd immersed himself in the restaurant business, just as he'd resolved he would do, and Argo's was running smoothly. His new life in a beautiful new town was moving forward. And he would soon be wealthy, once the estate sale and trust were finalized. Any other man would have been gleefully happy. Or at least upbeat.

It was yet another day, and standing in Argo's kitchen, Morgan felt nothing but emptiness. And he was too tired to be alarmed when he suspected someone was following him along Wilmington's streets as he grocery-shopped and dropped work suits at the cleaner's. He just didn't care. If the weird happenings were a result of his father's unethical eavesdropping, the people following Morgan would soon realize that he didn't know a thing. All their secrets died with Garland. The only tie to anything telling was the bugged Green Table, and that would be taken care of early tomorrow morning. Once he'd disassembled the setup, Morgan planned to smash the electronics before tossing the pieces in the trash compactor. He turned to see an employee watching him.

"Uh, hey, boss? Not to be disrespectful or anything, but you really don't look well. In fact, you look pretty awful." Even looking bad, Deanna thought, he was still gorgeous. The man was a visual masterpiece. She could stare at him all night long.

Morgan nodded at the woman in charge of Argo's wait staff. Deanna had caught him standing in the kitchen, zoned out, not doing anything other than watching the artistic plating of lobster-roll appetizers drizzled with Dijon-lemon sauce. He ran a palm down his silk tie and adjusted his jacket.

"Seriously. I mean, your suit and tie is meticulous, as usual. But you look like you partied all night long. I mean, you look sort of tired." She smiled long enough to make him uncomfortable. "Hitting Wilmington's night spots?"

"I'm not sleeping well."

She frowned and handed him a small tube, fantasizing that he was tired because he'd spent the night with her. "Here, dab some of this beneath your eyes. It's a skin tightener. Works wonders."

Did he look that bad? "Thanks, I guess."

"You can keep it," Deanna said. "It's a trial size. By the way, the Divine Image Group—all of them—are here, and they want to see you. Two of them are *the* go-to cosmetic surgeons if you live anywhere near Wilmington. That's what everybody says, anyway. The third one is a shrink. They're just finishing up an early dinner at the Green Table. What do you want me to tell them?"

To go eat somewhere else, Morgan thought, where the owner will do a better job of acting impressed. He hated dealing with uppity people who thought they were better than everybody else simply because they could put a few letters after their name. But then, that was probably a third of Argo's clientele. Lawyers and doctors. And these physicians had been eating at Argo's since it opened, he'd heard. He didn't care for doctors in general, since his mother died. If the medical community was so terrific, why hadn't someone diagnosed her heart condition before it killed her?

"I can always say you've stepped out," Deanna continued. She'd grown accustomed to the new owner's solitary tendencies. "Although they've wanted to meet you ever since you took over the restaurant. After all, you're Garland's *son*. You're a local celebrity just by association. And your dad was really good friends with them. Your mom was, too."

"Fine, I'll stop by their table."

Morgan held up the little tube of miracle cream next to the fluorescent lighting to read the directions. He didn't want any customers—especially plastic surgeons—to see him at his worst.

"Here, let me do it." Deanna squirted the cream onto a finger and, with the tip of her tongue stuck out, applied a dab beneath each of Morgan's eyes. "There! Better already."

He headed for the dining room, wishing he had a tiny bit of her enthusiasm so he'd be better in social situations.

"You're welcome," Deanna said under her breath, and went to collect a waiting food order. A tingle of excitement had coursed through her body during the brief moment of physical nearness to her boss. But he'd apparently felt nothing. He hadn't even bothered to thank her.

Spine straight and forcing a smile, Morgan caught the group of doctors as they were standing to leave the Green Table. Stepping up to the alcove, he felt as though he'd entered an alternate universe. It was an odd sensation. The elegant Green Table and its surrounding valuable artwork radiated an appreciable energy. But the table also held a secret, known only to him. Morgan felt powerful and important, like a stealthy undercover agent. Even though he would never spy on someone, the mere knowledge that *he could* gave him confidence.

He held out a hand to the man on his left. "I'm Morgan."

The man gripped his palm as though they were comrades, and the shake was more side to side than up and down. "It's so nice to finally meet you! I'm Dr. Haines"—he indicated the man next to him—"this is Dr. Rosch and Dr. Pratt. Please call us Leo, Jonathan, and Michael. Jonathan specializes in psychiatry, and Michael and I specialize in cosmetic procedures."

Morgan voiced something about it being nice to meet the men.

Leo stepped forward and palmed Morgan's shoulder. "You don't know how devastated we were to learn of your father's passing. He was a great man. A great friend. And I must say, you have Garland's eyes. Now I know why he was always bragging on you."

Garland had bragged on him? That was news. Morgan tried to smile.

Michael spoke up. "It does offer some consolation to see you taking up where Garland left off."

"Absolutely," said Jonathan the shrink, the word coming out a bit slurred. "Our practice is a few miles down the road, and we've been dining at Garland's place for years and years. We've come to think of him as family."

"Which means that you are family, too," Leo said. "Anything you ever need, anytime, you let us know."

"Thanks, I will," Morgan managed to say, even though they danced around his mother's death as though it were insignificant, the bastards. They hadn't bothered to mention Rosemary. Just because she'd passed almost a year ago didn't mean the pain wasn't still fresh to him.

The Divine Image Group threw out a few more pleasantries, but their voices blended into a single lump in Morgan's ears. He nodded and smiled and endured the social assault as he ushered them out Argo's front door with a reminder to drive safely.

He continued holding the door for an arriving couple, and when he realized who they were, he nearly stumbled into them. A wave of vertigo rolled through his brain.

"Morgan!" Maria acted delighted to see him, as though he were an old friend instead of a dumped ex-boyfriend. "I'm so glad you're here tonight. Remember Mark, my old boss? He flew in for a conference and has offered to drive me back to Dallas so I won't be on the road by myself. But he refused to go without first eating at the finest restaurant in Wilmington."

Her former boss was a married man with kids. And now he was playing chauffeur for an ex-employee? Morgan's smile froze as he fought to stay upright. His hand tightened around the door handle. Mark found Morgan's other hand and shook it.

"Great to see you again, and glad to hear from Maria that your restaurant is doing so well." Mark waited for Maria to move inside before following. "I'm really looking forward to dinner tonight, let me tell you."

The hostess determined that the Greer party was early for their reservation, but she could seat them shortly. They agreed to have a cocktail in the bar. Mark Greer, Morgan remembered. He'd met Maria's employer on a few occasions, at company functions. The man was a terrific boss, Maria told Morgan the day she'd given notice that she was quitting to move east with her fiancé. Mark gave Maria severance pay and her upcoming holiday bonus. Most employers would have bade Maria farewell and offered to serve as a reference. Mark Greer had given her extra money. And now he'd flown fifteen hundred miles to retrieve her.

Morgan watched them settle in at a cozy bar table, Mark tending to her comfort before finding his own chair. Most people wore upscale casual attire to Argo's, but Mark and Maria had decked out for the occasion. She'd worn her hair up. Long earrings dangled from her lobes and glittered every time the light caught them just right. Her lips were glossy red. He loved that shade of lipstick on Maria and wondered if she'd worn it for his benefit or Mark's. In a tailored suit, colorful tip of an artfully folded silk handkerchief sticking out of the breast pocket, Mark leaned back and smiled at his date. She returned the smile. They sure were showing a lot of teeth to each other, Morgan thought.

"Put them at the Green Table," he told the hostess.

"Josh Brown is coming, and he always sits at—"

"Just do it," Morgan growled, and stalked off.

"Fine," she mouthed to his back, wondering what had gotten into the new owner. He was more edgy than usual.

Repulsed at what he was about to do, Morgan locked himself in the private office, inserted the earbud, and fiddled with dials on the blue box until he could hear activity in the dining room. The audio came through so clearly, he envisioned exactly what tasks the busboy did as he cleared and reset the Green Table. Five minutes later, Deanna seated Maria and her former boss. Morgan heard the click of a lighter when Deanna lit the five fresh tea candles in the table's centerpiece. Recognizing that her customers were new to Argo's, she told them about the artwork surrounding the Green Table.

"You were right, Maria," Morgan heard Mark say. "This place is impressive."

"And romantic! Morgan put us at the best table in the house. I thought it might be weird to eat here, but I guess he's forgiven me."

Morgan shut his eyes tight. Now his employee would want to know who Maria was. And what he'd supposedly forgiven her for.

Deanna took drink orders, and then they were alone. The three of them: Maria and Mark and Morgan. He could see them on the monitor, from the overhead dining room camera. It was a wide shot, and although their features weren't clear, their body language was. Two heads, leaning toward each other. Maria's elbow on the table, her fingers playing with the stem of a water glass. The table's unique kidney-shaped design allowed for a couple to sit next to each other, and these two had positioned themselves as lovers would. Definitely not a simple employer-employee relationship. Mark reached for Maria's hand, the one that had previously held an engagement ring. Morgan's chair lost its legs, and the video monitor seemed to move. Nauseated, he yanked out the earbud and covered it with a stack of invoices. He didn't want to hear. He didn't want to learn how little he'd meant to Maria.

But he had to know. Rocking to ease the pandemonium in his stomach, Morgan twisted the earbud back into place.

"—doesn't matter now," came the man's voice. "She knows I want a divorce. I've already hired an attorney. We can be together and as soon as the divorce is final."

"No more sneaking around?" Maria said.

"Never again. I told her that we can do the divorce the easy way or the hard way. Easy is that she contests nothing and gets a very generous settlement. Plus the kids get to keep me in their life. They'll spend some weekends and holidays with me. With us."

Deanna arrived with a bottle of wine, and the table went silent while she opened it. Mark declined the customary tasting. Deanna filled two glasses and placed a small tray of bread and cheese in front of them. As soon as she'd gone, Mark continued.

"My wife is a smart woman. She chose the easy divorce. Which means that you and I can openly be together starting, well, right now."

The dark dot on the monitor that was Maria's head tilted back when she drank her wine. Morgan shut his eyelids tight so he wouldn't have a visual. Listening was all the input he could handle.

"Where will we live?"

That was his Maria, Morgan thought. Always practical.

"I've found a great condo and put an offer on it. You're going to love it. We can move in as soon as the deal closes in two weeks. Until then, I'll stay where I am, but we'll get you a motel room at one of those residence-type places."

Maria's voice, always soft and seductive when she was happy, drew Morgan into its depth like a cushy down comforter on a freshly made bed. He envisioned her mouth, glossy red lips, moving the way they did with a slight upturn at the corners, and he felt as though she were mere inches away. He fantasized that her velvety words were meant for him. "You are so brilliant," he heard Maria say, "and decisive. That's what I love about you. You want something and then you figure out how to make it happen."

He was brilliant. He was loved. *He* was the recipient of her compliments. Just one more time, for a few seconds, anyway, as long as Morgan could hold on to the fantasy.

"You flatter me too much," Mark said. Morgan wished the man would shut up.

Deanna arrived to take their food orders. Morgan opened his eyes, stared at the monitor. Saw the happy couple. Heard him order two of the seafood specials. Watched Deanna refill Maria's wineglass. Heard Maria thank the server. Watched Deanna retreat as Maria and Mark made a toast.

"To us," Mark said, "and our future."

Their words faded in and out as ripples of vertigo overtook Morgan. He sat perfectly still in his chair with both feet planted firmly on the floor, but still the office swayed around him.

"Well, I'm going to have to get a job, even so," Maria said.

"You'll work for me again."

"What will people think?"

Mark laughed, a confident, short laugh. "I own the damn company and don't really care what people think. Besides, once we're married, it will be your company, too."

Her sharp intake of breath and subsequent squeal came through the earbud like an ice pick. Muscles paralyzed, brain throbbing, Morgan endured the remainder of their meal from the confines of his small office. He discovered that Deanna was a professional and polite server and overheard that she was attending classes to earn a master's degree in education. He learned that Maria had been dating her boss, on and off, the entire time she'd been with him. Almost a year longer, in fact. He found out that it took Maria quitting her job and moving away to bring Mark to his senses and that Mark was apologetic about the way he'd treated Maria in the past. Morgan found out that his ex had always wanted to vacation in Maui, a factoid she'd never shared with him. He learned of a special chair, presumably one in Mark's office, that—according to Maria—was perfect for making love while sitting on his lap. She was eagerly looking forward to another *business* meeting, in fact, and planned to wear a dress without panty hose for the occasion.

The partially digested contents in Morgan's stomach rolled up his throat, and he heaved into a small trash can.

"By the way, I forgot to ask," Mark said. "How did your boyfriend take it when you told him you were breaking off the engagement? He seemed cordial enough to see you tonight."

"Oh, he's fine with it. His whole life is this restaurant, anyway. It's like he's obsessed with proving something to his dead father. And he wasn't even tight with the man. It's weird."

"Well, he's a very good-looking guy. I'd be beside myself with jealousy if you were still with him." Mark leaned forward, as though he weren't already close enough. "Anyway, I'm really glad that he didn't make things difficult for you, Maria."

"I gave him back the engagement ring and told him it was better to break it off now rather than later. He was cool with that."

Morgan felt like crying, the kind of let-it-all-out wail that a child in pain might give after falling onto a concrete sidewalk. Instead, he could only laugh as he thought of his MasterCard bill. Maria hadn't given the ring back, and he was still paying for the diamond she planned to wear around her neck. In a drop. To remember him by.

SEVEN

The Block is a laid-back joint that falls somewhere between "local dive with great food" and "happening happy hour spot." My two favorite things about the old converted warehouse are the river view and the wide-open feel. I was behind the bar, filling ice bins and restocking beer. I did it to be helpful, but on a selfish level, the chores made me feel closer to Ox, since his management style often puts him behind the bar. It might have been wishful thinking, but I detected the warm and fresh hint of his aftershave lingering around the cash register.

It didn't help that every other customer coming in wanted to know where Ox and Lindsey were. They'd gotten used to Lindsey's enthusiastic fist-bump greetings and Ox's good-natured chatter. The Block, I'd heard several regulars say, was like a second home to them. If I measured such things, I'd probably find the overall decibel level in my pub to be lower than usual.

"The kitchen didn't do a special for tonight," Ruby said. "Not that it really matters. People are going to ask for what they want anyway, I suppose."

"Anything wrong?" I asked her.

"I just told you. There's no special to tell people about."

"No, I mean with you. Are you okay?"

"It's just not the same around this place." She spied a beer can that had missed the trash bin and bent to pick it up. "Ah, well. It's only for another month or so."

So I wasn't the only one feeling the absence. Ruby patted my shoulder motherlylike and headed for the kitchen. Normally, the veteran server sashayed when she moved. Today, she walked. Even Cracker was docile, not bothering to circulate and beg for peanuts. Some people say that animals don't have emotions, but I know better.

Wiping down counters, I allowed my thoughts to wander to Morgan and his motivations. Most people, I'd learned, could be evaluated by whatever it was that motivated them. Profiles sketched, relationships discovered, and future courses of action revealed—all based on an individual's motivating factors. In Trish's world, a man's motivation boiled down to a sexual rendezvous with a mistress. The overriding constant in his daily routine was how, where, and when he'd next hook up with her. The window of opportunity could be quite brief, but still, it was the mark's main motivators that allowed Trish to get the goods on a cheating husband and collect a fat fee from the wife.

Of course, the cheating spouse is a simple example. Your average person is motivated by a much wider host of factors. Yet Morgan remained a mystery, and it didn't appear that *anything* motivated him, other than seeing Argo's succeed. I couldn't find anything outstanding or unusual or even commendable about the man, other than he'd been a law abider. No record. No arrests. Not even a traffic violation. Problem was, he didn't have *any* type of record. No social clubs, memberships, favorite vacation spots, or best friends. He drove an average car, had spent many years in an average job earn-ing an average salary, and had lived in an average neighborhood in Dallas. Why he'd decided to relocate his life to run a restaurant—an eatery previously held by a father he hadn't spoken to in years—remained a mystery to me. A shrink I'm not, but maybe Morgan's unremarkable past *was* his motivation. Maybe he'd grown weary of a dull life. The bigger question that spun inside my head was this: What did he know that he wouldn't share with his own sister? He'd obviously stumbled into something perilous, something he meant to keep a secret. Your average citizen would not so easily dismiss a home break-in.

I washed out my bar rag and went to work on the blender base. Sticky dried globs of something whitish had attached themselves to it, like barnacles on a pier post. Probably margarita. I never knew that lime juice and Cointreau, when dried, had concretelike properties. Seemed like the tequila would have counteracted them.

"Is this where the NABs are meeting?"

I straightened up from my scrubbing to see a woman in a tie-dyed turban. I couldn't tell whether she was fifty or eighty. "Excuse me?"

"The New Age Babes. Is this where we're meeting?"

I rinsed and wrung out my rag. "Sorry, ma'am, I think you're in the wrong spot. What's the name of the place you're looking for?"

A fellow NAB appeared next to Tie-Dye. She wore a knee-length flowing skirt and sandals. The hoops in each ear were the size of appetizer plates, and both thumbs were adorned with turquoise rings.

"This is the Block, right?" Tie-Dye said.

I nodded yes. A clump of people filed in and stopped to take inventory. I could tell without asking that they were part of the same group.

"Well, some dude named after a potato is our new president, and he said we could have our next meeting at his place," Thumb Ring told me.

"He told a women's group they could meet here, at the Block?"

"We just voted to start accepting men. That's why we elected the potato man our new president," Tie-Dye explained.

Before I had a chance to dial my number upstairs, Spud came clopping down the stairs, his cane running interference with each step. Wearing a blinding neon yellow hat and an untucked Tommy Bahama shirt, he blended right in with the ladies standing in front of me, hands on their hips. More people ambled in during the time it took my father to reach us, and the buzz of voices fired up as they greeted one another.

"Dammit, Spud, what have you done now?"

"Frannie told me I need to join some social clubs, so I did."

"Haven't you ever heard of the Lions Club? Or the Elks? Maybe the American Legion?"

He limped behind the bar and helped himself to an O'Doul's beer. "I ran into these delightful ladies at the flea market and they recruited me. Me and Bobby and Hal and Trip. All four of us."

His poker buddies. "And you volunteered to be their next *president*?"

Spud threw back his head to chug, gripping the edge of the bar for balance. "I'm on painkillers for my pulled leg muscle, for crying out loud. I ain't thinking real clear."

"Spud, you're as adorable as ever!" Thumb Ring said. "Where should we all sit?"

My father looked at me. His mustache twitched.

"What exactly does your group do, Spud?"

"Beats the hell out of me. I told you, I'm on painkillers," he said. "I might have taken two at the same time yesterday."

"We're a social club, sweet pea." It was Tie-Dye. "Retirees who want to find meaning in their lives."

"We do aura adjustments, tarot cards, astrological sign readings, Reiki therapy, dating nights," Thumb Ring added. "We're going on a cruise in two months. That's what we're doing today. Planning our cruise activities."

I glared at Spud, but like Cracker when he knew he was in trouble, my father wouldn't look at me. I saw Bobby, Hal, and Trip amble into the Block. They wouldn't make eye contact, either.

I clapped my hands. "Okay, all you NABs out there, listen up! Feel free to make yourselves at home over there"—I pointed to a far corner area of tables that were separated from the main dining area by a row of quarter-slot pool tables—"and welcome to the Block. Somebody will be by in a minute to get your drink and food orders."

Tie-Dye patted the top of my hand. "Oh, we always bring our own refreshments to our meetings. But Spud did say that all our drinks would be on the house."

Spud limped back around the bar to join the New Age Babes, still not meeting my look. Not only had he sprung a group on me, but the Block wasn't selling any food. And giving away free drinks.

"You want a veggie wrap, dear? We have plenty for everyone."

EIGHT

Immersing himself into other people's lives—albeit in hourlong chunks—busied Morgan's mind just enough to keep his thoughts off of Maria and her amazing abilities of deception. He'd been a blockhead, he knew. Used like a reliable but boring loaner car while Maria waited for the real thing—the sporty luxury model—to be fixed.

To keep from thinking about what a total loser he was, Morgan gobbled the Green Table's savory slices of life as though they were his favorite dessert: cheesecake. Plain cheesecake, caramel-drizzled cheesecake, chocolate-crust cheesecake, or vanilla-bean-coffee cheesecake. The varieties were endless. He knew that the Johnson couple was trying to spice up their marriage, for example, and that Nina Johnson regularly had intercourse with another man while Jamie Johnson watched. Morgan learned that Realtors from the Max-Sell Agency loathed their broker-in-charge, who happened to be afflicted with an enlarged prostate, and they brutally made fun of him each and every time he left the table to find a urinal. Morgan discovered that another couple of regulars, retirees in the design and printing business, had two grandsons in prison for arson, twins. He found out that a professional women's group of stock market investors were gleaning insider information from one of their members who owned a commercial cleaning business and had after-hours access to professional office buildings. And of course, there were the romantic dinners where futures were planned and dreams discussed. For those who'd already spent a great deal of their lives together, Morgan detected an intimate and overriding familiarity marred by the occasional fight. And gossip about others. Lots of gossip about neighbors, friends, co-workers.

Argo's drew its share of visitors, too, and there was always the random tourist group from Ohio, West Virginia, or a province in Canada who got lucky enough to score a seat at the Green Table because of a last minute cancellation. Morgan didn't find their conversations as tantalizing as those of the regulars, but still, cheesecake was cheesecake. Decadent calories for the mind.

Transients always brought a unique set of dilemmas to the Green Table: which attractions were worth the money, how they hated the thought of going back to work, in-laws and family issues, and guilt about spending so much money on vacation. Inevitably, their conversation always turned to food. The incredible food they were currently spooning into their gullets, a rehash of the food they'd eaten last night, and a discussion over where they might have dinner tomorrow.

Yes, Morgan thought, tourist conversations are usually predictable, and he was glad that the Green Table usually played host only to local VIPs. The current table's occupants weren't VIPs, however. They were parents of an employee. Just ordinary locals, one of whom was bitching instead of enjoying the food. He categorized their conversation as cheesecake of the key lime variety: bittersweet with an overriding aftertaste of sour.

The woman sitting at the Green Table lowered her voice, and Morgan automatically adjusted the volume of his earbud. "I don't care if this is Argo's," she said to her husband. They were the parents of a college student who worked in the kitchen, a kid named Brent who had given them an Argo's gift certificate for their wedding anniversary. "He's a glorified busboy, for goodness' sake. He should be doing something to get ready for a real career, something he can make a living at. Something he can list on a résumé."

Morgan watched the monitor and saw the man pat the woman's forearm. "Brent still has a year of college, Helen. A lot of kids his age work at restaurants. You should be glad that he has a job."

"Beth Plowden's son is a year younger than Brent and he's working an internship at the television station. A paid internship." The woman paused to chew a bite of food. "Even Laura's boy has a good job. He earns enough money to pay for his own apartment."

The soothing tone of the man's voice told Morgan that such conversations between husband and wife were commonplace. "If you want Brent out of the house, we can set him up in an apartment near the campus."

"That's not the point! I just . . . I just wish he had a little ambition. I wish he was more like his older brother."

"Honey, Brent is a great kid and I think we should enjoy this wonderful meal, which, by the way, is thanks to him. I love you."

"I love you, too," she said. "But I doubt Brent actually *paid* for the gift card. I'm sure he got it free since he works here."

Disgusted at her attitude, Morgan abruptly stood, almost knocking over his desk chair. The woman was like a female version of Garland, he thought. She didn't recognize her son's abilities and talents. She was probably always too busy berating the kid, just like Garland used to ride Morgan's ass when he was a teenager. Some people are effervescent, others aren't. But an outgoing or shy personality had absolutely nothing to do with ambition, he knew. Morgan would have bet money that the kid had ambition, and plenty of it. He could tell by Brent's work ethic, even if it was only a part-time job bussing tables. The boy was never late, did his job well, and never complained.

Compelled to intervene, Morgan pulled on his suit jacket and left the tiny office. The door's lock was designed to engage automatically any time the door was closed, and he was careful to check his pocket for the key before pulling it tight. He found Brent unloading one of the commercial dishwashers. The boy was tall and stringy, with red-dish hair and long bangs that almost concealed an acne-riddled fore-head. Once his skin cleared up and his body had a chance to fill out, Morgan thought, Brent would be a fine-looking man. He motioned the employee over, and they walked outside through a rear delivery door. Startled by the appearance of her boss, a server stubbed out a cigarette, popped a mint in her mouth, and hustled back inside. A small piece of wood was wedged into the frame of the door to prevent it from shutting fully. The air was refreshingly cooler than that in the kitchen, and the night sky held an early moon. Much more pleasant than the confines of his office, Morgan thought. Although not nearly as interesting.

"Yes, sir?" the kid said once they'd positioned themselves against the metal railing that lined the loading ramp.

Morgan looked into the kid's face. "What exactly is it that you want to do in life, Brent? Or, at least, what would you like to do for a career after college?"

"Uh, I'm not really, uh, into the restaurant scene," Brent said. "I'm working here to save money. With the tip share and all, it's more than a lot of my friends make, you know what I mean?"

Morgan knew he'd caught the kid off guard and Brent had over-thought the question. He tried again. "I'm not asking because I want you to move up the ranks at Argo's. I'm curious. What do you have planned for the future?"

Brent took a step back and squinted at his boss in the yellowish glow from the building's security lighting. "Honestly?"

"Honestly."

"I'm going to Alaska for eight months to intern for the Department of Fish and Game. They provide housing and everything." The kid studied his shoes for a moment, shuffled his feet. "It's a very cool deal. After that, I'll go through a criminal justice program while I work in their wildlife conservation division. And then I'll be set up to become a park ranger. I can stay in Alaska or apply to work at any state park in the country."

Morgan's instinct had been correct. The woman sitting at the Green Table was a dolt. "That's great. You're going after what you want."

"I guess so. I'm already accepted into the program."

"But you haven't told your parents?"

Brent's expression changed, and Morgan realized his mistake. "Just a guess. I know what it's like to deal with a demanding parent," Morgan explained. "I was afraid to tell my father anything when I was your age."

"Well, in my case, it's my mom. She's totally high-strung. I think I'm going to wait and tell them about Alaska, like maybe right after graduation. Or I guess I could tell my dad and let him tell her."

Morgan opened the loading door and food preparation noises drifted out: long-handled stainless spoons clanking against giant pots, oil sizzling, tableware being stacked, and the strange, barked sentences that constituted kitchen language.

"Not a bad idea." Morgan held the door for Brent and followed the employee back inside. "Maybe you should go somewhere with your father—just the two of you—and you can fill him in on your game plan." He looked into the kid's confused face. "By the way, thanks for the job you do here for us."

"Uh, sure. I mean, yes, sir. You're welcome."

When Morgan reached the Green Table, Brent's parents were finishing dessert.

"Hello, I'm Morgan. I understand you're celebrating twenty-five years together and wanted to stop by to wish you a happy anniversary."

"Oh, thank you," the woman said. "Are you the manager?"

"I'm the owner. But in the restaurant business it's all one and the same." Morgan produced a modest grin. "Manager, server, window washer, you name it." He still didn't enjoy doing it, but he had definitely gotten the hang of polite, meaningless chatter.

"You're Brent's boss, then," she stated.

"Yes, and let me say how thrilled we are to have your son working for us while he's finishing school. He's such a reliable employee, and so smart, too." Morgan lowered his voice for effect. "And how many kids ever treat their parents to a dinner at Argo's? Even with the courtesy discount, the gift certificate cost half his paycheck. He really wanted to make this night special for you."

The woman's already stretched face cinched up more, and her mouth puffed into an "O." Morgan left the table feeling good and realized that he was hungry for the first time in days. Ravenous, in fact.

NINE

Nestled in a vibrating chair and feet soaking in bubbling water, I studied up on the latest fashion trends in *Vogue* magazine—especially the undergarments and lingerie—and tried to ignore Spud and Fran. The day spa had a total of four pedicure chairs, but I had a feeling they were purposely leaving the last chair next to my father empty until Jersey and crew had left the building. It was my regular place for manis and pedis, and I hoped they wouldn't blackball me. After all, I didn't ask Fran to go. She'd invited herself and talked Spud into joining us. It was his first ever pedicure. And everyone within hearing distance knew it.

"That feels like you're trying to yank my toenail off, for crying out loud! What the hell are you doing down there? Using a pair of pliers?"

"Nope," the girl countered without missing a beat. "Somebody borrowed those and didn't give 'em back. These are cuticle trimmers. Very *sharp* cuticle trimmers. One time, I sneezed and snipped off the top of a little toe. Would've gotten fired, too, if I hadn't found it floating in the water."

Good for her. I made a mental note to leave a big tip. If only somebody were around to tip me for putting up with Spud on a daily basis, I'd be a wealthy woman.

I stretched my head from side to side to loosen up tight neck muscles. "Spud, a pedicure is supposed to be calming. Can't you just relax and let her do her thing?"

"Sitting naked on a blender would be more relaxing than this," he muttered. My father has a knack for offering visuals that people immediately wish they hadn't visualized. And he mutters in a way that is akin to shouting. A chuckle came from one of the massage rooms.

Fran's head appeared from behind an oversize fashion magazine. "Take a few five-count calming breaths, sweetie. You know, the kind we do in yoga class."

"That yoga crap landed me in the hospital, for crying out loud." Spud squinted at the girl working on his feet. "Ouch, ouch, and ouch! Can't you go ahead and paint them or whatever you do and let's be done with this torture?"

She smiled up at him. "What color would you like, Mr. Barnes?"

Wearing a pair of headphones—the noise-blocking kind with a hard plastic muff over each ear—my nail tech, Jenna, arrived. "Since you're reading, I figured I'd listen to a little R and B," she said with a wink.

"No problem," I mouthed, wishing she had brought me a pair. I slid my holstered Ruger around the waistband of my jeans to a more comfortable position at the side of my hipbone, instead of toward the back where I normally carry it, and readjusted the hem of my top to cover it.

Jenna caught a glimpse of the gun. She stopped patting dry a foot and removed one ear cuff. "Thought you retired, Jersey."

"I did. Sort of." Months ago, I'd confessed to her that I had every intention of leaving home without a weapon. However, strapping on a hunk of stopping power is part of my daily routine, a habit like flossing and putting in contact lenses and wearing a bra to push up my size D's. "There's a patch for everything else. Nicotine. Waning hormones. Back pain. But they haven't yet made a patch for retired security specialists."

Spud let out a sound like a wounded dog. "Holy bejeeezus! Are you into that maraschino crap, for crying out loud?"

"You mean masochistic crap, baby. Like masochism, the opposite part of sadism. Maraschino is the sweet cherry that goes into a drink."

"What?"

"Never mind," Fran said. "That's okay. It wasn't on the Word-A-Day calendar."

"Remind me to never come back to this toe salon," Spud muttered.

Jenna replaced her headphones and pulled my other foot out of the water. Fran went back to her magazine. Spud crossed his arms and squinted at his nail tech, who threw him an air kiss and kept filing. I'd planned to get a manicure as well but decided that it was more important to get my father out of the salon. My fingernails could wait.

We left the day spa—me in my hearse and Spud on the back of Fran's Vespa—and took off in opposite directions. Gathered inside the glass storefront, a group of heads watched us go.

I decided to pay Morgan a visit, for lack of anything better to do. The front doors were locked when I arrived, but his car was parked in back, next to a Gaffney Enterprises van. The door panel told me that the Gaffneys were in the safe business. I found a rear delivery door cracked open with a wedge of wood and stepped into a sparkling clean industrial kitchen.

"Hello? . . . Morgan?"

I followed the sound of voices to a small office. The office door was the kind with a hydraulic spring at the top, and it was held open with a chair. In jeans and a plaid shirt, a man—presumably the fellow from Gaffney Enterprises—crouched on the floor in front of a two-foot-tall metal safe.

"Morgan, hi, it's Jersey."

Morgan jumped at my voice. "What are you doing here?"

"Just out running errands." I glanced at my watermelon-colored toes that stuck out of wedge sandals. "Thought I'd stop in to say hello."

"I'm trying to get this safe opened," Morgan said through a small laugh. "Couldn't find the combination anywhere."

"Well, it definitely saved me time when you e-mailed a picture," the safe technician said. "You do the research in advance, you know exactly where to drill. This baby has a one-inch steel door and two different bolt systems."

I don't know a thing about safes, but the idea of breaking into one intrigued me. "Is the safe destroyed once you've opened it?"

He repositioned his large frame on the floor. "Naw, not if a person knows what they're doing. Once it's open, I'll put a new dial ring and lock on it and repair the drill hole. Nobody will ever know I was here."

"How long does it take?"

"I'll have this one open in another twenty minutes or so."

"Very cool." I nearly went into bimbette mode to cull information on the safe's contents but stopped myself. Morgan needed to trust me and open up, not blow me off more than he already had.

"You want something to drink?" He walked out of the office, waving me to follow.

"Water would be great, thanks."

We sat at a booth in the dining area, only the drilling noise of metal cutting through metal coming from the kitchen disturbing the silence. Morgan's knee bounced up and down. I asked how everything was going for him. Fine, he told me. Everything was fine. I drank my water. He fidgeted with his glass. I asked if he'd been getting out to explore Wilmington's popular sights. He sure was, he lied. Trish had already told me otherwise. The drilling stopped, and Morgan glanced over his shoulder. He really wanted to know what was inside that safe. So did I. We heard pounding sounds and then silence. More drilling. More silence. We made small talk about Argo's menu until the safe expert appeared.

"She's open. You want to take a look before I install a new dial ring and lock?"

"That's okay," Morgan said, fast. "You've got my credit card info, so just leave an invoice on my desk. Don't worry about fixing it right now."

"Cheaper for you if I go ahead and do it while I'm here. That way you can use the safe. Otherwise, it's a useless steel box."

Morgan shook his head. "I'd rather you come back later. The extra charge is fine."

"Your call." The fellow shrugged and headed into the kitchen. "I'll let myself out the back."

Morgan thanked him and turned back to me. "Look, I don't mean to be rude, but I've got a lot to do. And I'd like to check out the contents of the safe in private. There could be family stuff in there."

I nodded. There could be.

"So if there's nothing else, then . . ." He stood and waited for me to do the same.

Maybe I should have gone with the bimbette cover after all. Then I could have shouted something like "Finders keepers!" and raced him to the open safe. I decided that waiting in the hearse would be the next best thing. At least I could see if he hauled anything out when he left. I stalled a bit longer to see if he'd change his mind, but he didn't and I gave up. When Morgan walked me to the back door, we came face-to-face with a man and a gun, both aimed our way.

"Hold it! That's far enough." The weapon was a blued revolver, maybe a .38. Its owner was a stocky, light-skinned thug type with dirty blond hair, longish and tucked behind the ears. Well, one ear, anyway. The other one was half gone from the lobe up, as though somebody bit it off. A tattoo of a clock without hands surrounded by some sort of symbol—the kind of crude prison artwork created with a makeshift tattoo gun and ink from a ballpoint pen—decorated one forearm. His grip on the gun told me he was quite familiar with how to use it.

Hands up, I made my eyes go wide and stuck out my boobs. Morgan swayed and caught himself against a storage rack of foodstuffs. "Who are you?"

"An old friend of your father's," Earless said, and shrugged the gun my way. "Who's she?"

"Nobody." Morgan's face paled, as much as a black man's can. "Just a woman I know."

Earless's eyes roved over me and he grinned. "Like father, like son. You both go for the white meat."

"My mother wasn't a piece of meat." Morgan emitted something near to a growl and charged Earless. The man backhanded Morgan across the face with the butt of the handgun. Morgan went down but kept talking. "Don't talk about my mother that way!"

"Rosemary was a damn good salesperson, too. Your mother knew how to work the rich bitch crowd, I'll give her that."

Blood ran down Morgan's chin from a cut lip. He pushed himself off the ground. "What are you talking about?"

"Shut up and walk over there to that cooler, nice and easy. Both a you."

Morgan's entire body shook. "What are you talking about, working the rich bitch crowd? Answer me!"

The gun shrugged, just barely. "You really don't know?"

"Know what?"

Earless nodded to himself. "To the cooler. Now!"

The thug was going to lock us in the freezer? Pulleeze. He'd been watching too many bad-guy movies. Walking to the cooler, Morgan swayed but kept going, planting each foot carefully like a drunk. After kicking off my sandals, I followed with bare feet, wondering if he was an alcoholic. I hadn't smelled any booze on his breath. Strangely, his equilibrium was anything but settled. Maybe he had a medical condition.

"Go ahead, open it," Earless demanded. "Doubt you'll freeze to death. Somebody will find you when the restaurant opens."

Pretending to reach for the walk-in's lever handle, I spun and shoved his extended arm across his body—stepping into him so he wouldn't have the advantage of leverage—and forced his wrist into a reverse twist. In an instant, I had his gun. I swung open the cylinder, dumped the six rounds, and passed the empty gun to Morgan.

"What the hell?" Earless came at me with balled fists. I sidestepped the first punch and threw a heel into his chin. His head snapped back. He came at me again. My next kick made contact with his kneecap, and he went down, pulling another revolver out of his boot. I trained the Ruger on him, but he was quick and we ended up in a standoff. Keeping the muzzle pointed at me, he crabscooted backward on his butt. When he reached the back delivery door, he rolled through and slammed it shut. I went after him but couldn't get the door open. He'd wedged something under the bottom to hold it shut from the outside. It was the thick metal type of door that would have broken a bone had I tried to kick it open. By the time I went through Argo's front foyer and around the building, Earless was gone.

"Holy crap," Morgan breathed, catching up. "That was amazing, how you took his gun away and fought him!"

"No need to bruise my hands with a fistfight." We went inside through the back door. I found my sandals and slid back into them.

Morgan handed me the stranger's gun. "Who was that guy?"

"Why don't you tell me?"

"I swear, I have no idea. Maybe he saw the Gaffney van pull out and knew I was still here and wanted to rob me."

Earless's gun was an old .38 special that looked like it might have been purchased cheap at a pawnshop. Or stolen. I'd give it to Dirk and let his department send it through ballistics. That's the great thing about having a friend on Wilmington PD's payroll—getting things done without too many questions. "Morgan, I can certainly pretend to be an idiot when the situation warrants. But trust me, I'm not."

He breathed deep and emptied his lungs with a lengthy sigh. "I can only figure that Garland had some sort of relationship with him. And he obviously knew my mother, or wanted me to think he did."

"What do you suppose he meant about her working the rich crowd?"

Morgan made a clueless gesture with his hands.

"Let's go see what's in that safe," I said. "If it's private family business, then I'll leave you to it. If not, you might need my help."

"I don't need anybody's help!"

Arms crossed over my chest, I waited. A fat drop of blood rolled down his chin and plopped to the floor. His gaze followed it. "Okay, maybe I do need help. But I have no idea what I need help with. I don't know why somebody broke into my apartment or what they were looking for. I don't know why somebody searched my car. I don't know anything about my father, except that he ran this restaurant and everybody loved him. That's all I hear. How much everybody misses him. And my mother? Her thing was the garden club and volunteering. Working the 'rich bitch' crowd comment makes absolutely no sense. She was a schoolteacher, and when she retired from that, she helped Garland with the restaurant. She greeted people, and everybody loved her, too. Everybody adored both of them. They were like two of the most popular people on the planet. But they're dead. And other than restaurant employees, the only person I knew in Wilmington has moved back to Texas to live with her ex-boss. So she's dead, too, as far as I'm concerned. I don't go out, I don't have any friends, and I don't know who the jerk with gun was or what he wanted. I'm only trying to live my life and run this damn restaurant!"

Breathing hard, Morgan lurched forward and nearly fell. He found a clean dishrag and held it to his bleeding mouth.

Ruger drawn in case Earless had plans to return, I headed to the safe, staying close to cover. Spent of words, Morgan followed. The safe's door was open about an inch. Careful not to add my own prints to those already on it, I swung open the thick door with my elbow. The inside held two shelves. Both were empty. The entire safe was empty, except for a square of scrap carpet placed in the bottom. I found Gaffney's invoice on the desk, dialed the cell phone number, and asked if he could tell me the contents of the safe he'd just opened. Earless could have swiped something after the safe tech left, before he'd tried to put me and Morgan in the cooler.

"Lady, the contents of a safe isn't my business. I didn't even pull the door all the way open because he didn't want me to repair it."

"But was there anything in there? Papers or boxes or anything?"

"Like I said, it ain't my business to pore through somebody's belongings. I've been in this business probably more years than you've been alive, and if you're trying to accuse me of taking—"

"No, no," I interrupted. "That's not it. Did you see anyone else in the restaurant or parking lot when you left Argo's?"

"No. Everything was quiet. Empty parking lot, except for a hearse."

Morgan fell into the desk chair and shuffled stacks of newspapers, as though covering up something he didn't want me to see. I sat in front of the open safe and removed the loose remnant of carpeting at the bottom. Nothing there but a solid metal base and two round holes, where the safe could be bolted to the floor from the inside. That would definitely keep somebody from hauling the thing away with a hand dolly, but Garland hadn't bothered to bolt it down. I was about to replace the carpet when I spotted a tiny round pill. Half the size of an aspirin tablet, light blue, scored on one side, numbers on the other. I asked Morgan for a plastic bag and dropped in the tablet. Next, I removed both shelves. Both were covered with glued-on felt all the way around, except for the back edge. The top shelf was solid wood, about an inch thick. The middle one was the same thickness but made with two sheets of thin plywood, hollow in the center and open at the back. A large manila envelope was stuffed inside.

Inside was a handwritten list of names. Some had corresponding phone numbers. Beside the numbers were two- and three-letter abbreviations: PT, X, WL, and so on. Morgan took the papers, held by a snap clip, and flipped through.

"It's my mother's handwriting." His voice was soft, barely audible. "I'd recognize it anywhere. She used to send handwritten cards. Short notes to tell me to have a happy week, or to let me know she was thinking of me." He flipped through the pages again. "Some of these names . . . I'd have to check to be sure, but I think they're regular customers. I recognize maybe half of them, anyway."

I unfolded my legs and got off the floor. "Do you want my help to figure this thing out?"

"I don't know anything about you."

"And you *are* on familiar terms with plenty of other people in town who can help? Lend their expertise? Protect you? Find out why a man just tried to lock you in the walk-in?"

"Okay, okay. I guess you're right." His palms went to his face, covering what I suspected to be a frightened expression. "I admit it. I need help."

"Now that that's settled, you must quit lying to me."

Morgan's hands fell back to the desk as though his muscles were too tired to hold them up any longer. "I haven't lied to you, not really. Anyway, I can't pay you. It's not like I have a spare chunk of cash lying around. I'm still paying off the damn ring my ex took. And Garland and Mom's estate hasn't been settled yet."

I sat on a corner of the desk and studied his eyes for a moment to make sure he was listening to me. "This job, Morgan, is a favor for your sister. I want to help you, and I'm here for you. But for this to work, you have to tell me everything you know."

Eyes damp, he nodded.

I called Lieutenant Dirk. "I'm at Argo's restaurant and a Caucasian male just tried to rob the owner at gunpoint." The robbing part was a lie, but much easier than trying to explain the truth. "He took off, but I've got his gun. Maybe you want to shoot a bullet through it, see if there are any ballistics matches in the system? And if you could send somebody with a fingerprint kit, that would be great, too. Because he may have stolen something out of a small safe. Might be able to pick up a usable print from the door of the safe. That's all I've got. No name, no vehicle, no tag number. Oh yeah, and the guy is missing about half of his left ear."

"You bite it off?" Dirk said, half-serious.

"Really, Lieutenant. You should know that I don't scratch, pull hair, or bite. Well, not during a fight, anyway."

He made a snortlike sound.

"Will you do it?" I asked.

"The restaurant owner will need to file a report of a break-in."

"No problem."

Dirk agreed that he would run the weapon through the system and send someone to dust Morgan's safe for prints.

Meanwhile, Morgan was in a cooperative mood. Even if it was fear induced, I figured I might as well take advantage. "Let's go check out your folks' house, shall we?"

"Why?"

"You got anything better to do right now?"

He said he didn't.

"Good," I said, "because we might find something that will tell us what your mother and father were up to."

I offered to drive. Morgan wasn't overly taken aback at the sight of the hearse. He was still recovering from his eventful morning. We'd barely gotten to Oleander Drive when my mobile buzzed. It was Trish.

"That dark blue Nissan Murano? The one I caught tailing Morgan? Think I've found him again, except this time the Nissan is wearing a South Carolina tag. Probably another prop plate. Male driver, nobody else in the vehicle."

"Excellent," I told her. "Where is he?"

"Right behind you," she said. "Tailing Morgan, I'd guess."

TEN

I spotted the Murano about three cars back. Its sole occupant had both ears. I turned into a convenience store, pulled up next to a gas pump, and idled until the tail pulled in. He drove to the back corner of the lot where a coin-operated generator sold compressed air. After a beat, he got out and pretended to be checking his tire pressure.

I gunned it—as much as a hearse can be gunned—and pulled alongside the Murano, blocking him in. Unless he wanted to plow down the air compressor or back over thick shrubbery, he was going to have to talk to me. Tire gauge in hand, he stood, acted surprised. Produced a friendly smile. A charming smile, really, that filled an attractive face subtly covered with a four- or five-day beard growth.

After instructing Morgan to remain in the corpse caddy, I went to check out the driver. His hair and beard was a beachy blond, the natural kind of color caused by either genetics or lots of sunshine. Hazel green eyes that reflected the sunlight as though they held a bunch of tiny mirrors. Tall, lanky frame, wide shoulders. Strong hands and neatly trimmed, clean nails. Dressed in jeans, a good-quality T-shirt covered by a lightweight sports coat, and cowboy boots. The type of guy who'd help an elderly lady with her groceries or offer to carry her luggage in an airport.

I showed him my basic smile, the noncommittal, hard-to-read one. "Having a problem with your tires, are you?"

"Not at all," he said. "Out for a drive and noticed a little vibration in the steering, so I decided to check my tire pressure. Did you need some air?"

"I just got some air, thanks. A lot of *hot air,* that is."

"Excuse me?" He dropped the pressure gauge into a pocket and ran a hand across his chest. He was carrying concealed in a shoulder holster and subconsciously wanted to make sure it was there. I knew the move well because I'd caught myself doing the same thing in the past.

"Why are you following the owner of Argo's restaurant?" I asked.

The smile returned, and it was as charming as the first time he showed it. "Who are you?"

"You go first," I said.

"None of that ladies first stuff with you, huh? Must be one of those feminist types."

"Give me a break." *You jerk*, I almost added.

"And easily riled up, too."

I wanted to say something witty that would erase his grin, but nothing came to mind. Something about his attitude *had* riled me up. And that pissed me off. I just looked at him and hoped my face was more impassive than I felt.

"Okay, you win," he said. "My name is Brad."

"And your boss is . . ."

"Whoa, wait a minute there, babe. I went first, remember? It's your turn."

"Did you just call me 'babe'?"

"Give me a name, then." His stance and body language slid into smart-ass mode, just like mine can do when I want to get under someone's skin. "You don't," he continued, "I've got a lot more than *babe* in my politically incorrect vocabulary arsenal. Muffin. Sweet cakes. Honey. Cook—"

"Jersey," I cut him off, wondering if a left hook to his jaw would bring other names to mind.

He nodded. "You're the owner of the hearse, then. Unusual choice for an everyday car, Jersey Barnes. A bit grim reaperish, if you ask me."

So he'd already run my tag, probably when he first saw me and Morgan get into the wagon at Argo's. Which meant that he was either a cop or somebody else who had quick access to the DMV's database.

"I didn't ask you," I said. "And at least I don't drive around with bogus tags. How often do you change the fake plates on the Murano, anyway?"

"Wait a minute. *You've* been following *me?*" He pointed to the hearse. "In that thing?"

He didn't need to know that it was Trish who'd picked him up on the radar. I'd take the credit. I showed him my cocky smile. "There was even a funeral procession behind me. Police escort with the flashing lights and everything. Amazing you never picked up on the fact."

The grin left his face.

Finally. At least I had that. It was some satisfaction.

"Now that we've officially introduced ourselves to each other, I really need to get going," he said, real businesslike. "Would you mind moving your hearse out of my way?"

I took off my sunglasses and looked up at him, doing my best not to squint in the bright sun. "Yes."

"Yes what?"

"Yes, I would mind. The corpse caddy is staying right where it is until you tell me why you are following my client."

"I'm trying to be civilized here." Brad ran a hand over his almost-beard. "This encounter can get unpleasant if you'd prefer."

I dropped my shades back into place and let loose with a wave of laughter as though he'd just delivered the funniest joke I'd ever heard. At the gas pumps, a man filling up his tank looked our way. From the passenger seat, his buddy stared openly through a rolled-down window. Good. Brad needed to know that I wasn't afraid of attracting a bit of attention.

Once I managed to stop pretend laughing, I gave him a flirtatious touch on the arm. "*Unpleasant?* Now why on earth would you want to go and ruin a perfectly nice afternoon with *unpleasantness?* Especially in front of all these nice witnesses?"

Shaking my head, I laughed again just for show and ended the display by smoothing my low-cut cotton top, tugging it back into place. Brad's eyes stopped on my boobs for a split second before they caught a glimpse of the holster near the small of my back, beneath a linen jacket. It's my standard everyday attire: shorts, slacks, or a skirt paired with a scoop-neck top and some sort of lightweight jacket to cover a paddle holster at the waist. My collection of designer jackets is almost as impressive as my drawers full of racy lingerie. A girl's got to have some vices. Besides beer.

"Personally," I continued, "I'm not in the mood to shoot somebody today, Brad. It would be good if we could both keep our weapons holstered and avoid any *unpleasant* encounters."

The smile lit up his face again. He was great at playing it cool. "May I see your ID?"

"Show me yours and I'll show you mine."

He unfolded a leather wallet, produced a card. Brad Logan worked for the Drug Enforcement Agency.

I went to the hearse, found my wallet, and handed him a piece of plastic.

"Your identification is a *driver's license?*"

"I work for myself," I said. "Oh, wait a minute. I'm actually retired. So I don't even work for myself any longer." I pointed to my passenger, still sitting in the hearse. "Just helping out the brother of a friend."

Brad excused himself and walked out of hearing distance to make a phone call. Three calls, actually, if I counted correctly. He came back to stare at me, arms folded across his chest.

I gave him the once-over, blatantly, like men had done to me a thousand times. "Let me guess. You've just learned that I own the Barnes Agency in Wilmington."

"Already knew that. But now I know that you were a marine MP and you did a stint with the government. Pay grade, duties, and name of agency are, unfortunately, unavailable. I can probably find out, but it would be easier if you tell me."

"Basically, I did the same thing you do. The only difference was that I dealt with terrorists while you deal with drug suppliers."

"Hmmm," he said. "They're often one and the same."

"Yep."

Brad sized me up. And back down. It was appraising, not leering. At least he had some class. "You're like a female version of me. Too bad we never got the chance to work together. Could have been fun."

"Yeah, well, my assignments took me all over the place. Besides, as I said, I'm retired. And you, well, you're just a young thing, *babe.*"

"Touché, Jersey Barnes." His arms dropped to his sides. "Shall we meet somewhere to talk after you finish up with your client?"

"Are you going to keep following us?" I seriously doubted that I could lose him while driving the meat wagon.

"Depends. Where you going?"

"To take a look around Morgan's father's house."

Brad shook his head. "Nah, I'd rather go grab a bite of lunch. I've already been through Garland's place. Nice pad."

We agreed to meet for dinner at Dock Street Oyster Bar, one of my favorite downtown joints, and I had no doubts that Brad would show. I pulled out of the gas station and waved good-bye through the sunroof. As I said, it's a tricked-out hearse.

"What the heck was that all about?" Morgan said.

I told him that Brad was a drug enforcement agent.

"What does he want with me? I don't get it. I'm an accountant who inherited a restaurant. I didn't ask for any of this. Hell, I don't even know what *this* is."

"Neither do I," I told Morgan. "But I'm always up for a good challenge."

Brad was right about Garland's home being nice, and I told him so when I saw him later. We literally parallel-parked alongside the street at the same time, dropped coins into our corresponding meters, and walked the few blocks to Dock Street Oyster Bar together, like a real couple on a real date. The server tried to seat us in a corner booth, but neither of us would sit with our backs to the entrance. We ended up sitting side by side, in the same bench seat, but decided we looked stupid. Plus, it was difficult to talk. We moved to the bar area, where we both had a clear view of our surroundings, and asked for ice waters and beers. I ordered a dozen steamed oysters with a side of garlic bread, and Brad opted for the jerk-spiced grouper.

"When did you toss Garland's house?" I asked.

Brad reminded me that anything we discussed was off the record and asked for an assurance that I wouldn't muddle up his investigation. I assured him.

"We'd just gotten a warrant to search the home the day, he, uh . . . passed away," Brad said. "We've been tracking a pharmaceutical drug ring for more than a year and had reason to suspect that the owner of Argo's was involved by association. We'd identified several end users who ate at the restaurant on a regular basis. Initially, we thought an Argo's bartender or server might be involved, but by process of elimination, I ruled that out."

"And Morgan?"

Our waters and beers arrived, and after declining the mugs, we paused conversation to down the cold water before reaching for the beers. Our actions happened in unison, as though we'd practiced.

"Good grief," I said, "you're a male—"

"Version of you," he finished my sentence, and threw the dazzling smile at me. "I was thinking the exact same thing about you. We're very much alike, I'd bet."

We clinked the mouths of our beer bottles together.

Brad studied my face for a beat. "Okay, here's the deal. We—my boss—could care less about the individuals who are getting prescription drugs to have a little fun. At least when it comes to criminal prosecution. We want the sellers. The traffickers. If we can nail down one of the middlemen, it will lead us to the top dog. That's my big picture. That's my job, to track this thing to the top."

"How does this involve Morgan?"

"I'm not sure it does. We don't know whether or not Morgan is aware of the drugs that were filtering through Argo's. But we are certain that Argo's is a link in the puzzle." Brad blew out a long, heavy sigh. "This is turning out to be the most frustrating case I've ever worked. Believe it or not, it's actually easier to bust people dealing cocaine, pot, or methamphetamines. The prescription drug market— painkillers and such—is a whole different ball game."

I took a swallow of my Red Stripe, noticing with amusement that our bottles had exactly the same amount of beer left in them. We even drank at the same rate. "Out of curiosity, where do the pills come from? I thought it's a regulated industry."

"Unethical overseas pharmacies. Burglaries of pharmaceutical hot zones by employees of nursing homes, medical clinics, mom-and-pop drugstores. Pilfering from military medical supplies and hospitals. Valid prescriptions written by crooked doctors. Even individuals. Another DEA agent found a caregiver who, using her employer's health insurance card and a fake driver's license, was visiting walk-in clinics. She'd see six or eight different doctors in one day and fill prescriptions for muscle relaxers and painkillers, paying in cash. She had a standing group of customers ready to buy the pills from her."

"Wow. And I thought our drug problem in the U.S. was mainly drug cartels."

He shrugged. "This is just another piece of the pie, and I happened to draw the short stick to get this assignment."

Our food came and we dug in, not talking for a few minutes. We may have made food appreciation noises.

"I can't give you any further details," Brad told me. "I do think Morgan is clean. But there may still be activity at the restaurant, and weak though it is, it's a thread."

The garlic bread was perfect, and my oysters were fresh and tasty. I shelled one and dunked it in cocktail sauce. "Why not tell Morgan what's going on and enlist his help?"

"I didn't want to put him in unnecessary danger," Brad said. "Of course, now that he knows DEA is keeping an eye on him, who knows what could happen? If he mentions something to the wrong person, one of two things will happen. Either the person bolts and I lose my thread, throwing yet another dead end at a yearlong investigation. Or Morgan unwittingly puts himself on the firing line."

"Far as I know, he keeps to himself. No friends, no girlfriend, doesn't socialize with the restaurant help. To play it safe, though, I'll stress to Morgan the importance of keeping quiet about this."

"Thanks."

"You're welcome," I said. "I wonder what Morgan plans to do

once the estate is settled. It's just him and his sister, and from what I gather, they stand to inherit a big chunk of change."

"I doubt it."

"You doubt what?"

Brad finished chewing a bite of fish, swallowed, wiped his mouth, drank water. "Let's just say that Morgan won't be getting an inheritance anytime soon."

"His father was broke? Or in debt?" I'd checked the tax records, and Garland's house didn't have any liens on it. And the place was amazing. Loaded with collectibles, artwork, and antiques. Not to mention a room full of wines from around the world. Morgan made me take several bottles as a thank-you gift for my help. I'm not big on wine, but a few of my friends are. And in my world, freebies are a good thing.

"No, no, it's nothing like that." Brad shook his head. "I've already told you much more than I should have, so now it's your turn. What is your involvement with Morgan?"

I told him that I was friends with the judge and she'd enlisted me to introduce her brother to Wilmington and basically keep an eye on him while he got settled. The explanation sounded reasonable enough to my ears, but Brad didn't seem to buy it. He gave me a look.

"Hey." I gave him a head tilt. "It's the truth." *Sort of.*

I felt sure that Brad was withholding pertinent information, so I didn't feel too bad about holding out on him. He didn't need to know about the one-eared man. He certainly didn't need to know what I'd found in the safe, which I now decided might be a list of Argo's drug customers. And I didn't mention to Brad that somebody had searched Morgan's apartment and car. Heck, for all I knew, it was Brad who'd done it. We changed the subject and ordered two more beers and finished our meals and split a single piece of pie.

Dock Street had filled up by the time we were contentedly full. We gave up our table and went for a walk. The fall days were growing shorter, and the post-sunset hour had thrown a pinkish cast over the river. If we kept going, we'd come across the Block. I wasn't up for bringing Brad to my bar. My home. He seemed to sense that I didn't care to walk farther. We found an empty bench and settled into it, staring at the Cape Fear, the glow of lampposts and storefronts casting a golden glow over the evening.

"Tell me about you, Jersey."

I gave him a sideways look. "You've already done a background. What else do you want to know?"

"Cut me some slack here." He turned his head to look at me. "You know what I mean."

I looked ahead, leaving him to stare at my profile. "I retired from the government to open my own agency. Then I got great people to run the agency and I retired from that. I'm hoping to play and enjoy my retirement, but I'm finding it difficult to leave home without a weapon. I love this area. My father lives with me, in an apartment that is attached to mine. I have a white Labrador retriever named Cracker. I like to work out. I drink a lot of beer but am trying to cut down. My favorite food is everything. And I have an unreasonable fear of dead people." I smiled. "That's pretty much it."

Brad laughed. "Are you married?"

"No."

"Engaged?"

"No."

"Committed?"

Was I committed? I wanted to be, if Ox and I could keep the special bond we've had since high school without allowing sex to get in the way. If we could be together romantically, as a couple, and not dominate each other. Separately, we complemented each other in a beautiful way. Together, either we'd meld into something incredible that was off the charts, or the relationship would turn volatile and explode into a hundred pieces that could never be repaired.

"It's complicated," I finally said.

ELEVEN

Morgan didn't know if the hidden microphone had served its purpose for his father, but it had certainly opened his eyes. He was glad he hadn't destroyed it on first impulse. Truth was a good thing, and the tiny wireless microphone in the Green Table's candleholder had served up the truth about Maria. Now it was time to set things right and remove the peppercorn-size electronic. Especially since a drug enforcement agent was snooping around.

Each time Morgan made an early morning trip to Argo's, though, he got sidetracked. Once he'd even unfolded the ladder and pulled out a couple of tools. Maybe the phone rang, or he might have gone shopping for new restroom light fixtures, or perhaps some tables in the main dining area needed rearranging. He couldn't recall, specifically, what diverted his attention every time he arrived at Argo's with good intentions. Like any addict, he justified his lack of action by thinking of the next day. The Green Table's secret wasn't going anywhere. He could always get rid of it tomorrow, in the day's maiden hours. Tomorrows were a great thing. They kept coming.

Meanwhile, he found himself ensconced in the small office more and more. A sympathetic friend, the office was his second home, his private domain. He felt hidden and safe from the world. He made it a point to be seen coming and going from Argo's and sometimes told employees that he'd be out running errands when he was really nestled in his swiveling leather desk chair like a moviegoer playing hooky from work, snatching a break from reality. He came and went through the rear delivery door, and when the restaurant buzzed at full capacity, everybody was too busy to pay him much attention anyway. The thrill, the high, the sheer addictiveness of eavesdropping on strangers, had crept up in baby steps until it enslaved him like an opiate. The gratifying rush was the high point of his day. Some conversations were more interesting than others, but all were good escapes. Even the garden-variety birthday dinner groups proved more interesting than his own life.

"Have either of you ever wondered what would have happened if there were air bags back then?" Morgan heard one of the doctors say. He thought it might be Jonathan but couldn't be sure. It was one of the Divine Image Group doctors. He squinted at the overhead view on the monitor. Yep, Jonathan, the one with the bald head who was the psychiatrist. The one who probably made his living by matching his patients' symptoms to the current popular three-letter abbreviated disorder of the day. The three men were in for their usual Friday night meal. On Fridays, Morgan knew, the Divine Image Group closed shop at three o'clock. Which gave the doctors plenty of time to have a drink somewhere before hitting Argo's when the doors opened at five.

"Man, oh man, this fish is good," Leo said. "The only fish my wife knows how to cook is salmon, and she smashes that up into patties that taste like plasterboard."

"I'm serious," Jonathan said. "Think about it."

Checking the monitor, Morgan noticed that the man's food hadn't been touched, although he was near the bottom of his third Scotch and soda. "Simple air bags could have changed everything when that car ran off the road and wrecked. If the driver had been cushioned"— he had trouble pronouncing the word—"he wouldn't have been so disoriented. And if that were the case, he might've shot us straight out. Without bothering to talk first."

The third member of the Divine Image Group, Michael, refilled wineglasses. Ordinarily the server would have hovered near enough to know exactly when the glasses were less than a quarter full. But earlier, the group had told Deanna they'd like privacy during their meal. "If you want to bring up today's technology," Michael said, "what about fiber samples and DNA matching and all that high-tech forensics garbage? Surely they'd have found something to tie us to the scene. For that matter, what about 911? If everybody had cell phones back then, one of us would have called for help right off the bat."

"That might have been a good thing, if the cops came." Jonathan's chin arched up as he waited for the last of the Scotch to roll into his mouth. He spotted Deanna and motioned her with an empty lowball glass. "Maybe then we wouldn't be in this mess."

Leo scraped up the last flakes of salmon with a chunk of bread and stuffed the wad in his mouth. "Yeah, well, we wouldn't be where we are, either. I rather like where I am. I like my Mercedes and my mountain house and the fact that my wife doesn't have to work and my boy is going to Princeton and my girl will be going to Europe next summer with her senior class. If you want to start playing the weepy what-if game, take a minute to stop and think about how much we've given to this community."

The table quieted when the men saw Deanna approach. She served a fresh Scotch, refilled water glasses, scraped crumbs from the table, cleared plates, disappeared.

"Whoopee," Jonathan said. Thick and slurred, the single word traveled slowly through the thin wire in the ceiling. Morgan adjusted his earbud. "I listen to pampered people bitch about their lives and dole out antidepressants. And then you two give them new noses and suck out their fat. How . . . *meaningful*."

"What we give our patients is *confidence*, and don't you ever forget that." Leo's finger went up. "And anyway, as far as giving back, I was talking about all the donations we make for good causes. New playground equipment at three parks. State-of-the-art kennels at the animal rescue. Landscaping around the low-income housing. The orthodontics program for needy kids. Shall I keep going?"

On the monitor, it looked like the boozed-up doctor shook his head no.

"He's right, John," Michael said. "You're a good doctor, and you help your patients deal with their lives. And Leo and I are good cosmetic surgeons. We make our patients happy. The three of us do more for this community than any medical group I'm aware of." He downed some water. "Besides, it'll all be over soon. Another year and we can get out."

Leo burped, wiped his mouth, drank some wine, shook his head as though confused. "I still can't figure out how he found us. It's never made any sense. How did he know it was us, and how did he track us down after all these years?"

"You sound like a damn broken record," the shrink said. "How many times are you going to bring that up? How did he know? How did he find us? How did it happen? How, how, how?"

Leo's head rolled back and to one side in a "whatever" gesture. "It's a valid question. It was pitch black that night. Nobody saw us. The only two witnesses were dead. It doesn't make sense."

Jonathan sucked some Scotch and slammed the glass onto the table. Morgan jumped in his office chair.

"My ID card. It was my ID card, okay? My freakin' student ID card."

Michael's voice dropped a few octaves. "What are you talking about, John?"

"The next day, after it happened? I couldn't find my student ID. It was in my shirt pocket the night before, at the party. I know I had it. And I searched everywhere. Your car. The frat house. Our apartment. Everywhere."

"Son of a bitch," Leo said. "You were staggering drunk that night. You were bent over puking your guts out, you drank so much."

"It must have fallen out of my pocket," Jonathan said, sounding far away.

"He had to have been following that car, then, when we ran it off the road," Leo said. "He saw the wreck and stopped, but we'd already gone."

"Yes," Jonathan agreed, as though he'd already been through the scenario a thousand times in his head. "He caught up with the car all right. The money was gone, but he found my ID."

Riveted, Morgan held his breath.

"And he waited all these years to come after us," Leo said. "Son of a bitch, John."

The shrink swirled his melting ice, tried to get the remaining traces of liquor from them. "So sue me. *I'm* not the genius who took the duffel bag."

Leo sighed, and the sound seemed to last forever in Morgan's ear- bud. "Look," Leo reasoned. "We're all in this together. Another year, everything will be paid back. We'll be done with this lunatic. We'll get out and get on with our lives."

Jonathan laughed, but it was an ugly sound. "If either one of you thinks it's going to be that easy, you're both idiots. He might not let us out."

TWELVE

I held out the pill to the pharmacist, the single light blue pill I'd found in Morgan's office safe. The fellow seemed friendly enough, and the pharmacy chain's advertisements boasted a caring, helpful staff. Maybe their TV commercials were true.

"I was hoping that you could identify this for me," I said. "It has numbers there, on one side."

"Is this one of your prescriptions?"

I gave him a story about my elderly father combining his prescriptions into a weekly pill dispenser box—I'd just spotted such a device hanging on a counter display—and explained that he'd thrown away the original prescription bottles.

"Are his prescriptions filled here?"

"Yes." I figured it to be the right answer.

"I'd be happy to pull up his information and help you out," the pharmacist said. "But your father will need to be here. The data on an individual is confidential."

I argued that I didn't want confidential information. I only needed a single pill identified. He spouted another roadblock answer.

"Your television commercials are completely wrong." I snatched the tablet off the counter.

I found another drugstore two blocks away, one whose pharmacist was much more accommodating. She examined my pill, flipped through a reference book, and was back at the counter in less than five minutes. "It appears to be alprazolam, one milligram. Generic substitute for Xanax."

"What's that for?"

"Mostly anxiety or conditions of nervousness."

I looked at the single pill. "Prescription only?"

"Absolutely," she said. "It's a controlled substance."

"So this is something that people might abuse?"

She put the pill back in its plastic bag and handed it to me. "People can abuse pretty much any drug known, including over-the-counter stuff. Alprazolam is one that can be addictive, like painkillers."

I chewed on that information as I drove to the Barnes Agency. Had Garland been dealing prescription drugs to restaurant customers before he died and storing his product in the small safe? If so, that could explain the list—they were his buyers. But the earless thug had mentioned the wife, and the list was in Rosemary's handwriting. Rosemary passed away a year ago. Brad said the DEA had been working on his current case for more than a year. The time frame fit. But if Garland or Rosemary were selling dope, where had the drugs come from? I recalled the photo in Morgan's office. Garland had the appearance of a man who could be into anything: name-brand silk shirt, smooth black skin, great smile, bushy eyebrows over mischievous eyes. An ex-athlete, college professor, banker, or crime lord. But Morgan's mother looked like a well-kept, classy woman with warm eyes. Rosemary had one appearance, and it wasn't that of a drug pusher.

Then again, I know as well as anybody that looks can be deceiving. During my days with SWEET, it was my job to deceive.

I thought again of the blue pill. It could have come from a valid prescription, written by the family physician. But who would keep a personal prescription inside a locked safe? Spud's massive portfolio of drugs was kept in plain view, on the kitchen counter.

I pulled in to find the agency's small lot packed with nine vehicles. Four belonged to Rita, JJ, Trish, and Andy. I didn't recognize the others. I opened the front door to lots of happy chatter. And moaning. The latter sounds came from a woman sprawled facedown on Andy's massage table. He worked on her lower back.

"Hiya, boss," he said, glancing up. "You here for the party?"

"I retired, remember? I'm not the boss of anything. And I wasn't aware of a party."

Andy leaned back and made a face as though he'd been hit with a mean comment. My response probably had sounded petty, defensive. But it was true. Nobody had invited me. I felt left out and was reminded of how much I missed having Ox around. Probably I was a different person without him. Probably I was a downer to be around. No wonder they hadn't told me about the party.

"Don't mind her," JJ said from behind a desk. Her feet were up and she sipped something from a champagne flute. Real glass. Probably real champagne. "All those shuffleboard games at the senior center have made her grouchy. Jersey hates to lose."

"Ha, ha." I scanned the front office to see several unfamiliar faces, all women, all smiles and gossip, as though they were at an Avon party.

"We've started having a little get-together every few weeks," Rita said, and introduced the strangers to me. "We sample wines. We let Andy work his magic. Everyone gets fifteen minutes on the table."

"Really." Rita's management style certainly differed from mine. On the other hand, billing hours had remained steady since I'd turned over control. And my two partners certainly looked relaxed. Not stressed, considering the types of clients and assignments the agency takes on. Maybe the addition of Andy to our small team had been a good thing.

I eyed Trish. "Have you had your fifteen minutes of shame yet?"

She nodded, a circular sort of neck roll that resembled a dance move. "Just finished. He worked on my shoulders. I feel like rubber."

"Okay, Gumby. Think you can focus long enough to discuss business? You know, that stuff you do called *contract work,* for which I pay you? The reason we are meeting here"—I checked my watch—"in five minutes?"

"You rarely ever pay me in actual cash," Trish reminded me. "Personal use of the agency's old clunker of a surveillance van is hardly monetary compensation. For that matter, it seems that every time I climb behind the wheel, the fuel gauge is sitting on empty. Hello? Have you looked at the gas prices lately? I'm actually *paying* to work for you each time I fill the tank."

We moved into the blue room, out of earshot. I noticed the addition of new toys: a lightweight night vision scope, a wiretap detector, and a colorful sports watch. A pang of curiosity made my fingers twitch, and I picked up the watch. It was a videocamera. The stem to set the time was actually a miniature lens, and the square faceplate was the screen. I'd always loved checking out new gadgets and weapons. I supposed I still could, although it didn't make much sense to be up-to-date on the latest covert camera equipment when I'd never use it in a practical application. It would be like learning to shift the gears of a race car, knowing I'd never drive on a real track. Pointless.

"Don't take this the wrong way," Trish prefaced, "but you're like . . . really tense or something. Lighten up, will you?"

"I'm fine," I said, but the barb hooked my subconscious and hung there, a seed that might sprout into something for me to think about later. Any conclusions would probably have to do with Ox. Or rather the absence thereof.

Trish did the head roll thing again. "Here's what I've got on your new DEA friend."

Brad Logan had been with the DEA for eleven years, she said. After graduating college, he successfully sold high-end real estate before—in a strange new direction—he applied for a special agent opening and got in. He had a clean bust record. He worked well both solo and in teams. He was single when he went in, married a nursing supervisor, divorced six years later. One male child, eighteen, in his freshman year at UNC Charlotte. Brad owned a town house, rode a Harley, liked to surf. And he was most likely coming to the end of his undercover days.

Brad's was a high-danger position. For that very reason, Trish said, field agents often get assigned to a different position after ten years. Or they retire and find a new career. If the formula held true for Brad, the current drug ring case he worked might be his last hurrah before changing career paths. For his sake, I hoped he'd go out with a win. For the judge's sake, I hoped the DEA's interest in Argo's restaurant would quietly go away.

Trish cleared a space on a table and sat, feet swinging. "I think you've found yourself a basic DEA guy who also happens to be a hottie. No ulterior motives. No personal ties to Argo's or Morgan's family. Just a man doing a job."

Thinking I should put a few chairs in the blue room, I copied Trish and slid my butt onto the opposite table. Although the Barnes Agency wasn't typically a party pad. Meetings were normally held in the front main office. "I sure would like a few specifics on the case he's working. Other restaurants, if there are any, names, types of drugs."

"Then you'll need to get it directly from Brad. Why not seduce him and then search his place?"

"That's a thought." Seducing him might be fun. And get my mind off Ox.

"Or use Soup." Trish did an imitation of our friend Soup sitting at his electronic command center, like an orchestra conductor, blissfully happy in his element. "Soup could probably hack into their system and have a full report to you by tomorrow."

"Sadly, Soup is in Amsterdam. Vacationing. Even the best hackers in the country need to cut loose and take a break once in a while." Soup is an ex-fed who now worked for himself and, thankfully, represented only the good guys. I missed having Soup on call. I was missing Ox and Lindsey and, now, Soup. I needed to get a grip.

Trish shrugged. "Well then, that leaves the option of getting it directly from the source."

"I sense that Brad is not one to leave stuff lying around. Probably doesn't even keep anything to ID him at his place. In fact, if I were him, I'd have a second place somewhere. Rented with cash under a fake name. A personal safe house of sorts."

"Yeah, you government agent types are always borderline paranoid."

I shook my head. "Not paranoid. Cautious and prepared. Big difference."

Trish jumped off the table, ready to return to the festivities. "Need anything else from me?"

"No." I followed her out of the blue room, and a burst of shrill laughter greeted us. I almost wanted to join the women. Have some quality girl time and forget about Morgan and Argo's and the fact that I felt oddly disassociated without Ox in my daily life. I left the Barnes Agency without getting my fifteen minutes on Andy's table. Driving to the Block, I decided to follow the only leads I had: the list of abbreviated names from Morgan's safe and the list of dinner reservations I'd taken from the hostess stand. Surely I could find some matches between the two. It would be a start.

I also needed to scope out the autopsy report for Morgan's mother. If drugs were running through her restaurant, she might have been a user. And if she was using, there might have been traces in her system when she died. Not only that, but I found it too coincidental that two people were dead, neither had apparent health problems, and both owned Argo's. Ignoring curious looks from neighboring drivers, I rolled down all of the hearse's windows and opened the sunroof. It was a perfect day for a window-down drive. If only the corpse caddy were a convertible. Wind whipping my hair, I dialed Dirk's mobile number. "Trade you lunch at the Block for a copy of an autopsy report," I said when he answered.

"Is this simple morbid curiosity coming from Jersey Barnes? The one who melts down at the sight of a dead body?"

"Doesn't bother me a bit to look at a picture, Dirk. Just can't stand to be *near* a dead person. Huge difference. Besides, it's not politically correct to make fun of one's phobia. Mine even has a designated name."

"Yeah, well," he said, "it's also not politically correct to distribute copies of autopsy reports to civilians."

"It will be a really good lunch," I told him. "Or dinner. I'll even spring for drinks and dessert. You can bring the wife."

"Kids, too?"

"Yup. All of 'em. The whole clan."

"You know that teenagers won't go anywhere without their friends."

"Fine," I said. "We'll call it the Dirk Thompson Family Reunion party. Bring your friends and neighbors, too. Heck, bring your whole damn street. Just get me the autopsy report."

"Wow, Jersey Barnes has a grumpy side," he said, and paused for a beat as if trying to figure out why. "Give me a name of the deceased and a date."

I did. "You get anything back on that gun from the Argo's attempted robbery? Or prints from the safe?"

"The thirty-eight only had a partial serial number. Somebody filed most of it off. We fired a round through it, but no ballistics matches in the system. Dead end. A hunk of metal for the scrap pile. As for the safe, lifted a few clean prints. One belongs to a safe technician. His prints are in the system for a conceal carry, among other things. He's clean. The other is unidentified. Nothing that leads us to your earless man, the one who *allegedly* tried to rob the place."

I didn't argue with his use of "allegedly." Turning a corner, I passed a Jeep-load of young men with military buzz cuts sitting at a stoplight. Spotting me at the wheel of the hearse, they let out a chorus of catcalls and honked their horn.

"It wasn't really a robbery attempt, was it," Dirk said.

"It might have been." I adjusted the Bluetooth headset hanging over my ear. "He was definitely a bad guy."

Dirk chuckled, changed the subject. "How's Spud? We haven't had any public disturbance calls lately. He sick?"

"Spud is on a self-improvement kick. He's grown a mustache. And he's been hanging out with his new girlfriend, Fran."

"The old lady on the scooter that plowed into his mannequin?"

"Yep."

"Only in Jersey's world," he said, and hung up.

THIRTEEN

It wasn't the same walking into the Block without seeing Ox there. I said hello to a few regulars before climbing the stairs to my home. I beeped myself through the security system to find Spud in my kitchen, staring intently at a ficus tree. Even his mustache was perfectly still.

"You okay, Spud?"

He continued to stare at the plant, as if in a daze.

Alarmed, I moved in to examine him, thinking he might have suffered a stroke. "Spud? Can you hear me?"

"I'm practicing reading an aura, for crying out loud. Do you mind?"

I found a bottle of Dos Equis beer in the fridge. Somebody had been to the grocery store. "Is this for your NAB group?"

My father explained that, yes, he'd learned the skill of aura reading from the New Age Babes. Every living organism had an energy field radiating around it, he told me, animals and plants. Learning to see the color of the aura was one way to enlighten the mind. A red aura around a person meant they were angry, he said, while a blue aura indicated calm.

"What color is the ficus tree's aura?" I asked.

His head tilted to the side. "I detect a large aura, sort of a whitish yellow." He broke his gaze and looked at me. "Healthy plants have a large, bright aura."

"That ficus tree is fake, Spud. It's a silk plant."

"What?"

"It's not real. So it can't possibly have an aura."

"Oh, for crying out loud! I been working on reading the stupid plant's aura for fifteen minutes now. I thought I finally had it!"

"Better stay calm, Spud. Your energy field might go red."

He turned the Barnes narrow-eyed glare on me. "Here I was all ready and set to impress Frannie with my new talent, and you go and ruin everything!"

I asked if Fran was a member of the NAB.

"No," he said. "What does that have to do with anything?"

She'd probably be curious as to where he'd learned to read auras, I told my father. When she discovered his involvement with the New Age Babes—a group of all women—she probably wouldn't be too pleased. She might even be jealous.

"I hadn't thought about that," Spud muttered. "She's the one who told me to join some social clubs!"

"Social *men's* clubs, Spud. Not women's clubs."

"I'll quit, then. This aura stuff is a bunch of crap anyway."

"You're their newly elected president, remember?" I said.

"Oh, right. I shouldn't quit." His mustache twitched from side to side. "I'll get Frannie to join!"

My father, always the deep thinker.

"She's good people," he continued. "We might be in love."

I looked more closely at Spud. I'd never before heard him utter the L-word about anyone, ever. Not even to me, at least not that I could remember. He may have told me he loved me when I was a toddler or maybe when I'd begun to form whole sentences. But never after I had an understanding about what the word meant. And certainly not before he vanished from my young life.

"I think I need another pain pill," he said.

So that was it. The pain medicine for a pulled leg muscle. I thought about taking advantage of Spud's unguarded state of mind. I could ask why he'd left me and my mother. I could take a deep breath and do it, right now. Just ask him. Why.

He saw the question on my face. His wrinkles deepened for a beat, and he appeared much older than his eighty years. What I saw in my father's eyes was very similar to the emotion I had detected in Ox's eyes a few months back when I'd asked if he'd slept with his ex-wife: *Don't ask if you don't want the answer.*

Did I really need to know? Did it even matter now, why my father walked out of my life some thirty-five years ago?

Cracker howled at the sound of a passing siren, breaking the spell, instantly erasing the question on my lips. "Well, if you want to impress Fran with your aura-reading abilities, Spud, you might want to practice on the people downstairs in the Block," I said. "At least you know they're alive."

"Why didn't I think of that, for crying out loud? I'll call the boys over so we can all practice together."

Exactly what my pub needed. A group of crazily dressed geriatrics staring silently at the customers. And I'd put the idea in his head. Stupid me.

Spud found his cane and plodded downstairs. I called the judge. Luckily, she was out of court and answered her personal phone on the first ring. "Jersey, I was just thinking of you! Have you found out what's going on with my brother?"

Sort of, I answered, but first I wanted to know about Rosemary's death. The judge told me that her mother had died of an unexpected heart attack. Those were her father's exact words. She remembered where she'd been and what she'd been doing when he called her, the judge said. She'd flown to Wilmington for the funeral and spent a week with Garland before returning to Columbia.

"That's basically it," the judge finished. "Mom was the picture of health. It was a total shock to hear she was dead. But what does she have to do with anything? And what's going on with Morgan?"

I didn't have anything concrete to report, I said. I had to give her something, though, so I let her know that the DEA was looking into Argo's as part of an ongoing investigation that involved several Wilmington restaurants. I inferred that Morgan was simply caught up in the aftermath of previous happenings at Argo's. And most likely not in danger. It was a lot of noncommittal double-talk and she knew it. She wanted to jump in her car immediately and make the drive to Wilmington.

"There's no need for that, Judge. You don't want to get involved by association. Besides, there's nothing you can do by being here."

"You'll call me as soon as you know something more?"

I said I would.

Two hours later, Rosemary's autopsy report arrived in my e-mail in-box. Her heart had stopped beating all right, but not from a heart condition. Five different drugs were detected in her system, and the official cause of death was a drug overdose. Garland chose to protect his wife's integrity by going with the heart attack story. I wondered if I'd be able to do the same. A small favor for my judge friend was turning into a giant dilemma. Did she—and Morgan—have a right to know how Rosemary died? Was it my place to tell them?

A shrill electronic tone sounded, interrupting my thoughts. I couldn't tell where it came from.

Spud clamored through the door, Bobby and Trip on his heels. Bobby held a hand to the side of his face. "The old biddy slapped me."

"We need an ice bag, for crying out loud," Spud said.

I retrieved a cold compress from the freezer and handed it over. Bobby held it to his forehead.

"A customer slapped you?" I asked.

"She slapped him across the top of the head," Trip clarified.

"Gave me a headache, she did," Bobby said. "I was only trying to read her aura."

"You were staring at her boobs," Trip said.

I tried not to smile. "Bad idea."

"You told me to practice reading auras on real people," Spud said.

The three men looked at me, accusing. Bobby's headache was my fault. The shrill electronic ringing started up again. I tracked the sound to a kitchen cabinet. A blinking cell phone lay atop a stack of plates.

Spud snatched it. "I been looking for this thing everywhere! Frannie gave it to me."

The thing continued to ring. Loudly. The sound—similar to that of feedback through an amplifier—made my shoulders hunch up. "Maybe you should answer it, Spud."

Holding the phone at arm's length, my father squinted at the faceplate and punched a button. The phone kept ringing. He punched another button. The ringing continued. My father can barely manage a one-touch cooking code on the microwave. He retired from the cops before the age of the Internet and enhanced forensic science. He still hasn't figured out how to use an ATM.

Spud shoved the phone at me. "How the hell do you answer it, for crying out loud?" The phone stopped ringing.

"You answer it by hitting this green button." I showed him. "To hang up, hit the red button."

Spud took back the phone and held it away from his body, as though it gave off an offensive odor. It beeped. "Hello?" he shouted into it. "Hello? . . . Is anybody there, for crying out loud? . . . Somebody say something!"

The phone beeped again.

"There's nobody there," Spud said. "Why won't it shut up?"

"I believe you have a text message, Spud."

"What?" A vein popped out in his temple.

"A message, dummy," Trip said. "You have to open it to read it. Like a letter, but it's written on the little screen."

Muttering, Spud punched tiny buttons with a thick, knobby forefinger.

"Your aura is bright red," Bobby told him.

"Aura this," Spud said, and gave him the middle finger.

FOURTEEN

I let myself into Ox's place and looked around. Everything was as it should be, neat, tidy, sparsely decorated in man fashion. I mixed a tablespoon of powdered fertilizer in a jug to water the plants. As I was moving past the bath, the familiar scent of his aftershave stopped me. Not sure if it was real or imagined, I filled my lungs and let his nearness envelop me. And then I wondered if somebody else was currently enjoying the real thing, the freshly applied cologne clinging to his skin. A server, maybe, or a camerawoman, or an ESPN associate. The disconcerting feeling might have been jealousy. I didn't like it.

Shaking off the vision of Ox enjoying his days with somebody else—of course he was spending his time with *somebody* while Lindsey was busy with classes—I finished watering the plants, flushed the toilets, did an exterior walk-around, and headed out to have a one-on-one with a few select Argo's customers.

I'd compared the safe list with the hostess stand list and found three names that were a positive match with both first names and phone numbers. I called the first number and made up a story about having a gift basket delivery from a local wineshop.

"You've got the wrong number," a woman said. "I didn't order anything."

"You're Karen, right?" I said before she could hang up.

Hesitation. "Yes."

"Well, I've got a delivery for you. The sender is Argo's. Isn't that a restaurant? Anyway, it's a gift basket. I spilled a soda on my delivery sheet clipboard and half the addresses are smeared. Will you confirm your address, so I can get on with my route?"

She didn't say anything.

"Look, I don't care one way or the other. I'm just a driver. I can take it back to the store and they'll make the calls and it'll go out again tomorrow. But if there's perishable food in there, it could go bad."

She gave me an address. "Leave it on the front porch, please."

"You got it."

My Garmin navigation system directed me to a gated neighborhood with sprawling brick homes and lots of professionally landscaped lawns. I told the gate guard that I was making a delivery.

"Of a body?"

I've gotten so accustomed to tooling around in the corpse caddy that I sometimes forget what I'm driving. "Nope, not a body. Just a gift basket." I sat up straighter and turned toward the window to give him a better shot of cleavage. "The hearse makes a perfect delivery vehicle. Lots of room in the back. Of course, we're going to repaint it a bright yellow and put the store logos on there."

He waved me through without bothering to check inside the back of the wagon. Lucky me. I parked in a cul-de-sac in front of a home under construction and hiked three blocks to Karen's house. A two-story contemporary, it had a circular drive lined with flowering bushes. A yard crew of three crouched in the hedges, spreading mulch and trimming and weeding. I waved and followed a brick pathway to the rear. A woman sat on the covered patio, reading a paperback. A half-empty frozen drink was on the table beside her, next to a cell phone.

"Karen?"

She looked up with a start. "Yes?"

She wore a cloth visor—the expensive kind with a designer logo stitched on the bill. Her face was smooth and flawless, and her hair was pinned up in a twist. Manicured fingers and toes. Gold earrings. Casual skirt and top-quality sandals. Store-bought boobs, about the same size as mine. Giant rock on the ring finger.

"My name is Jersey. May I sit and talk with you for a moment?"

She put down the book. "Your voice sounds familiar. You just called, didn't you? About a delivery."

"Guilty," I said. "I lied. There's no delivery."

"What do you want?" She picked up the cell phone, ready to dial someone. A neighbor. Or the police, maybe.

I helped myself to a chair and propped my elbows on the table so she could see my hands. Friendly, nonthreatening. "I just want to talk, Karen. I want to know about the special items you've gotten at Argo's. You know, the ones that come in pill form and aren't on the menu?"

Her posture went rigid. "I don't know what you're talking about, and I'd like you to leave. You're trespassing."

I studied her melting drink. It looked like a margarita. "Here's the thing, Karen. You can either talk to me, right now, a simple chat. Or you can talk to the DEA agents when I bring them back here with a warrant to search your house. Imagine what the neighbors will say. Not to mention your husband. What's he going to think when he gets home from work to find the law crawling through his belongings?"

She went to an outdoor summer kitchen, rummaged in a drawer, and returned with a pack of cigarettes. She lit one with shaky hands and inhaled deeply. "Who are you?"

Somebody helping out a friend, I told her. Not a cop. But there would be troubles for her, I said, if she chose not to help me. She chugged her drink and stubbed out the barely smoked cigarette into a wet napkin. After a beat, she lit a fresh one. Probably a closet smoker, I guessed, since she didn't have an ashtray and stashed her nicotine sticks in a drawer next to the gas grill.

She exhaled a stream of smoke. "What do you want to know?"

"I already know that you were illegally buying drugs," I lied, "but I need the details. Not only what you're using, but what else is available." I'd learned long ago to let the person I'm questioning think that I knew much more than I did. If I backed up my approach with the right attitude, a guilty person's imagination often went into overdrive. Fortunately for me, it worked with Karen, and I caught a glimpse of fear as her mind fast-forwarded through all sorts of potential repercussions.

"I'm not *using* anything," she finally said. "You must think I'm a druggie or something."

I did a hands-out gesture. "Hey, I'm not here to judge you. I'm after information. Your personal life is your business."

She inhaled, sighed out the smoke. "My father-in-law, Daniel, passed away recently. Before he died, he was housebound. Confused and angry. Liked to throw things. On oxygen and insulin, among other things. Wouldn't take a bath. Going deaf and blind." She flicked cigarette ash into the makeshift ashtray. "My husband refused to put his father in a nursing home. Instead, he hired a private nurse to help me out." She spat out a laugh. "Problem is, the nurses would never stay because they couldn't handle Daniel. My maid wouldn't even clean his room anymore after he threw a lamp at her. So guess who got stuck doing everything?"

"You," I answered, because it was what she was waiting for.

"Exactly. Me. I had to sedate the man to brush his teeth and clean him up and give him his shots every day. Oh, the nurses would come and go. But who was tied down to this damn house as a caretaker? Me, while my husband headed off to work each morning for his important meetings and power lunches. I couldn't deal with it. I started taking the old man's medications, to cope."

"So you were sedating yourself, too, so to speak."

She nodded. A woman—presumably the maid—came out of the house to ask Karen if she wanted a drink refill. Karen did, then asked me if I wanted anything. I declined. The maid returned in an instant with a fresh, full glass and left with a promise not to tell "the mister" that Karen was smoking again.

"Yes, I suppose I was sedating myself to keep from shooting myself. Or Daniel."

"Why didn't you go to your family doctor and ask for a prescription?"

She laughed. "There's a limit to what you can talk a doctor into giving you. It was easier to take Daniel's drugs. Pain pills and sleeping pills, mostly. And sedatives. When a patient is as bad off as my father-in-law was, the doctors keep the prescriptions coming. Anything I asked for. All in the name of keeping him comfortable while everyone waited for him to die."

Karen's backyard was spacious and loaded with creatively placed garden beds. The faint sound of a pump drew my attention to an inground hot tub surrounded by teakwood chairs. The lawn crew appeared and went to work with hand trimmers.

"Then he died," I said.

"Yes."

"And you lost your supply of prescription drugs," I said.

She nodded. "I thought my life would get better. That I wouldn't need the pills anymore."

I waited.

"Things didn't get better. I found out that while I was stuck at home caring for his father, my husband was in Puerto Rico with one of his clients."

"Business?"

"Apparently more pleasure than business. They shared a hotel room."

"That had to hurt," I offered.

She eyed the cigarette pack, decided against a third. "He's had affairs before. But not since he brought his father into our home. I was so angry, I couldn't stand to look at him."

I asked Karen how she discovered Argo's.

"I had a massive migraine one day, at the hair salon, when I was getting my color done. A woman in the next chair offered me a Vicodin. We ended up having lunch together and I told her all about my jerk of a husband and we got to bitching about men in general and she told me about the network."

"Network?"

"That's what she called it. The network. Theresa told me to buy one of those cell phones that are preloaded with minutes? So we bought one at a convenience store after lunch and I gave her the phone number. A few hours later, a guy called me. He gave me a phone number to call whenever I needed 'party supplies.' Anyway, I'd call the number and tell them what I wanted. Then they'd call back, tell me how much money, and when and where to go to pick the stuff up."

"There were other places besides Argo's?"

Karen went to Argo's only twice, she said. There were other local restaurants. Once, the pickup place was a coffee bar, where she was supposed to enter the drive-through at precisely one o'clock in the afternoon. When she asked for a latte with seven shots of vanilla and put three one-hundred-dollar bills in the tip jar, the barista handed over a bottle of amphetamines, complete with a label detailing usage instructions. And as far as the choices, Karen told me, the network had whatever she wanted. She didn't even have to name a specific drug. She could say she was feeling tired and depressed, and the person on the other end said they'd take care of it. Prior to completing an outpatient rehab program—she'd told her husband it was a photography course—Karen had purchased a variety of painkillers, sedatives, and uppers. She would swallow an amphetamine with her morning coffee and toast, pop a few painkillers during the day, and take a sedative to help her sleep at night.

A worker appeared to ask Karen if she wanted the hedges around the hot tub trimmed.

"*Sí*," she told him, and finished her second drink. At least it was the second since I'd been there.

"Who did you ask for when you went to Argo's?"

She removed the visor and rubbed her eyes. "Started with an 'R.' Rose, I think. That was a long time ago. She was blond, I remember. Really pretty. I made reservations for me and my husband at the designated time. We ate dinner. Before we left, she met me in the bathroom and gave me the stuff. Anyway, she's not there anymore. I ate at Argo's a few months back with friends and, just out of curiosity, asked about her. They said she died."

"Rosemary?"

Karen nodded. "That was it. Not Rose. Her name was Rosemary."

We watched the young men in the yard. Each wore widebrimmed hats, and although the day's air was pleasant and tinged with a Confederate jasmine-scented breeze, their shirts clung to their torsos. And they didn't look as though they were enjoying the smell of the blooms.

"What is the network phone number?"

"I'm not using the network anymore. I do outpatient rehab visits, and I'm working on getting sober. I threw out the most recent number. Besides, it would have been changed by now anyway. It changed all the time."

"When you used to call the network, who did you talk to?"

"I would talk to whoever answered the phone. They never gave a name. And the people changed, at least by the sound of their voices."

"So you would call the designated phone number. You never got the name of who you were talking to, but they would tell you who to ask for at the pickup location."

A leaf blower fired up, but Karen didn't offer to take me inside. "One place I went," she said loudly, "they told me to sit at the bar and that either bartender could help me. At Argo's, of course, you can't get in without a reservation. So I had to call in advance and make a dinner reservation, then see the hostess lady."

Karen waved at the yard crew, mimicked putting her hands over her ears. The leaf blower stopped. "I don't know how you got my name," she said, "but I don't use the network any longer. And I really would like for you to leave now."

I nodded, stood. I'd gotten more than I'd hoped for. But not enough. "Are you still friends with Theresa?"

"I never saw her again."

"The name of your hair salon?" I pushed.

She stood with crossed arms. "CC's Hair Boutique. Please go."

I waved when the gate guard did a double take at my exiting corpse caddy. Long gift basket delivery, he probably thought.

On a roll, I tried the second phone number on my list, only to learn that it connected to nothing except a service provider error message. Bad number.

I chugged a bottle of water and tried curtain number three. Its owner, Pat, hung up on me when I told her I had a delivery. I dialed again. "Don't hang up on me, lady. I'm just the driver and I have a network delivery for you. I need an address."

"That's not the way it's done," she said. "I've already been given instructions."

"Yeah, well, things change. People get fired. People quit. Your pickup location is no longer valid, so they're having me make deliveries today." I laughed. "Hey, you ought to appreciate the special service. No extra charge."

The line remained silent.

"You want the stuff or not? Makes no difference to me."

"Not at my house," she said after a beat.

"Fine, pick a restaurant."

"Boca Bay on Eastwood?" she asked. I knew the restaurant and, based on the selection, guessed that she probably lived in Wrightsville Beach. It was close to her home, but not too close. And a relatively upscale, busy place. Lots of tourists.

"Sure," I agreed. "I'll be at the bar. I'm wearing a red tank top and tan jacket. And be there in half an hour. I've got four deliveries after you."

Boca Bay is a basic seafood and pasta restaurant with great Mediterranean dishes, fresh sushi, and a unique tapas menu. I sat at the bar and ordered some Spanish brochettas and a Beck's Light. A lone woman slid into a bar stool right on time, to my right, leaving an empty stool between us.

"You Pat?" I said.

Frowning, she nodded yes and slid a pack of Dentyne Ice chewing gum my way. It was the kind of gum sealed in a blister pack, and I could see folded bills stuck between the chewing gum and cardboard wrapper. "I'm in a hurry."

The bartender appeared. "My friend will have a glass of wine." I looked at Pat. "White okay?" She looked like a Chardonnay kind of woman. Late forties, maybe fifty. Different color hair and plumper build than Karen, but the same designer labels, manicured fingers, pampered skin, and expensive jewelry. Sizable emerald-cut rock on her ring finger. Another well-kept, upper-class druggie.

"I told you I'm in a hurry," she said when the bartender moved away to pour her wine. "Give me my stuff."

Her wine arrived. I thanked the bartender. Ignoring the wine, Pat stared at me. I finished my last tapas and decided against ordering more. My clothes were starting to feel snug.

"Here's the thing, Pat." I took the pack of chewing gum and leaned over so I could speak without being overheard. "I can pretend that you didn't just give me money to complete an illegal drug transaction, if you decide to talk to me. Or you can talk to somebody else in an interrogation room." Hey, it was all I could think of. And it worked.

"Son of a bitch," she said, breathing fast. Her body instantly went jittery. "Are you going to arrest me?"

"No." I didn't correct her assumption that I was a cop and purposely adjusted my linen jacket to give her a peek at the Ruger holstered behind my hip. "Enjoy your Chardonnay. Have a bite to eat. Let's talk."

Either Pat wasn't too bright or her brain was foggy from all the drugs. She should have realized that if I were a cop and I knew who she was, I'd know where she lived. I'd have just shown up at her house. Her elevator didn't seem to be going all the way to the top, but that meant progress for me. Another piece of the big picture that might explain Morgan's dilemma. And the fact that Pat had shown up for a delivery meant that she still used the network. While she certainly didn't look like your average junkie, she was desperate enough to meet a stranger to score her dope.

Pat's fingers drummed the bar top as she shifted in her seat. She eyed the door, thought about darting, thought better of it. Studied me. Pushed aside the wineglass and asked the bartender for vodka on the rocks.

"If I tell you what I know—which isn't much, by the way—do I get immunity? I'll stay out of trouble?"

I had to work at keeping a straight face. She'd been watching way too much television. And she'd never even bothered to ask who I was or who I worked for.

"Yes," I told her. "That's the way it works."

Pat's details of the network confirmed what Karen had told me earlier. The difference was that this woman was hooked on Oxy-Contin, a powerful painkiller. She made a buy about once every week, she said, using grocery money. I guessed that she bought more than just the pain pills, but I didn't push it. I was happy that I'd lucked out with the timing. Pat confessed that she was supposed to pick up her latest supply later in the evening, at a convenience store. She told me which one and what time.

"I have to ask the clerk for a can of dog food," Pat said. She'd moved into the high-backed bar stool next to me. "The people always change so they don't know what you look like. The dog food thing is how they'll know it's me."

The bartender cleared my plate, and I asked for an ice water. No more beer until I'd jogged at least two or three miles. Maybe four. The wheels continued to spin furiously inside Pat's head. If she kept thinking so hard, I might be forced to order another beer to wait it out.

"You're going to go and pretend to be me, aren't you," she finally said. "Then you'll arrest that person."

I didn't say anything.

"Or you'll get them to talk so you can find their boss," she said, and downed half the vodka as though it were iced tea.

I stood to go to the restroom and knocked Pat's handbag off the back of her bar stool. It fell to the floor, scattering contents. Makeup, tissues, hairbrush, and a clear plastic aspirin bottle that held multi-colored pills.

"Whoops, sorry!" I bent to scoop it all up before she had a chance. I found her wallet and glimpsed the driver's license. The woman gulping straight vodka was Pat Viocchi. It was an out-of-state license. She was either a part-time resident or a full-timer who hadn't bothered to get it changed. And I still needed her local address. I could try to tail her, but the hearse would make that nearly impossible.

Squatting on the floor, I continued to hand Pat's stuff up to her when I spied a checkbook. Standing up, I slid it in my back pocket. She may not have bothered to change her license, but she would most likely have put a local address on her checks.

"I've told you what I know, and I'm not going anywhere near a convenience store tonight. Can I go now?" Pat couldn't sit still. "I've got to get going."

"Sure, take off. But just out of curiosity, why don't you see a doctor to get your prescriptions?" The same question I'd asked Karen.

Her nostrils flared. It was an unflattering look. "It's easier and cheaper to get what I need myself."

"Cheaper?"

"My husband is self-employed, so we don't have traditional insurance. By the time I pay for a doctor's visit and the cost of the drugs I need for my back pain, it's about the same. Besides, the network doesn't ask questions."

I returned the pack of Dentyne, bills intact, to her. She left without paying for her drink. I finished my water, dropped a couple of twenties on the bar, and headed to the hearse. It was time to enlist help from my DEA friend.

FIFTEEN

Nice place you've got here, Jersey Barnes. Laid-back, open. Interesting decor. Great view," Brad said. He'd agreed to meet me at the Block, and we sat in a booth, one with a wide-open view of everything. He ordered a flounder sandwich with pineapple slaw. We both drank beers. To heck with running first. "And your business partner is Duke Oxendine. He a Wilmington local?"

"Been doing more checking up on me?"

He held up his beer and we clinked mugs. "I have high-tech resources at my disposal," he said. "May as well put them to good use."

"Find out anything else interesting?" I seriously doubted he'd be able to determine which agency I'd been with. SWEET flies so low under the radar, a snake couldn't limbo beneath it.

Flashing the captivating smile, he shook his head. "Nope."

"Good," I said. "Then let's talk about prescription drugs."

Brad's sandwich came out quickly, and while he ate, I told him what I'd learned about the network from the two women I'd questioned earlier in the day. All of it. His expression didn't change, but something flared in the hazel irises. Probably admiration. He was impressed.

"And you got the names of these people how?"

I told him.

He took another bite, chewed evenly, drank beer. "Do you realize how much you have compromised this investigation by running around playing Nancy Drew?"

Nancy Drew? What a jerk. So much for the look on his face being admiration.

"If I were you," I said, "I'd be thankful for the information. And by the way, I'm a simple citizen helping out a friend. I can talk with whomever the hell I want to. I don't have to clear my day's itinerary with you first."

His voice remained level, but the look flashed in his eyes again. "First of all, don't sit there and tell me that you approached these women claiming to be helping out a friend," Brad said. "Who did you impersonate? DEA? Local cop? Somebody else with a badge?"

I drank my beer. I hadn't officially impersonated anyone. I just hadn't corrected Karen's and Pat's assumptions.

"And second of all," Brad lectured, "yes, you do need to clear your itinerary with me when it involves a yearlong investigation of mine, dammit."

I showed him my heartfelt smile, to throw him off base. "Sorry."

"That's it? Sorry?"

Ruby came by the table, and I knew she was soaking up every word she could hear without being blatant about it. She removed Brad's plate and delivered two fresh beers. I thanked her and purposely didn't introduce the two of them. There was enough local gossip flowing through the Block without me adding to it. Not getting her scoop, Ruby flounced off.

"Yeah, that's it," I answered. "*Nancy Drew* is sorry."

His posture relaxed. "Okay, okay, that comment was uncalled for."

"Well, I apologize, just the same. I should have told you what I was up to." Probably.

He frowned, but only one side of his mouth went down. It was kind of cute. "You're only saying that to pacify me."

"Did it work?"

Brad smiled, both sides of his mouth up. Like that, the anger was gone. He looked at his watch. "I don't have time to chew your ass any longer anyway. If Pat was telling the truth about the convenience store, I don't even have time to get a team in there. This is not a good situation."

"What do you mean?"

"An informant like this—if she's the real thing—is too valuable to screw up. If I knew in advance, we'd have done some O and S before approaching her."

"Understandable."

"Once I had a line on her next pickup, I'd take precautions to make sure nobody was tipped off," he lectured. "Plus, we'd have several eyes and ears on the minimart. A soda or bread delivery van. A broken-down car across the street. A vagrant walking the streets." He shot me a disapproving glance. I felt visually scolded. "For starters," he added to make sure I knew that was just the beginning of how he'd have handled things much differently.

"You told me you kept hitting dead ends," I said. "At least now you've got something to work with."

"Let's hope." He made the lopsided frown again, checked his watch. "And let's roll."

He retrieved a gym bag from his SUV and changed in the restroom, emerging in a Carolina Panthers T-shirt, shorts, and ball cap. We headed to the convenience store in his vehicle.

"How come you get to dress undercover and I don't? Shouldn't I have a Panthers shirt on, too?"

"There's no game today, and women only wear the duds to support game days, if then. Guys will wear this stuff anytime." He looked sideways at me and grinned. "Besides, that skirt and low-cut top works quite well. Nice legs, by the way."

"Thanks."

"You carrying?"

"Of course." I lifted the edge of my skirt to reveal a thigh holster. Similar to a stretchy bellyband holster, it holds the Ruger SR9 snuggly to the inside front of my left thigh. The pleats of my Liz Claiborne skirt concealed it perfectly.

"For some reason, that was a total turn-on. Wow. Show me again?"

"You flirting with me, Agent Logan?"

"Yes."

"Still mad at me?"

"I'm not sure."

"You need me, if I'm going to pretend to be Pat," I said, feeling a touch guilty about the fact that I was enjoying the flirtatious banter. Sure, I had felt it right away when Ox left for Connecticut: scathing emptiness. But our longtime connection and more recent exploration of each other's bodies had never been verbalized into a commitment. Besides, flirtatious banter with another man was just that—talk.

"I don't feel good about this," Brad said. "I ought to throw you out of the car right now and get a female undercover to go in with me."

We both knew there wasn't time for that, and I didn't bother to irritate the situation by reminding Brad of that fact. We arrived fifteen minutes early and backed into a parking slot at the side of the building. Two people were filling up at the gas pumps. A single car was parked off to one side, probably an employee. And a motorcycle was parked on the other end of the building, partially hidden by outdoor ice machines. Our plan was to act like a happy couple and shop for beer and snacks while we scoped things out inside. At Brad's signal, I'd inquire about dog food, and if all went according to plan, he'd grab the clerk. Absolutely nothing was to go down if there were customers present.

I first hit the restroom and took a quick glance around the rear storage area. It was dark and quiet. No signs of activity. The manager's office door was open, and it was empty as well. Both restrooms were empty. Brad had ducked inside the walk-in cooler, where all the beer and sodas were stocked into sliding racks that opened to glass doors inside the retail area. When he emerged, a nod told me it was empty, too. Far as we could tell, the clerk behind the counter was the only employee in the store. A single customer came in, bought two energy drinks and five dollars' worth of quick pick lottery tickets, and left.

Brad and I approached the counter with a six-pack of beer and a bag of Doritos. A ruffled-looking man tinkered with a roll of paper tape in the cash register.

I smiled. "Long day?"

"Sorry, I'll have this fixed in a jiff." He looked up, returned my smile with bright white dentures through a frazzled expression. "I'm brand new. Haven't even finished training yet. I wasn't supposed to work tonight."

"No rush," I said. "How'd you get stuck working on your day off?"

"The other cashier no-showed. Manager's husband is having a birthday party, so she's not coming in. Guess that left me."

A burly, darkly tanned, tattooed man in jeans and a leather vest came through the front doors and seemed to be more interested in checking me out than browsing through the rack of magazines in front of him. And he didn't look like the type to read a magazine. Not one without nude pictures, anyway. Something was off.

I made sure to keep my face turned away from the man and pretended to look for my wallet. Brad hugged me to him and planted a kiss on my cheek. "I just realized we forgot the Cokes. And we probably ought to get another six-pack of Bud for the party."

I returned the kiss, thinking that it wasn't all that unpleasant. It felt rather nice, actually. "I'll run to the bathroom while you get the rest of our stuff," I said.

Leaving our purchases on the counter, we made our way to the back of the store. "Let's get out of here," Brad said. "Back door."

We found the rear door obstructed by a stack of flattened cardboard boxes and locked by a keyed dead bolt. I wondered what the fire marshal would have to say about that but didn't get a chance to ponder too long because I saw Leather Vest weaving his way through the aisles. His hand gripped something beneath his vest.

"He's on to us." I drew my weapon. The store's front-door chime beeped and a group of giggling teenagers herded inside. "Crap. We can't chance a stray bullet. Get us out of here."

With a grunt, Brad threw a kick into the door right below the dead bolt. The frame cracked and splintered, but the door held. Leather Vest was hustling now, a visible handgun leading his way. "Thank God for rotten wood," Brad said, and threw a second kick. The door busted loose from its frame.

"Pick me up!" I yelled, and ran in the opposite direction from where we'd left Brad's Murano. I found the parked motorcycle—a Harley Softail with a custom paint job—and fired two rounds into the sidewall of its front tire. Cussing, Leather Vest rounded the corner of the building and took aim at me. From the other direction, Brad sped into the line of fire and slowed enough for me to throw myself into the passenger's seat. We peeled out of the convenience store lot, taking a couple of hits in the rear of the SUV.

"Here I was," I said, returning the Ruger to my thigh holster and strapping myself into the seat belt, "thoughtful enough not to ruin his twenty-thousand-dollar bike when I shot out the tire. I mean, I could have put some lead into the engine. Or the cowhide seat. And he thanks us by shooting up your car."

"No biggie," Brad said. "'Long as we still have all our body parts.'"

In unison, we pulled out our cell phones, looked at each other, and laughed. I put mine away. Brad could call it in. He was the officially working person between the two of us. He dialed and identified himself as an agent, recited a number, and gave brief details of an unidentified shooter at Bob's Mini-Mart. Suspect believed to have been riding a motorcycle, which was currently disabled.

"Hold for the description of the motorcycle," he said, and waited for me. I recited the make and tag number, hoping it was registered to the man riding it. It would be nice to find out who'd been sent to intercept me at the minimart. And who'd sent him.

We drove erratically for five or eight miles, Brad taking lots of last minute turns to make sure we didn't have a shadow. We didn't. He pulled into a strip mall parking lot, did a quick walk-around to check out the damage on the Murano, returned to the driver's seat.

"Vehicle's fine," he said.

"We need to get to Pat Viocchi's house, don't we."

Brad nodded, thinking the same thing. *Somebody* had tipped off the network to the fact that an agent was going to try to make a pickup at Bob's Mini-Mart. If that someone was Pat, she could be in danger. To them, she was now a problem.

"Give me the address from that checkbook you lifted," Brad said.

I did. He entered it into a nav system. After calculating our route, the device told us we'd arrive in fourteen minutes. We got there in eleven. Pat's address belonged to a quiet neighborhood consisting of two-story brick town homes woven along golf course fairways. Brad headed to the back while I knocked on the front door. A lapdog—by the sound of it—started yapping. Nobody answered. I knocked again and rang the bell. Nothing. After a minute, Brad opened the door to let me in, a terrier bouncing around his ankles.

"Back slider wasn't locked," he said. "Looks like somebody jimmied it open."

Weapons ready, safeties off, we searched both levels, starting downstairs. We found Pat Viocchi on the upstairs master bathroom floor, her head twisted at an unnatural angle. Grayish skin contrasted sickly with the white terry robe wrapped around her body. Milky, unseeing eyes stared up at the vanity.

"Oh, crap," I said, panic crushing my lungs. "I'm out of here."

Ten minutes later, Brad found me outside, sitting in Pat's small courtyard behind the town house, watching a foursome of men hit golf balls off the red tees. "You okay?"

"It's the dead body thing," I said.

He almost laughed but stopped himself. "You were serious about that?"

I nodded. "Strange considering what I used to do for a living."

"And yet you drive a hearse."

"It's a long story," I said. "What happened to her?"

He joined me at the patio table. "Broken neck. Shower is damp, so it probably happened when she got out. Her place was searched. Neat job of it, but whoever killed her was looking for something."

I felt my spine crumple and I slumped in my seat. "She doublecrossed me, didn't she."

"Junkies are unpredictable, Jersey. After she had a chance to think about it, she decided that she didn't want to lose her supplier of drugs."

"So she called the network and tipped them off about me going to the minimart," I said. "Guess you can't trust a drug addict, regardless of how well groomed and coiffed they are."

Brad nodded. "Probably thought she'd score some brownie points. Earn herself a freebie or two. Teacher's pet syndrome."

"But the network had other ideas," I mumbled. My actions had resulted in the death of a woman. "They couldn't chance her talking."

"Look, in an operation like this one, *everyone* is disposable except for the person or people at the very top," Brad said. "That's the reason it works so well, and that's the reason this case has been frustrating the hell out of me. They operate by using *disposable people*. The buyers, the stationary runners who make the deliveries. The brain running the network will never let any one person know too much. That's why the pickup locations rotate and the phone numbers constantly change. If a user gets too needy or problematic, the network drops them. Simply doesn't give out the new phone number. Same thing with the runners. They start demanding more of a cut or steal product, they're dropped. Anyone talks too much, they're dropped."

"Or in this case, killed."

The golfers finished taking turns from the tee box and headed noisily down the cart path. Brad gripped my chin and turned my face toward his. "Question for you. Say you're at home and a hyped-up junkie breaks in to search for something he can pawn. He needs forty bucks for his next fix." He stared into my eyes. "You yell for him to stop, to go away. Instead, he keeps coming at you. He has a gun. What do you do?"

"I shoot him," I said. "He probably dies."

"Right. But *you* didn't kill him. Bad decisions killed him. Same goes with the woman in there. She made a string of bad choices."

I understood what Brad was trying to do, but it didn't make me feel better.

"Stop second-guessing yourself," he said. "We've got work to do."

"We?"

"If I know you, you're going to stay on this thing, right? Get some answers for your judge friend?"

I nodded.

"Well then, we may as well help each other and work together. Unofficially, of course."

I nodded again.

Brad made a phone call. Within minutes, we heard the wail of approaching sirens. He had to make a report to his boss, he told me, but my name wouldn't be on it.

"Thank you," I said, and headed out on foot, leaving Brad to wait for the police.

"Jersey," he called. I stopped and turned. "Have you told me everything you've found related to this case?"

"Yes," I answered, close enough to see his eyes in the fading daylight. *Mostly everything.* "Can you say the same?"

The sirens grew closer. "You'd better go," he said.

SIXTEEN

The Divine Image doctors were back at the Green Table, and Morgan couldn't resist learning more. A secret from their past had come back to haunt them, and Morgan wanted—no, *needed*—to know what it was. He craved the information and justified his action of eavesdropping by telling himself he might gain insight into Argo's mysterious secrets. The doctors' past could explain why somebody had rummaged through his apartment and searched his car and why the Drug Enforcement Agency was keeping tabs on the restaurant. After all, the doctors had been good friends with his parents. Garland was "like family" to them, they'd said. And if that was true, then Morgan had every right to learn what the doctors were up to. He had a vested interest. Even though he and Garland never acted like family, he still carried the man's DNA. And now he owned Argo's. His father's legacy, really. The more he learned about the restaurant and read past reviews, the more he realized that Garland had left his mark on Wilmington. At first, Morgan wasn't sure what he planned to do with the eatery once the estate was settled. Now, he knew he'd keep it. Maybe even expand. And once he learned what he needed to know, he would destroy the hidden microphone. Until then, Morgan told himself, he was going to do something that would make Garland proud. Perhaps his father had put the microphone in place at the Green Table *for a reason.* If so, Morgan was the only person left to figure it out.

The earbud practically pulsed in his ear when Morgan shut himself in the small office and settled in to eavesdrop. Out of habit, he hit a combination of keyboard strokes to tab through the various security camera views on his monitor. He paused on the front-entrance camera when he spotted a bum walking in. The man bypassed the hostess and went to the bathroom. The doctors were talking about their receptionist—nothing that interested Morgan—so he kept his attention focused on the monitor. The bum came back into view and stopped, as though looking around the dining area. His pants were baggy, held up by a tightened belt, and his shirt appeared dirty. A line of unkempt curly black hair escaped from beneath a baseball cap, and when the man turned to go, Morgan caught a glimpse of a face that looked just like his father's. This man was much thinner than Garland had been, and his posture was slumped instead of robust, but he could have been Garland's double. Or brother. Except Garland didn't have any brothers.

Morgan braced himself on the desk as a blast of vertigo rolled through his core. When he opened his eyes, the bum was going back outside. Morgan's mind was playing tricks on him. He had hated his father. Yet he'd decided to keep Argo's once the estate was settled, in memory of Garland's accomplishments? And now he was seeing the dead man in a stranger's face? He wondered if the bum was hungry and thought about taking a container of food outside. But he knew the man had already disappeared.

Once his dizziness passed, Morgan switched the monitor back to the dining room view and located the doctors. He probably needed sleep, Morgan figured. And exercise. Sleep and exercise would do him good.

"Seriously, John, you really need to lay off the booze," Leo was saying, "and whatever else you've been prescribing for yourself."

Jonathan told Leo to shove it.

"He's right," Michael said.

Michael seemed to be the peacekeeper of the group, Morgan thought, while Leo was their leader. Jonathan was the resident drunk.

"It may or may not have been your student ID that allowed him to track us," Michael continued. "Either way, it doesn't matter. We've been a team since the beginning, and we'll still be a team when we decide to retire. That means we've got to stick together to get through this mess. And *that* means that you keep your act together and keep treating patients as usual."

Jonathan mumbled something indecipherable, but on the monitor he appeared to nod his agreement. Then he took a long swig of whatever he'd ordered on the rocks. He kept his head back until the glass held nothing but ice.

"You could always take a leave of absence," Leo suggested. "Sign up for a continuing education course, someplace warm and tropical. Get your head clear."

The shrink said something about paying the monthly fee. "Plus, who's going to write the scrips if I'm not around?"

A server, Hank, delivered a calamari-and-artichoke-heart appetizer along with three small plates. He asked about drink refills. Everyone declined except for Jonathan, who ordered a double Scotch, neat. On the monitor, Morgan saw Leo and Michael exchange a look over their partner's drunken binge.

"First of all, we can swing the monthly payment with or without you. It's just one more office expense. And as for the scrips, Leo and I can write enough to keep him happy," Michael said. "Besides, it's not like we're the only physicians he's got. I told him right off the bat that we wouldn't do anything to jeopardize our licenses. That means no excessive scrips, other than the standard painkillers that our plastic surgery patients need anyway."

Jonathan let out a sloppy laugh. "Right. So I refer my patients elsewhere and take off for a month. Which of you is going to prescribe the psychotropic stuff like Ritalin and Adderall? Might seem odd to the medical board that a lipo or bleph patient would need stimulants."

The men ate their appetizer in silence, Jonathan picking at the same piece of calamari for several minutes. His Scotch arrived. Without ice it was easier to gulp, and he did.

"I miss Rosemary so much sometimes I can't stand it," Jonathan suddenly said.

Morgan's spine tingled at the mention of his mother's name. How many Rosemarys could the doctors know?

"We all miss her." Leo pushed back his appetizer plate. "Her and Garland both. It's not the same around here without them. What's your point?"

The psychiatrist sucked down more Scotch while the two cosmetic surgeons waited for an answer. After a beat, Jonathan realized his glass was empty and put it down. He wiped the back of a hand beneath both eyes. Was the man crying? Morgan wondered.

"Oh, sweet Jesus," Leo said, his voice filled with disgust. He leaned across the table and forced Jonathan to look at him. "Tell me it's not true."

"What?" Michael asked. "What's not true?"

Leo pointed at the shrink. "You were screwing Rosemary, weren't you, John."

"No, of course not. She would never have been unfaithful to Garland," Jonathan said. "But we could talk to each other, tell each other anything."

"So then, you were counseling her as a patient?" Michael asked.

The shrink's slight nod of confirmation was visible to Morgan on the monitor. The office walls started spinning around him like an amusement park ride.

"We always met somewhere outside of the office and just . . . well, we just talked. We talked about the baby ducks and the weather and relationships and life in general. It started as patient counseling, I guess, but turned into something much more. It was an affair without the sex, I suppose. I've never been as intimate with anyone else, ever."

"You stupid idiot," one of the doctors said. "You were seeing Garland's wife away from the office? She was almost old enough to be your mother."

Through the hot buzzing in his ears, Morgan could no longer tell which man was saying what. He closed his eyes to steady the walls.

"I told you, it wasn't like that." Jonathan's words were slurred but sharp with anger. "First of all, we were best friends—not lovers. And second, our age difference was irrelevant. I could make her laugh. And she could talk to me without worrying that I was listening just so I could get into her pants."

"All those times you were out meeting someone for lunch, we thought it was another of your bimbos." Leo's head shook from side to side. "Nobody that mattered enough for us to meet. But *Rosemary?*"

Jonathan tried to drink from an empty glass.

"It was a tragic thing that happened," Michael said after a while.

Jonathan shook his head. "I never should have gotten Rosemary involved."

"What?" somebody demanded. "Rosemary knew about the blackmail? Why, you're just an outpouring of revelations today, John."

Jonathan's voice was close to a whisper now. "She was dealing with menopause. Tired all the time and depressed. The hormones her doctor prescribed weren't helping, so I gave her something that would. Then she wanted more. I realized much later that I had used her addiction to keep her reliant on me. To keep her close."

"And?"

"And once, when we were talking, I told her about the network. I told her everything. When she found out what we were up against, she wanted to help."

Michael wasn't eating or drinking, and his stare was fixed tight on the shrink. "Okay, I'm trying to get this straight. First, you *counsel* Rosemary away from the office. Then you become best friends *without* benefits. Then you get her hooked on drugs and turn her into an addict under the pretense of helping her through the physical symptoms of menopause. Then you spill your guts about the mess we're in and convince her to help."

Jonathan nodded.

"Help how?" Leo demanded.

Jonathan's head was down. "She was one of his runners. People picked up right here, at the restaurant."

"You dumb drunk." Morgan had his eyes shut now, but it sounded like Leo's voice. "Did Garland know?"

Morgan opened his eyes in time to see Jonathan shake his head no. "Rosemary never told him. She adored Garland. Told me right up front that they would be together forever. She made it very clear that there would never be a chance for us. . . ." Jonathan's voice trailed off again, and this time the sounds of sniffled crying traveled through the wire in the ceiling to land in Morgan's ear. "But I loved her so much."

Ignoring the nausea that pressed against the back of his throat, Morgan remained shut in the office for the duration of the Divine Image Group's meal. Leo had dessert. Jonathan had more Scotch. And Michael tried to keep the two of them from verbally attacking each other.

At the end of the hour, Morgan had a mess of information floating in his head, unsettled, disturbing. His mother had been having one-on-one intimate chats with one of his father's supposed best friends—a best friend who turned Rosemary into a drug addict. The doctors were illegally writing prescriptions for patients who didn't exist. Their practice was in danger of shutting down if they lost their medical licenses. They'd paid out a large sum of money to somebody but still owed a lot more. Hundreds of thousands more. None of it made much sense to Morgan, and when he felt that he might faint, he put his head between his knees.

He awakened hours later, cheek smashed against the desktop, neck muscles feeling like cast iron. Argo's was dark and empty. It was after two in the morning. In a daze, Morgan slipped out, thinking that he needed to tell Jersey Barnes what he'd learned.

SEVENTEEN

I'd tackled an early morning run along the Riverwalk and was surprised to see so many people milling about at the breakfast hour. Every year, tourists seem to stick around longer than in previous years. Wilmington and the area beaches used to be a summertime destination, but now, out-of-towners keep visiting all the way through the holiday season. The day's summerlike weather had drawn a good weekend crowd, and these folks were early risers.

When I returned to the Block, Brad was at a table with Spud and his friends. And they were playing poker. Nothing like an early morning game of five-card draw. Bobby and Hal were dressed in a polyester version of Tommy Bahama tropical shirts and shorts. Trip wore all white, except for his socks, which were black. Spud's wiry legs stuck out of blue-and-green-striped shorts that might have been swimming trunks. He wore a muscle shirt beneath a blinding yellow short-sleeved-button-down, unbuttoned and untucked. His feet were stuffed into orange neoprene slippers, the kind of shoes people sometimes wear on the beach so shells don't cut their feet. Once I got beyond the collage of loud duds, I noticed an assortment of stuff in the tabletop's center, and it didn't consist of money or poker chips.

"Morning, Jersey." Brad used his hand of playing cards to point at his opponents. "The boys are breaking in their new clothes for the cruise."

The boys? They looked like lost old men who'd wandered into a Ringling Brothers dressing room. I shook out my leg muscles and almost bent over to stretch before I realized Brad was watching me watch *the boys*.

"Uh, good morning," I said, straightening. Spud's friends took turns acknowledging me. Eyes on his cards, Spud grunted his greeting.

"I'll raise a brand-new sleeve of Titleist golf balls and a sample pack of Viagra." Bobby fished around in a plaid backpack for a moment before tossing the goods into the pot.

"None of us play golf," Trip reminded him. "Besides, the balls are pink."

"Yeah, well," Bobby said. "You win this hand and get the Viagra, you might start hanging out at the driving range to meet some ladies. Then you can use the pink balls as a gift. They're a good conversation starter. I read that in the AARP newsletter, that it's important to start conversations if you want to make new friends."

"I've already got me a lady," Spud announced. "And by the way, that Viagra ain't cheap. Use the sample pack and then you've got to go buy some more. Although it does work pretty good, so it's probably worth the money. Problem is, you don't know exactly when it'll kick in."

"I *so* did not need to hear that," I said to nobody in particular. No wonder Fran had been spending a portion of her nights sleeping above my bar. Or rather, not sleeping. Cracker sauntered over to greet me and nuzzled my legs. On the other hand, I thought, at least somebody around here is getting some.

Brad folded his hand of cards. Trip fished around in a fanny pack and tossed in a coupon for two free China Buffet early bird specials, arguing that they easily matched the raise value. Spud spread out his cards and fanned his face, looking sweaty and goofy at the same time.

"Hey, kid." My father gave me the once-over. "In that getup, you look like one of those chicks on TV, on the exercise channel." He fanned his face again, newly grown mustache twitching from side to side, its tips still aspiring to be handlebars. "I'd bet that people would watch you jump around on TV."

I looked more closely at my father and instantly recognized the zoned-out look in his eyes. He was still taking the pain pills. I wanted my old father back. The cantankerous, loud, unreasonable one who didn't spurt out off-the-wall compliments. I held out my hand. "Let me have them, Spud."

"Have what, for crying out loud?"

"Your pain pills." The plastic prescription vial had disappeared from my kitchen counter, and I thought he'd finished the pills and thrown it away. Apparently not. "Hand them over."

"I hurt my leg," Spud explained to Brad. "Had to go to the hospital ER."

"You keep taking those pain pills, Spud, and you're going to do something crazy." I kept my hand out. "Like ask Fran to marry you."

"Funny you should mention that," Spud said dreamily.

"Fran is mad at him," Hal said. "She found out that we joined the New Age Babes and we're going on a cruise with a gaggle of women."

"Yeah, we went shopping for our cruisewear, and Spud brought Fran to help us pick out clothes," Bobby said. "She wasn't too happy when she found out what the clothes were for."

"So your daddy took her next door to the jewelry store to look at rings," Hal said. "Told Fran that they could have an engagement party on the ship if she'd join the NAB and go on the cruise with us."

"What happened?" I heard myself ask.

"Frannie told me I could take the cruise and shove it you-know-where." Spud cocked his head. "Although I don't see how you could actually shove a big ship anywhere, much less up there."

"Fran was wound up tighter than a rattlesnake on a highway," Trip said. "Said she wouldn't stand by and watch a bunch of women in swimsuits fussing over your daddy out in the middle of an ocean."

"I wasn't thinking right or I'd never have talked them into accepting men into their club," Spud said. "I don't even remember being inducted as their president, for crying out loud."

"My point exactly," I said. "Give me the pills."

Muttering, my father produced a prescription container and dropped it in my outstretched hand. The label told me there were no refills left. Thank goodness for that. I dropped the remaining four pills into a glass of water. Spud eyed the glass and licked his lips, much like Cracker when staring at a bowl of peanuts.

"Don't even think about it," I said.

Spud harrumphed. "Killjoy."

"You'll thank me later."

Brad extricated himself from the poker game and we went to the outside patio. After I explained my father's use of pain pills due to his recent brush with yoga, the conversation progressed to more important things. Like whether or not Argo's was still being watched by the DEA. It would be nice to have something good to report to the judge.

"Every location we consider suspect is still potentially under surveillance," Brad said, careful in his selection of words. "Argo's is just another on the list. We're certain there was a link in the past."

"Meaning Rosemary?" The earless thug had first mentioned

Morgan's mother. The list of names I'd found in the safe was in her handwriting. And Karen, the housewife I'd questioned, had said that Rosemary met her in Argo's restroom to trade drugs for money. Then, of course, there was the telling fact that she had died from a drug overdose.

Ruby brought us two glasses of iced tea and moved off, ears straining for tidbits.

"Yes, meaning Rosemary," Brad said.

"Obviously you've seen the autopsy report," I said. "You know she died of an overdose. So she was selling *and* using. Okay. But why stick with this now? She's dead, Garland is dead, and Morgan obviously doesn't know anything."

Brad positioned his chair to stay in the umbrella's shade. "You got part of that right."

"What are you talking about?"

"Never mind."

I drank half my tea with one tilt, rehydrating after my run. Brad was just doing his job. Obviously he had kept certain details from me, but there was no need to get overly irritated about it.

"Was it you who searched Morgan's car and apartment?" I asked.

Brad shook his head no. "We've watched him closely. Listened to his phone calls. If we decide to search his place or the restaurant, we'll do it with a warrant."

"I don't think so," I said.

"Excuse me?"

I reminded Brad that my interest was to protect the judge's family, namely Morgan. I didn't think that people traipsing through the establishment would be good for business or for employee morale. Not to mention Garland and Rosemary's postmortem reputation.

"Are you trying to tell me what I can and can't do?"

I smiled, studied my nails, noticed some chipped polish. I needed a manicure. "I'm simply noting the fact that you don't have nearly enough to convince a judge to sign a search warrant. All you have is hearsay, from me. And I'll deny the list ever existed. For that matter, I'll say you've misunderstood the retelling of my conversations with Karen and Pat."

Brad's arms folded across his chest. He repositioned his chair again, this time moving into the sunshine. The muscles in his jaw worked.

"Besides," I continued, "didn't you conveniently leave me off the incident report from Bob's Mini-Mart? How will you explain that to your bosses when they find out that not only did I tip you off, but I was there helping you?"

"If it came to that, you'd end up contradicting yourself to cover your ass."

I gave him my best, most brilliant smile. "So? *I'm* not the one with a career on the line. I'm simply a concerned citizen."

He mumbled something to himself that might have been "bitch."

"Did you just call me 'babe' again?"

The arms came uncrossed, and the hazel eyes seemed to be reassessing their initial impression of me. "Hardly."

I used the Block's kitchen to make sandwiches, and when I returned, the early-arriving lunch crowd had begun to claim patio tables. Several regulars waved at me. A woman I didn't recognize wore a tee with a message imprinted on the back: "I ain't from the South, but I got here as fast as I could." Her companion wore a New York Mets baseball cap.

I spread out two identical plates: sliced turkey with provolone and horseradish mustard on whole wheat with a side of fruit salad. I felt like eating healthy. And I enjoy a nontraditional breakfast sometimes. Brad seemed the type to eat just about anything at any time.

"Your resourcefulness continues to impress me." Brad stabbed a chunk of cantaloupe and chewed. "One minute I want to see that enchanting thigh holster again, and the next I wish you'd never dropped into my life."

"Thanks," I said. It may have been a compliment. "So what did your people find in Pat's place?"

Whoever killed the woman had searched her place afterward, Brad said. If there were any drug stashes, they'd been taken. Pat had no criminal record, not even a traffic violation. The DEA was interviewing her social clubs, friends, and husband. Took her computer and BlackBerry, but so far, nothing except old, invalid phone numbers.

"It doesn't make sense." I wondered how somebody like Pat got caught up in such a mess. And how a woman like Rosemary became involved with a criminal drug operation.

Brad finished a bite of sandwich, wiped his mouth. "Still having trouble with the fact that this tree's branches lead to wealthy, accomplished people?"

"I'm not one to stereotype, but if I hadn't seen the evidence, I never would have imagined that somebody like Rosemary could be into this."

"Niche marketing at its finest. People like her have reputations to protect, so they're typically not going to do anything stupid to get themselves caught. Nobody would ever suspect them as users or runners. We're talking lawyers, business professionals, wealthy housewives. They have the cash to spend." He ate more fruit, scanned the patio. "Plus, they justify what they're doing because the drugs are manufactured by pharmaceutical companies. Medical grade, FDA approved."

The early October day had stretched its way into the eighties. I wiped perspiration from the back of my neck. "In other words, they're not shooting up with something manufactured inside an abandoned building, or standing on a dirty street corner to score a rock of crack cocaine. So they don't categorize themselves with the junkies you see on TV or read about in the newspaper."

"Exactly."

The last time I recalled sitting on the Block's outdoor patio discussing a case with a hunky man, Ox was the person across the table from me. It was a few months ago, mid-August, sticky hot. The nearness of Ox made the humidity seem sensual and sultry and he must have felt the same way. Maybe we'd waited long enough and the timing was right, or maybe we were both sun-drunk. Regardless, the day turned into an afternoon I'll never forget. Hours of pure bliss. We connected on every possible human level. Finally—after first meeting in high school when I taught him the eleventh-grade ropes and he taught me how to box—we slept together. And then his ex-wife showed up. To reclaim him. True, Louise had gone back to the West Coast solo, so that was something. But shortly after that little issue was settled, Ox had stepped into role of chaperone and headed to Connecticut for Lindsey's internship.

"Hello? Anybody home?"

I looked up to see Brad watching me stare at the river. "Sorry, just thinking about something. I'm back."

"So where are we on this thing?"

"Other than whatever it is you're withholding from me?"

He smiled. "Other than that."

"I've got another name for you." I told him about CC's Hair Boutique and Theresa, the woman who first told Karen about the network.

"Been there yet?" he asked.

"Nope."

"Going?"

"Yep."

Ruby arrived at the table with the pub's cordless phone tucked under one arm. She gave me the handset and left with our empty plates.

"Hello, this is Jersey," I said.

"Still missing me?" Ox said, and the air instantly grew hotter. My cheeks warmed.

I excused myself from the table. Outside on the sidewalk, I watched the cars and bicyclists and pedestrians, careful to stay close enough to the building to keep the cordless telephone signal. We talked for ten delicious minutes, condensed updates of our separate lives. I hit the off button and returned to the patio table, thinking the conversation hadn't been nearly long enough.

Brad eyed the phone. "Was that your complication?"

"Come again?"

"You said that your love life is complicated," he explained. "Was that your complication?"

I didn't answer. Things with Ox were complicated, but it wasn't any of Brad's business.

Brad stood, stretched, stuck some money beneath a plate, and kissed me on the cheek. "I'll send somebody in to get a haircut at CC's. Meanwhile, let me know if you manage to scrounge up something they don't." He joined the stream of people walking along Water Street.

EIGHTEEN

Morgan was waiting beneath a picnic shelter when I arrived at Halyburton Park. Even wearing everyday clothes, the man looked like a million bucks. It occurred to me that he blended beautifully with Wilmington's beautiful-people crowd. If only he had a social life.

"Are you sure you weren't followed?" he asked in greeting.

"Pretty sure." I wondered why the clandestine tactics all of a sudden. Morgan had called shortly after Brad left the Block, demanding to meet at a public place, but one that didn't have a lot of people milling about. Unless the city's Parks and Recreation Department has a scheduled class or event, Halyburton Park is more of a nature preserve than anything else. It's usually relatively quiet. Today, even the playground was barren.

"I took a roundabout route getting here to make sure nobody was behind me," Morgan said.

I nodded. *Good for you*. I'd planned to take the day off. I wanted to relax and catch up on my magazines. Check out the new fashions, see where the current hem length was supposed be. Maybe grab a matinee movie. Or else find some beach sand and stick my bare toes in it. One nice thing about Wilmington is that you can wear sandals almost year-round, as long as your toes look good. My toes still looked good from my last pedi, and I was ready to go *somewhere* and do *something*. Something to remind me that I really am retired.

Yet here I was, sitting at a picnic table with the judge's brother. Before, I had to practically hook Morgan's words and reel them out of his mouth. He didn't want to talk. Apparently he had a change of heart, because now I'd been summoned. And it certainly wasn't to pick up a paycheck, because nobody was paying me. To make myself feel better during the drive to the park, I started making a mental list of everything I planned to do sometime soon. Learn to ride a horse, for starters. It's something I've always wanted to try, and there are nearby stables that give lessons. And paint. I might turn out to be a decent artist if I were ever to throw some colors on a canvas. And travel. I want to travel without toting weapons. Well, maybe just one weapon would be okay. I could always take my first official retirement trip on my boat, *Incognito*. Perhaps a nice long cruise to the Florida Keys, stopping to collect mile-marker souvenirs along the way.

"There's a group of doctors who eat at the restaurant," Morgan began.

I sighed. Back to reality. "My restaurant or your restaurant?"

"Argo's," Morgan said. "Their practice is called the Divine Image Group. They do plastic surgery, and one of them is a psychiatrist. Anyway, they have a standing reservation for dinner every Friday night. Lately, they've come in more often than that."

"Okay."

Morgan fingered a large splinter of wood on the corner of the picnic table, as though trying to press it back into place. "They uh . . . well. There's something going on with them."

"Would you like to tell me what that might be?" *And how it involves you or me?*

"I think they've been prescribing drugs for patients who don't really exist." The words rushed out, as though he wanted to talk before he changed his mind. "One of them was in love with my mother. And they owe somebody a lot of money."

Now, he had my attention. I garnered as much information from him as I could: full names of the doctors, how long they'd been friends with Morgan's parents, whether or not they ever dined with anyone else at their table.

A couple arrived at the playground with a three- or four-year-old. The woman sat on a bench while the man helped the boy climb a slide. I guessed them to be the boy's grandparents—nobody who had an interest in Morgan or me.

"When did you first meet these guys?" I asked.

Morgan explained that he hadn't embraced the social aspects of restaurant ownership, but that his head server, Deanna, "made" him go meet the doctors because they kept asking about him. It was the same night that his ex-fiancée had come in with her old boss, he recalled.

"You ever hear anything more from Maria?"

"No," Morgan said. "She was using me, the whole time, while she waited on Mark Greer to come around."

"Her old boss?"

"Yeah. He's getting a divorce so he can marry Maria."

"You okay with that?"

Morgan removed his shades and looked at me. "Don't have much choice, do I?"

Something about the judge's brother was much different from when I'd first met him. Heartbreak? Acceptance? Experience? One month ago, Morgan had seemed tired, deflated, and nervous. Now, he emanated a sort of quiet confidence. He appeared more *capable*.

"Wilmington is a great place to meet people," I offered. "Lot of young professionals here, lots to do."

He smiled. "I'll get around to that in time."

An elderly man arrived at the playground with a pair of binoculars and what appeared to be a bird identification manual.

Seeing him, Morgan pitched sideways and nearly fell into me.

"You okay?"

"Sorry," he said, holding himself upright, palms against the top of our picnic table bench. "I get vertigo every once in a while. Had it on and off since I was a kid."

That explained why Morgan sometimes had balance issues. The bird-watcher settled onto a bench and opened his book. Morgan stared. I asked if he recognized the man.

"No, it's . . . well, it's weird. It's no secret that I haven't spoken to Garland in years and years. I'm sure my sister told you. The only reason I even came to the memorial service is out of respect for her."

"And?"

"And all of a sudden, I'm thinking about him a lot. My father. I keep seeing people that remind me of Garland. Like at the restaurant, a stray bum came in to use the toilet. He could have been Garland's double, in the face, anyway." He looked again at the man on the playground, who'd gotten up and went strolling into the trees, binoculars pointed at the branches. "And that man there. Something about him made me think of Garland again. My mind is playing tricks on me."

"Let's walk," I suggested, and we made our way to a short nature trail. Naturally, Morgan would begin to wonder about his father, now that he'd taken charge of the restaurant. I had constantly wondered about my father, growing up, during the marines, and later, while chasing down bad guys. I wondered what he looked like, and if he'd married, and if I had any half sisters or brothers, and if he'd be proud of me. And most often, why had he left? Blood relationships are a strange and powerful thing.

I asked Morgan if he could tell me anything else about the doctors and their prescription-writing activities. He shook his head: No, nothing.

"How did you get this information?"

He didn't answer for several steps. Finally, "I overheard them talking."

"To whom?"

"They were talking to each other. The three of them."

A pair of squirrels darted up a tree in front of us. "In Argo's?"

Morgan scooped to pick up a stone, tossed it into the trees. "Yes."

I asked if anyone else overheard the doctors' conversation. *No.* I asked if Morgan had discussed the subject with anyone besides me. *No.* I asked if he'd been waiting on their table himself. *No.* I asked if they ever mentioned the name of the person or people they owed money to. *No.* I asked if Morgan was certain he'd heard things correctly. *Yes.*

We stopped at a clearing and stared at a flock of twenty or thirty American goldfinches feeding in the bushes at the edge of a pond. About the size of a sparrow, they're hot lemon yellow and beautiful. They always migrate south in the fall.

"Exactly how did you manage to overhear such a private conversation, Morgan?"

"I just happened to be in the restaurant at the same time they were, Jersey. That's it. When I heard my mother's name mentioned, my ears perked up and I kept listening. I heard everything perfectly clearly. And no, they obviously didn't know that I could hear their conversation."

"So you were in the dining room, then?"

He gave me a look that translated meant, *Well, duh.*

We headed back to the visitor center, where we'd parked our cars. His nondescript sedan and my shiny black hearse. Morgan said he was going to the restaurant. I wanted to interview Deanna and asked him if Deanna was scheduled to work at Argo's.

"Not tonight, why?"

"Just wondering if the head server gets to take off on weekends," I fibbed.

We pulled out and pointed our vehicles in opposite directions. I dialed Argo's and, claiming to be Deanna's next-door neighbor, asked for her cell number. I waited on hold for less than a minute before getting the information.

When I dialed Deanna, she sounded almost breathless. "Hello?"

"Deanna, hi, it's Jersey. I'm a friend of Morgan's."

"My boss, Morgan?"

"Right. Listen, can I meet you somewhere to talk for a minute?"

She was getting dressed to meet friends at Level 5 for drinks, she said. Afterward, they planned to see a musical comedy at City Stage. I needed only a few minutes, I told her, and I could meet her at the bar. She hesitated. I mentioned that I'd buy their first round of drinks.

"Sure thing, then," she said. "See you there."

Level 5 is, as its name suggests, located on the fifth floor of a hundred-plus-year-old Masonic building. It has an outdoor rooftop bar with an energizing view of downtown, an inside bar, and a two-hundred-seat theater. Interestingly, the building's fourth floor consists of condos, the third floor is suite rentals, and the remainder of the building is occupied by businesses. If you're ever in the area and want to check out Level 5, you'll have to purchase an annual membership. One of those weird alcohol control things. The state of North Carolina says that to obtain an Alcoholic Beverage Control Commission permit to serve booze, an establishment must either have at least 30 percent food sales or become a private club. Since

Level 5 doesn't have a kitchen, they charge patrons five bucks each year to join. Some area bars only charge one dollar.

Deanna was beneath the rooftop's canopy with a cluster of hip, exfoliated, oiled, gelled, and scented friends. A quick introduction told me they were all hospitality people and a few were also up-and-coming actresses. The two of us moved away from the rest of the group, Deanna carrying a pineapple martini and me a Bass Ale in the bottle.

"So what's up? Are you another cop?"

I should have known. "Fellow named Brad already talk to you?"

She sipped, smiled. "He can interview me anytime. He's the kind of guy I could bring home to Mom and Dad's for dinner. And *cute.*" She stretched the word into three syllables for emphasis.

"When did *Officer Brad* talk to you?"

"Yesterday. Said he had to interview employees at a bunch of area restaurants. Dumb questions, really. Like he wanted to know if anyone still comes in asking for the previous owners. Garland and Rosemary. I mean, come on. Everybody knows they died."

I let the ale roll over the back of my tongue and breathed in the lively evening: freshly groomed people, drifting food smells from somewhere below, jasmine blooms, and a hint of earthy river scent.

"I'll try not to ask the same dumb questions," I said. "Tell me about your new boss."

"Well. He's like crazy shy. Or maybe you'd call it introverted. At first, he hated talking to people, but that's sort of what a restaurant owner has to do, you know? He's getting better about it, and every once in a while he seems to enjoy talking to the customers. I actually saw him smile the other day."

Her eyes went sparkly talking about Morgan. "What else?" I asked in my girl-to-girl voice.

"I've had a crush on him since he first walked into Argo's and introduced himself as the new owner. I keep hoping he'll ask me out, since his fiancée broke it off with him." She let out a dramatic sigh. "He's not interested. He doesn't go out with anybody, far as I can tell. I invited him to join us tonight, but he said he had to catch up on paperwork. Yeah, right."

"You think that was an excuse?"

She ate the wedge of fresh pineapple from her martini glass. "Let's just say he spends a lot of time locked in that office of his. The private one. Nobody's allowed in there. Garland was the same way. But it can't possibly take that much time to do restaurant paperwork."

"Why not?"

Deanna's people started laughing. She glanced their way. She was missing the party. I needed to speed it up.

"Our head chef schedules his people, plans the menu, and does all the food ordering. I schedule everybody else and keep track of reservations and the hostesses. An accounting firm does our payroll and accounts payable." Pinky outstretched, she got to the bottom of her martini. I caught the server's attention and held up two fingers. I needed to keep Deanna talking for at least another five minutes.

"Really," she continued, "all Morgan has to do is keep an eye on things, approve payroll and invoices before they're paid. Tend to the advertising and marketing. Though Argo's is so well-known, we don't do much advertising. So is he home catching up on paperwork tonight? Doubtful."

"Do you know the Divine Image Group?"

"Sure. Everybody knows the doctors. They always sit at the Green Table, best seat in the house."

"You wait on them?"

"Anytime I'm working, the Green Table is mine. Talk about kick-ass tips."

"You ever overhear people's conversations in Argo's?"

"Of course. We hear people talk all the time. But they stop as soon as you walk up, you know? If it's something private. Or romantic."

Somebody called her name, and Deanna said she'd be right there.

"One last question. Is there anybody else, any other customers, who always sit at the Green Table?"

She shrugged. "The people who know about the GT ask to sit there when they call, but it's always reserved for VIPs. Of course, we have plenty of regulars we put there when they call for a reservation. But the docs are the only ones who have an ongoing, standing reservation, every single Friday. Been that way for years and years. Anytime they call for an additional reservation on a different day, chances are that whoever's at the GT gets bumped. We'll bump people from the GT for celebrities, too." She shrugged again. "You know, whatever. The more special people think they are, usually, the better they tip. So hey, I don't mind."

We walked back to Deanna's friends and they immediately enveloped her to gossip about a pair of guys inside. I said my good-byes, paid for everyone's drinks, and became their new best friend. I don't customarily pick up the tab for people I don't know, but Uncle Sam had reimbursed me nicely for my last assignment, when I was called back to active SWEET duty and forced to work on a roach coach, cooking egg biscuits on the side of the road. It's a long story. But it did leave me with a bit of pocket money. Amid a chorus of well-wishes, I departed the rooftop with some interesting tidbits to contemplate.

Driving to the Barnes Agency, I envisioned Argo's dining room layout, focusing on the famous Green Table. Morgan said he'd simply overheard the Divine Image Group talking to one another—an obvious lie. You had to go up two steps to get to the table. Glass windows were on one side and walled artwork on the others. The GT, as Deanna called it, had its own cozy alcove. Morgan could not have overheard anyone sitting there, short of utilizing audio surveillance.

The lights were on, and JJ's car sat in the driveway of the Barnes Agency. I found her in the blue room, testing a laser range finder.

"You're working late tonight."

"Hey, Jersey. I'm part of patrol duty for an event in Seattle tomorrow. Threats of an assassination attempt." She did a curtsy. "They're even sending a jet for me."

"You should be honored," I said. JJ replaced me at the Barnes Agency when I officially retired. She shoots a high-powered rifle better than anybody I know—male or female.

"Honor doesn't put gas in my tank," she said. "But this job comes with a sweet paycheck."

"I'm down with that." The Block rarely shows a profit. The Barnes Agency, on the other hand, pulls in some high-dollar contracts. "Hey, do we still have that fountain pen?" I asked. "The vibrating one?"

"Missing Ox, are you?"

"Ha, ha." I made a face at her. "I need an audio bug detector. Something small and inconspicuous. Don't we have a pen that vibrates when it detects specific wireless frequencies?"

JJ rummaged through a shelf, found a case, produced the black fountain pen. It looked like a Montblanc. "It only has a range of three or four meters," she said. "Good for checking whether or not an individual is wired when you're talking to them. It actually writes, too."

"It should work for what I need at Argo's." I dropped the pen in my handbag.

"How do you always manage to get the assignments with good food?"

"It's not an assignment. I no longer have assignments, because as you might recall, I am retired."

JJ laughed. "Better put a new battery in the pen. And make sure it's not turned on until you're ready to use it, or it'll run out of juice."

"Thanks," I told her. "Be careful in Seattle."

"That would be absolutely no fun at all," she quipped.

When I arrived home, the bar had an average crowd. I climbed the stairs to my apartment, once again thinking about Ox. How much I missed him. And Brad. How much he irritated me. Cracker was sleeping inside the kitchen door, waiting for me, and gave me a sleepy greeting. Spud's apartment was dark, and I guessed that my father was spending his night at Fran's place, which meant no fresh-baked goods for me. Hungry, I peered into the fridge. It was so empty, it nearly echoed when I opened the door. A jar of mustard, some olives, deli meat, and a gallon of milk. No beer. I got the shaved turkey to make a sandwich, only to realize I was out of bread, but Cracker was happy to have the meat plain. He swallowed each slice without bothering to chew.

If I went downstairs for food and beer, I'd have to be social. I didn't feel like being sociable. And I couldn't very well ask one of the employees to deliver. One last search through the fridge revealed a bottle of Chardonnay in the bottom vegetable drawer. Neither Spud nor I drink wine. The Chardonnay was probably a gift. No telling how long it had been in there. Good thing is, wine doesn't have an expiration date.

I went to bed with the chilled bottle and a glass and watched an old black-and-white movie with Cracker snoring beside me, and I drank until I fell asleep, dreaming that the leading roles in *From Here to Eternity* were played by Ox and me.

NINETEEN

Trying to eliminate an obnoxious headache that wouldn't go away, I swallowed three Excedrin tablets and drank a glass of tomato juice, standing behind the bar. I'd woken up feeling as though I'd been beaten up and immediately remembered why I don't drink wine. I had the mother of all hangovers. It was midday, and I was bartending for the afternoon to help take up the slack in Ox's absence. As long as a group of tourists didn't come in and ask for silly-sounding drinks like a Dixie Stinger or a Buttery Nipple, I'd be fine.

Thinking about dunking my pounding head in the ice bin, I heard something strange coming from the ceiling. Ruby elbowed me and pointed up. She'd heard it, too. We stopped what we were doing to listen. Faint scuffling sounds filtered intermittently through the Block's PA system. Staring at a ceiling-mounted speaker, we definitely detected muffled voices.

The only two places where an employee can address the Block's patrons using the built-in public address system are from the hostess stand at the main entrance and from the back office, which is really a desk tucked into one corner of the kitchen. But nobody worked the hostess stand. The Block's customers know to seat themselves. Even on busier weekend nights when there is a hostess working, we never use the PA system. With a foggy brain, I stared curiously at the ceiling, willing my headache to ease up.

"Oh, for crying out loud, Frannie!" my father's voice suddenly boomed through the speakers, all ten of them. A smattering of customers looked around to see what was going on. "I ain't never gonna be able to do this."

"Come on, baby," Fran crooned. "You said you'd try. It'll be fun once you get it going!"

"I can't get it up," Spud's amplified voice complained to the entire Block. "It won't come up."

A ripple of laughter rolled through the bar. Whatever my father and his girlfriend were up to, they'd managed to turn on the PA system and lock the button in the on position. A screech of feedback sounded, and from somewhere, Cracker let out a loud, soulful howl. I felt like joining him. Trying not to roll my eyes—because it would probably hurt—I poured two draft beers and served them to a couple of off-duty firefighters.

"It's like riding a bike," Fran told about twenty-five people, not including those sitting on the outside patio and any passersby who'd stopped to listen. "It seems impossible, but then all of a sudden, there you go! Pedaling down the street with the wind in your hair."

Sloppy kissing noises filled the Block. "I know you can do it," Fran said. "Come on, sweetie. Try it again, for me."

Amplified shuffling noises filtered through, along with what sounded like a computer keyboard. "Dammit, woman, it won't come up!"

The Block had fallen into a stunned silence. A few laughed out loud. I hustled into the kitchen, wondering why the cook hadn't put a stop to my father's exploits. Oddly, it was business as usual in the kitchen. Nobody paid a bit of attention to my father and his girlfriend. I moved around the food prep area to see Spud sitting at the desk in front of the Block's sole computer, Fran leaning over his shoulders.

"What are you doing at my desk, Spud?" I yelled.

"Trying to check my e-mail, for crying out loud. But it won't come up."

Laughter filtered in from the dining room, and I remembered that the PA system was engaged. I found the switch and clicked it off.

"I bought your daddy a computer," Fran told me. "They're delivering it tomorrow. So I'm giving him a lesson on how to do e-mail."

"I'm putting in the stupid password and it still won't come up!" Fran told him that the caps lock key was probably turned on.

"What's a damn catslock tee?"

She patted him on the shoulder. "Maybe we should work on using your cell phone first, before we do computer lessons."

"Fine." He scowled at the computer. "But I want to Google myself first."

By the time my shift ended, my headache had disappeared and I'd only had to make one round of Banana Boat shooters. I felt perky enough to hit CC's Hair Boutique in search of the elusive Theresa. But first, keeping my fingers crossed, I dialed Soup.

"Yo, Jersey," he answered. "You calling to welcome me back?"

"How was Amsterdam?"

"Fantastic. At least what I can remember of it. I brought you some happy pops. Sort of like a lollipop, but these have a special ingredient, only for adults."

"Are they legal here?"

"Probably not," he said. "And since you only call when you need something, go ahead. Lay it on me. Don't worry about the fact that I haven't even unpacked yet."

I told him about the Divine Image Group doctors and gave him what little information I had on them. "I need everything you can find. Upbringing, where they went to med school, any patient lawsuits or warnings from the state medical board. Employees. Marriages, divorces, kids. Financial records. The works."

Soup blew out a sigh of displeasure. "You *really* need a happy pop. I thought you retired."

Soup was right. I probably *could* use a happy pop, although I don't do drugs. I have my moody days, but overall, I think I'm pretty well-adjusted. Even as a kid, I rarely cried and never threw tantrums. When I learned of my father's departure—I remember the day clearly—I shrugged at the injustice and went outside to play hopscotch. I figured he had a good reason for leaving, and my young brain assumed he'd be back. I've never been one to overreact. Not even the time I fell out of a tree and split my knee open and all the boys ran at the sight of gushing blood. I used my teeth to rip a sleeve from my shirt, made a tourniquet with the fabric and a stick, hobbled home, and passed out on the front porch.

Things are what they are. As an adolescent, I always held out hope that my father would come back. Now, all these years later, *I knew for a fact* that Ox would be back. In a matter of weeks. But my upbeat, can-do attitude had faltered without him, and I wondered if it had something to do with our afternoon in bed together. I wasn't sure I liked my mood at all—or the realization that I'd come to rely on Ox much more than might be healthy.

"The retirement jokes are getting old," I said to Soup, knowing how bitchy it had to sound. "I could also use a record of all the prescriptions the Divine Image Group has written over the past year or two. Is there a database for that?"

"There's a database for everything, if you know where to look," he said, "and how to obtain access."

Luckily for me, Soup is one of the best hackers in the country. "Excellent," I said. "How soon can you do it?"

"This job pay anything?"

"Free food at the Block," I offered.

"I already get that," he reminded me.

"Don't you owe me a favor?"

He laughed, once. "No."

"Then I'll owe you a favor," I said.

"You already do. Two or three of them."

I had to think of something better. "A state supreme court judge, for whom I am doing this favor, will be much indebted to you."

"Which state?" Soup asked. Foolish, he's not.

"South Carolina."

"And that helps me how?"

"Look, North Carolina and South Carolina are practically one and the same. You ever get in trouble, my judge friend can probably help you out. She has a lot of pull."

"I had more friends like you," Soup grumbled, "I'd be so broke I couldn't buy advice."

"So how soon do you think I can have that?" I asked, but he'd already hung up.

CC's Hair Boutique was a mod-looking joint done in stainless and white. Lots of white. White tile floor, white stucco walls, white furniture in the waiting area, white faux marble tables to hold the magazines.

A guy—thankfully not wearing all white—greeted me and asked if I had an appointment.

"No appointment, although I probably do need a trim," I said. "I'm out of conditioner, and a friend of mine said that you sell the PureOlogy products."

"We carry PureOlogy," he said, reaching out to feel my hair in a way that only a hairstylist could get away with. "Which conditioner do you use?"

"I can't remember what it's called," I said, deciding to go with my bubbly, girly, bimbette role. And I really did need conditioner. Spud had swiped mine to use on his mustache. "It's pepperminty and makes your scalp kind of tingle?"

He pulled a bottle off the shelf. "Here you go. It's the one for color care."

I hadn't realized the shampoo and conditioner I used was for color care, but my hair *had* seen the blond-to-brunette spectrum over the years. "Great, thanks."

"My next client doesn't come in for forty-five minutes," he said. "I have time to trim off those split ends and shape you up."

I had split ends? "Oh, that's perfect. Shape away!"

His name was Alex, and he led me to one of the hair-washing sinks. I'd left the Ruger and paddle holster in the corpse caddy, so I didn't mind handing over my short-sleeved collared jacket. Lying back, I relaxed and enjoyed the warm water and scalp massage while Alex chatted about his previous client's Persian kittens.

Head wrapped in a towel, I moved to another chair, where Alex proceeded to comb out my wet hair and ask about my plans for the evening. I babbled on about partying with my friends at Level 5—it's what came to me on short notice—and decided to toss out the name Theresa.

"My friend who told me to come to CC's to buy conditioner?" I began. "She said there used to be a stylist here named Theresa, who was really good. Is Theresa still around?"

It may have been the placebo effect, but I thought I detected Alex's attitude go defensive. "You're a local, right? Who's your stylist now?"

There are a lot of hair salons in Wilmington. I threw out a name and made up a story about Shawna, my current stylist, suddenly quitting because she landed a role in an independent film to be produced in Wilmington. "Nobody from the salon even bothered to call her customers to let them know!" I said. "So I thought, To heck with them. I'll have to find a new place."

Alex pulled a strip of wet hair straight up from my head. "I hope she's a better actress than she is a stylist." Wilmington is, after all, an East Coast hotbed of television and movie production. It was a good story. He bought it. And he answered my question about Theresa. She used to cut hair at CC's but just recently left. Not only that, Alex confided, but she'd worked at the salon for only a couple of months.

"Was she trying to be an actress, too?" I think I made the question sound believable.

"I don't think that boyfriend of hers would let her hang out on a set all day." Snip, snip. "Besides, Theresa wasn't the actress type."

"Men can be such jerks," I said, watching pieces of my hair fall to the ground. "Was he, like, real controlling or something?"

Alex spun my chair so I faced the mirror. He snipped and shaped. "All I know is her boyfriend was scary. Looked plain mean. Stopped by here one afternoon—supposedly to take Theresa to lunch—and that's the last we saw of her. She called a few days later to tell us she quit."

"That's weird," I said. "What was his name?"

"We never knew. But he had a mangled ear on one side," Alex said.

TWENTY

The Divine Image Group partners sat in their conference room, a spread of freshly delivered deli sandwiches and bottles of flavored teas in front of them. They didn't normally eat lunch in the office and they rarely ate lunch together, but today was an exception. Two of the men were worried about the third. They knew that a tripod couldn't stand on two legs. Their strength had always been a foundation of three, and their practice could be in danger of collapsing if Jonathan didn't get his act together. Not only that, but Leo had some interesting news to share. He wanted to blurt out the discovery but held back. They needed to get a take on Jonathan's emotional state before giving him something else to worry about.

Michael poured dressing over his blackened tuna salad, and Leo dug into a grilled pastrami. "Gotta love the three-month-cycle patients, like Leona Atkins," he said. "I saw her again this morning. She's a walking annuity. Gets her Botox, alternates site injections with Restylane, does IPL on her chest, and loads up with product on her way out the door. Writes us a check and schedules the next appointment before she leaves."

"Yeah, but life would be dull without surgeries." Michael ate a forkful of salad. "Transforming somebody's figure—now that's a satisfying day at the office. One- and two-week follow-ups, they look like crap and they still hurt. By the four-week follow-up, I'm their newest favorite person on earth."

Jonathan rummaged through a container, found a dill pickle spear, took a small bite. Usually, he'd jump in with a funny tale or an update about one of his patients. His partners waited, but he had nothing to contribute to the conversation today.

"You're losing weight, buddy," Leo told John. "Better eat something. If you don't start taking better care of yourself, you're not going to be in any shape to take care of your patients."

"You should consider taking a vacation," Michael added. "You aren't having fun anymore, John. You used to enjoy coming to work. You used to play golf and go antiquing and compete in trap-shooting tournaments. What can we do to help you start having fun again, John?"

Jonathan tossed the half-eaten pickle back into a Styrofoam container. "I can't do this anymore."

Michael ate a chunk of tuna. "Do what?"

Jonathan reclined in the leather executive chair and stared at the ceiling. His arms went out. "This. Pretending to have a psychiatric practice when my life—our lives, are being controlled by some gangster as though we're puppets on strings. We don't even know who this asshole is, yet he's ruining our lives. Some idiot who goes by D-man—what stupid kind of a nickname is that, anyway—some idiot whose name is a *letter* is running our lives."

Leo and Michael exchanged looks. They had to get their partner under control. Michael put down his fork. "Look, John. It's not *that* bad. He just wants his money. That's all. We're almost there, and when we've paid everything back, this will all go away."

"I agree," Leo said, thinking back to that night when the three of them were still in school and he took the duffel bag from the car. Back then, everyone called him Will, short for his middle name, William. "I don't like being blackmailed any more than the next person, but this guy just wants what he figures he's entitled to, right? So think of it as a business deal. We don't like it, but we do it anyway. We stick together and ride it out. Besides, I have some news. I know who he is."

Michael dropped the pile of lettuce he was about to stuff in his mouth. "What? You know who's been extorting money and prescriptions from us? Who?"

"Ray Donnell Castello."

"It can't be," Michael said after a beat. "He's in jail. He went to jail for life."

There had been no witnesses to the shootings except for the three of them, Michael remembered, thinking back to that life-changing night. They were students in med school. It was pitch black and raining. There weren't even any nearby houses or other cars on the road, except for the single car coming at them. They'd spotted its faint headlights in the distance and had taken off in their own car before the vehicle got close enough to see them.

Later, when the incident was merely a fading nightmare, the boys learned the identity of the person in that car, or at least the person they assumed was the driver. A man named Castello. As kids, they never bothered to read the local daily newspaper. They barely had time to read all their textbook assignments. After the crash, though, they'd scanned the news every day. The very first day after it happened, they saw a brief blurb about two unidentified men being found in a wrecked car. Both were dead, the journalist reported, but the article didn't give details, other than to say gunshots were involved and a suspect was in custody. Two days later, the suspect was identified: Ray Donnell Castello. The cops termed him a "career criminal" who had several outstanding warrants for his arrest. The boys debated as to whether or not they should come forward and tell police that Castello didn't kill the two men in the car. It would be the right thing to do. And they could always do it without mentioning the money. But ultimately, they justified their silence by knowing that Castello would go to prison regardless. His past record would see to that. He was a wanted man.

Days later, another newspaper story caught their attention. Police still didn't know the identity of the dead men. But Ray Donnell Castello, the lead suspect, had been jailed for a prior armed robbery offense. He had been serving time in a New York prison when he escaped during an inmate riot, the article said. Not only that, but a stack of charges were pending against him from other states, including a homicide. Castello was going back to jail *for life*, the lead prosecutor said.

The boys convinced themselves that they'd made the right decision to not get involved. Castello would be off the streets forever. Besides, they'd taken the money from two dead men. Not Castello. They didn't owe Castello a thing. They forgot about the local news and quit buying the daily paper. Will, John, and Mike got back to the business of being medical students. And of course, planning how they would hide—and later use—the money.

"He did go to jail for life," Leo told his partners. "When this asshole appeared out of nowhere demanding money, it never occurred to any of us that it could be Castello. But last week, on a hunch, I checked it out."

"And?" Michael prompted.

"And he apparently worked some sort of a plea deal a few months into his original sentence. I guess he had information that the prosecutor's office wanted. He snitched. So all this time, we're assuming he's in for life, when really he was just serving twenty years," Leo said. "In any event, he's out. I don't know for sure that Castello is D-man, but it makes sense."

"It does make sense. It's the *only* answer that makes sense." Michael's eyes were wide. "The two men in that car thought we were sent by some man named Denny. They thought we ran them off the road on purpose. Before he accidentally shot himself, the driver told you to tell Denny to go to hell. Remember, Leo?"

"Of course I remember," Leo said. "Those headlights we saw coming? That must've been Denny, chasing the two guys in the car. That's why they were going so fast—they were running from him. That's why they lost control when they swerved to miss us."

"Right," Michael agreed. "But none of our theories mattered after we knew Castello was in for life. He couldn't bother us. So nothing about that night mattered at all."

"It matters now, Mike." Leo pushed away his plastic container and threw a used napkin over it. "It matters now because the animal is out of the cage."

Michael was done eating, too. He found a roll of Tums in his pants pocket and chewed a handful. "So Denny was a nickname for Donnell. And so is D-man, the name he goes by now."

Jonathan had a wad of napkin back to his nose again. "He must've found my student ID at the crash scene before the cops got him. And then, when he pleaded out to twenty years, he decided to come up with a revenge plan while he counted off the days. He knew he'd be getting out."

"For that matter," Michael said, "he could have been keeping track of us from prison. They get all sorts of privileges, I think. Television, magazines, Internet."

"While we're speculating"—Leo finished his tea—"tell me this. How did the police just happen to pick up Castello right after the wreck? Maybe none of this would have happened if Castello found

Jonathan's ID and came after us at school. I mean, we were kids. We could have claimed we didn't know any better. We would have just apologized and given him the money and that would have been the end of it." Leo eyed his partners and spoke slowly, emphasizing each word. "So how did the police get to the scene fast enough to nab Castello? There was nobody around to see or hear the car crash or the shootings, except Castello himself, who was chasing the two guys in his car."

"I called them." Michael's voice was flat. "*I* called the police."

Leo's head snapped around. "What?"

"John passed out on the sofa. You headed straight to the shower to get the blood off you. And none of us had even looked in the duffel bag yet. We didn't know what we had. Anyway, I went to the pay phone across the street from our apartment and called the police station to tell them about the wreck. That's all I said. I told them that we were driving home and passed an overturned car, but that we didn't see any people."

Leo's face went red. "Why, for God's sake?"

"I couldn't go to sleep with the thought of two dead men sitting in that car all night long. What if some innocent kid riding his bicycle the next morning came across that awful scene? Would you have wanted your little brother to see that?"

Leo let loose with a string of cusswords, directing the last few vulgar sentences personally at Michael. No longer concerned about avoiding a feud, Michael met Leo's furious look dead-on.

"Like Jonathan said earlier, *I'm* not the genius who took the duffel bag."

The men sat rigid in the thick silence, nobody eating or drinking, for several long minutes. Eventually, Jonathan leaned forward and pressed a folded napkin below his nostrils. Drops of bright red dotted the white paper when he removed it.

Michael sighed. "That was uncalled for, and I'm sorry, Leo. We all equally shared in the money that was in that duffel bag. What's important here is not whose fault this is, but the fact that we've been best friends since college." A partnership was like a marriage, Michael figured. You take the good and the bad and make it work. Well, maybe that's not the best example, he realized. The group had seen their share of divorces. He thought of a different analogy. "When you are partners, you share in the good times and help each other through the bad ones. And at least now, thanks to you, Leo, we know the identity of this jerk."

Jonathan sniffed several times to control the blood trickling from his nostrils. "You're naive, the both of you."

"And you've got to get yourself together, dammit." Leo's eyes narrowed. "You drink too much. You prescribe meds for yourself. And now you're getting *nosebleeds*? Have you been snorting your troubles away?"

Jonathan held a fresh napkin beneath his nose before looking at it to see if the blood had stopped. "If you still want to place blame, Leo, fine. I'll take the blame. Everything is my fault. It was *me* who caused this whole mess. If I hadn't gotten so drunk at that frat party, I wouldn't have been vomiting and I wouldn't have lost my ID." His voice dropped to a near whisper. "If I'd ever been able to make *any* of my personal relationships work, I'd be happily married. I wouldn't have pursued Rosemary. And if I hadn't given her the drugs . . . if she hadn't become addicted . . . if I hadn't confided to her about this big pile of shit we stepped in, she'd still be alive today." His head moved back and forth like a kid throwing a tantrum: *No, no, no!* "This isn't going away. Rosemary is dead. And I don't care if we do know his name. Blackmailers don't ever stop once they've gotten their talons into you. Don't you people watch TV?"

"Cop shows are fiction, John." Leo popped the cap on a bottle of tea and drank. "And yeah, this whole thing with Castello probably is your fault. But it's Michael's fault and my fault, too. Hell, maybe it's nobody's fault. Maybe it just is what it is. So we deal with it. We stick to the game plan. Are we all on the same page?"

Leo took the silence to mean agreement. He stood, checked his watch. "I've got a two o'clock consult and a three o'clock surgery, so I'm out of here. And John? Either you clean up your act or you're out of here, too, permanently. We still have a practice to run."

Jonathan nodded without bothering to look up. Leo stalked through the door. Michael gave John a squeeze on the shoulder and followed Leo out of the conference room.

After watching his partners head back to work, Jonathan cleaned up the mess from lunch. Paced the conference room. Sat down to stare through the windows at passing traffic. Tried to think. Asked God if there was a way to redeem himself. Got no answers, nodded off, and didn't move until a vivid dream of Rosemary awakened him. She was beautiful, laughing, holding hands with Garland. It was a party. And when Jonathan greeted her with a kiss on the cheek, Rosemary imploded into nothingness, leaving behind a puff of sweetly scented powder.

TWENTY-ONE

The great thing about working from home is that I can do so while wrapped in my lacy, silky jammies. They feel good against my skin. If more people slept nude and wore their pajamas around the house, the world might be a happier place.

I'd spread out my notes on the kitchen table and pored over the few facts I had, to see if any of the pieces would slide magically into place, like one of those giant magnetized picture puzzles for kids. When none of my index cards moved together on their own accord, I took a break from thinking and called Ox. His voice—both the deep tone and the unique Lumbee dialect he'd retained despite all the military moves—comforted and energized me. Lindsey was in heaven, he said, and convinced now more than ever that she wanted to work as a television sports personality. I already knew that the teen was dancing on top of the clouds. I wanted to know about Ox.

"So how are you?" I asked.

"Busy. Having a ball spending time with my daughter. Missing you."

He asked about the Block and the employees and Spud and Fran, and then I filled him in on the small favor for the judge that had taken on a life of its own. He listened without interrupting.

"Any thoughts on what might be going on?" I said.

"Other than the obvious conclusions, no."

"What about your guiding spirits? Do they have any input for me?" Ever since I'd first met him in high school, Ox has had a knack for sensing things that other people miss. I don't understand it, but I fully believe in the gift his Lumbee heritage has given him. I've also witnessed the man experience tokens—or, as his people call them, toat'ns—which are signs that a spirit is present.

He chuckled. "Let me check and get back to you."

"I miss them. Your helpful spirits. And you. I miss you." There was a lot more to talk about, but not now and not over the phone. We said good-bye.

The bad thing about working from home is that Spud has a habit of turning to me for his fill of daily entertainment when there's nothing more interesting going on.

"Hey, kid," he said, coming into the kitchen. "Frannie and I have decided to help you out on this thing you're working on, since Ox ain't here."

"Yeah, sweetie," Fran said. "We know you really miss him."

Of course she knew I missed the man. Obviously, she'd been eavesdropping. "Thanks for the offer, but there's not really much you can do."

"Well, what are you doing today?" my father asked. Standing at his feet, Cracker cocked his head as though he wanted to know, too.

Good question. "I'm not getting anywhere sitting around staring at my notes. Maybe I'll hit the gym before I take a shower.

Check on things downstairs." I studied my nails. The chipped polish had not miraculously repaired itself since the last time I'd noticed it. "And I really need a manicure." Jersey Barnes, supersleuth in action.

"Why don't we go to that fancy eatin' house and have dinner?" Spud suggested.

"That's a great idea!" Fran cooed. "Maybe we'll pick up clues." Jersey Barnes *and crew*, supersleuths in action.

I needed to hit Argo's anyway, to determine if the dining room had been bugged. It was the only theory that made sense, if it was true that Morgan had simply heard the Divine Image Group doctors talking. I phoned to make a reservation and left a message requesting the GT. The answering service assured me that someone would return my call by two o'clock.

I did my own nails—a quick fix by removing the polish and filing them short—before tackling the gym. Afterward, I let Cracker take me for a walk. Spud and Fran tooled off on her scooter to hear a lecture at the Cameron Art Museum on South 17th Street. We planned to meet back at the Block at five-thirty.

Our reservation was confirmed for seven-thirty. It was a perfect evening to be on the water, so we piled into the corpse caddy and drove to the Cape Fear Marina, where I keep *Incognito* docked. My one extravagance, she's a forty-eight-foot oceangoing sportfishing yacht. She was a gift from an appreciative past client, and I didn't think it would be affable to tell him that I don't fish. Although her outriggers have never been used, she does make a perfect party boat and is excellent for long weekend trips.

Thanks to a dockhand who works cheap, *Incognito* was clean and ready to go, cabin air-conditioning on, toilet paper in the head, and refrigerator stocked with water and beer. We left in plenty of time to make our reservation and cruised south on the Cape Fear River, used Snow's Cut to reach the waterway, and backtracked north to intersect with Bradley Creek. It took much longer than if we'd driven, but being on the water was rejuvenating. I hadn't run my boat in a while. It felt good.

Spud and Fran, after making a big production of climbing the ladder, joined me on the covered fly bridge. Like me, Fran seemed to relish the fresh air and passing sights. In contrast, my father wouldn't stop grumbling. Wearing one of his newly purchased outfits—the clothes for his upcoming cruise with the NAB—he fidgeted with the buttons of a lime green polka-dot shirt. The dots were the size of drink coasters. And pink. Lime green and pink top, navy-and-white-striped slacks, all accented by a yellow-enameled walking cane.

"This shirt has a flaw in it," he said.

"If the flaw is *in* it, then take it off," I told him. "Problem solved."

"What?"

"Never mind, it was a joke." I decided against trying to explain my attempt at humor. "What's the problem with your new shirt? Besides the fact that people need sunglasses to look at you."

He said something about it buttoning in the wrong direction.

"Oh, my." Squinting, Fran studied the shirt. "I think you bought a woman's shirt."

"The saleslady told me anybody could wear this. It's a uniplex shirt."

"Uni*sex*," Fran corrected.

"What's sex got to do with anything, for crying out loud?" The breeze had flattened out his mustache, but it still twitched from side to side, as though annoyed. "I can't go around in a girly shirt, especially not to Argo's."

"I like your shirt," Fran said, and fluffed her hair. "It's perfect for our cruise."

I think my eyebrows went up. "You're going on the NAB cruise with Spud?"

"Of course I am, sweetie. All those man-hunting women need to know that your daddy is already taken."

Spud grinned like a cocky teenager. "I still can't go around in no girly shirt tonight."

There were men's shirts hanging in the master stateroom closet, I told him. Last time Soup and his friends had taken a trip on *Incognito*, somebody had left clothes behind. Making a symphony of old-age noises, Spud and Fran maneuvered down from the fly bridge and disappeared into the cabin. Ten minutes later, Spud emerged and shouted up to me, "What do you think about this?"

He wore a black Led Zeppelin T-shirt. And the same navy-striped slacks.

"Oh, that's much better," I answered.

"You think so?"

"Absolutely. I especially like the lyrics on the back. Not everyone knows all the words for 'Stairway to Heaven.'"

Fran and Spud enjoyed the remainder of the trip from the open cockpit below, Spud stretched out like a retired rocker on the fighting chair—which on my boat had never been used to reel in a fish—and Fran fussing over him like a groupie. I had to slow down for no-wake zones in the waterway, but our cruise proved enjoyable as we studied the backyards of expansive waterway homes and fantasized about what it would be like to live with the rich set. I found Bradley Creek without having to consult my navigation system and backed into a vacant public slip without hitting anything. So far, so good.

When we'd tied off and were walking up to Argo's, I noticed the restaurant's large windows, artistically placed up-lighting, and mature shrubbery. I could actually see the Green Table and its occupants. Theoretically, somebody in one of the nearby houses or boats could use a laser microphone and audio-enhancing equipment to eavesdrop. Since Morgan was an accountant by trade, my bet remained on a much simpler, interior setup.

The hostess didn't flinch at my father's odd attire, but several other customers stared openly. Good thing Argo's didn't have a dress code.

"Is Morgan here tonight?" I asked.

"He was earlier," she told me. "But I believe he's gone for the evening."

I'm trained to notice details, and without having to go back outside to double-check, I knew that Morgan's sedan was in the parking lot. On the other hand, maybe the hostess told everybody that the boss was not available.

I inquired again about the Green Table, and as she seated us, the hostess discreetly mentioned that it was occupied by some top dogs from the set of *One Tree Hill*. I don't watch much television at all—especially not teen drama series—but I pretended to be suitably impressed. The popular show is produced at EUE/Screen Gems Studios, a full-service motion picture facility in Wilmington. The three of us settled into a booth, and I found myself wishing that Ox were around to make it a foursome. We ordered drinks and a braised rib appetizer and three of the chef's fish specials.

"Okay," Fran whispered. "What do we do now? Should we go question people?" She whipped out a small digital camera. "Or take pictures?"

"You can't go pokin' around and taking pictures while people are trying to eat, Frannie," my father reasoned.

"Good point, Spud," I agreed. "I'm going to do a quick walk-around to see if I find any bugs."

Fran stopped playing with Spud's knee. "They've got *bugs* here?"

"She's not talking about crawly bugs, Frannie. Listening bugs, for crying out loud. You know, like tiny microphones."

"Oh." She shivered. "How can I help?"

I realized that it might be less conspicuous for her and Spud to wander around the restaurant than it would be for me to do so. And I knew for a fact that my father could play a role. I'd seen him in action several times before. We came up with a game plan while we ate our hickory-and-ginger-spiced ribs.

Before the entrées were served, I turned on the pen, passed it to Spud, and sat back to watch him and Fran in action. Their first stop was the GT. I couldn't quite make out her words, but Fran chatted away while Spud hung behind her, pen in hand. The head server, Deanna, appeared instantly and gave an "I'm sorry" gesture to the Green Table's occupants. When Deanna noticed that Spud and Fran were wandering rather than returning to their own table, she offered to escort them.

Spud declined.

I heard Deanna ask if they were looking for the restrooms.

"Oh, we don't need a bathroom, sweetie," Fran near shouted. "His prostate is just fine. I can vouch for that."

Deanna's face remained impressively blank.

"We want to walk a bit before we eat," Spud said. "My legs cramp up if I sit too long."

Deanna moved off but continued to keep an eye on them.

They ambled through the restaurant, stopping periodically so Spud could "rest" on his cane.

It wasn't long before Deanna found me. "Hey, you're Jersey, right?"

I confirmed that it was indeed me, Jersey Barnes, asker of questions and buyer of drinks at Level 5.

She pointed at my father. "Is that couple dining with you?"

I confirmed that they were.

"They're sort of making people uncomfortable. You know, walking around like that and stopping next to tables."

"I imagine they'll sit back down as soon as our food shows up," I told her.

Deanna disappeared. Three chef's specials were delivered approximately four minutes later. The kitchen must've moved our order to the top of the list. Seeing the food, my father and his girlfriend meandered back to our booth, his yellow walking cane leading the way.

"Looks like a piece of fish served at any other restaurant," Spud said, bouncing up and down a few times to settle in on the booth seat. "Only they've squirted a sauce over it and the vegetables are stacked into a little pyramid."

"Fine dining is always a bonny experience," Fran said.

Spud and I looked at her. "What?" we said in stereo.

"That's a calendar word today. Bonny. It means pleasing to look at."

"Well, for crying out loud. That word doesn't even sound pleasant."

Digging in to my pyramid of vegetables, I asked what they'd learned during their tryst through Argo's.

Spud proffered my RF signal-detecting fountain pen. "It only vibrated when we first stopped at that big corner table, where the TV people are sitting."

"Nowhere else?"

"Nope," Spud said, and dug in to his plate of fish. "This plate has a boner, too."

"The word is '*bonny*,'" Fran corrected. "The presentation of the food is bonny, as in artistic."

"It's still a stupid word, for crying out loud."

While they ate, I headed for the bathrooms, special fountain pen in hand. I pretended to walk into the men's room by accident. No bugs. I checked the women's room. No vibration. The pen detected nothing until I moved past the hostess stand. It vibrated, much like a silenced cell phone. That meant two bugs so far: the GT and the hostess stand. I walked through the kitchen, pretending to look for Morgan. Nobody paid me much attention. And the fountain pen remained still. Morgan's office door was shut, but I sensed him inside. I knocked. He didn't answer. I found a server and asked for a piece of aluminum foil. She pointed to a shelf that held stacks of dispensing boxes. One of them held foil. I tore off a tiny strip, returned to Morgan's office, and slid the foil a few inches beneath the door, shiny side up. It served as a crude mirror, and I detected movement—just barely—on the other side of the door. Probably the desk chair rolling on the hard floor. Who else would be sitting in the chair if not Morgan? Of course he was in there. Why he refused to answer the door was puzzling, though. Unless my budding theory about the big corner table surrounded by Jonathan Green's artwork was correct.

Back at the booth, I ate my fish. It was tender and flaky and topped with an exotic fruit sauce and toasted pine nuts. The GT's occupants appeared to be getting ready to leave. On a hunch, I slid out of my seat and went to the Green Table.

"Hi," I said. "And so sorry to interrupt. Just want to apologize if my father disrupted your dinner. You know, the elderly couple who came over earlier?"

A group of four—two men and two women—eyed me. There were cocktail glasses on the table, as well as a bottle of red wine. Not to mention two empty dessert plates and two coffees. I imagined their tab to be at least three hundred dollars, if not more.

One of them waved a hand as if to say, *No big deal.* "Don't worry about it. They wanted to know how they could get into the business as on-camera extras. Cute couple. Not rude at all."

"Good," I said. "That's good. By the way, the new owner of this restaurant, Morgan, is a dear friend of mine. And his daughter is a *huge* fan of *One Tree Hill.* He just told Deanna, your server, to completely comp your tab. Food and bar."

"Wow, that's fantastic," said one of the women. "We'll have to be sure to send a thank-you note."

"You folks dine at Argo's anytime, and keep in mind that Morgan simply *won't* take your money," I said. "Oh, he might like a logo T-shirt or a day pass for his daughter to get on the set during filming. But in all honesty, he's just thrilled to have you in his restaurant." They stood and gathered belongings. I reminded them to leave a tip before returning to my booth. The group exited happily without paying for their meal.

Morgan appeared instantly. "What the hell do you think you're do—" He stopped in midsentence when he realized what he'd done.

"Let's take a walk," I suggested. "I'll show you my boat."

Spud and Fran were content to stay inside Argo's and share a dessert special: bananas Foster served with a spiced rum raisin sauce. Morgan caught Deanna's attention, and after inquiring about the GT's tab amount, he told her not to worry about the dine and dash— that he'd comped them.

"Thanks so much for giving away three hundred and eighty-four dollars," Morgan said once we were outside.

"It worked, didn't it? I got you out of that office of yours."

"I couldn't let you go around telling the whole restaurant their food is free. I do have a business to run, you know. And my *daughter* loves their TV show? Nice touch."

"Thanks." The evening sky had darkened considerably since I'd docked *Incognito*, and Argo's was beautifully lit up from our vantage point on the water. We sat in the air-conditioned salon, the boat rocking just enough to remind us we were on water. Morgan declined anything to drink.

"How does it work?" I asked.

His shoulders slumped. "There's a hidden microphone."

"Yeah, I figured that much. Tell me how it works. And why it's at the GT."

He went to the galley and returned with a beer. "Changed my mind."

After a few beats of silence, I asked again: "How does it work?"

"It was already in place when I took over the restaurant." He told me the story of how he'd found it accidentally, how there was a wireless microphone in the Green Table's centerpiece along with a receiver in the ceiling that was wired directly to his office, and how something would divert his attention every time he went in early to dismantle the setup. He wanted to get rid of the microphone, he said. He just hadn't done so yet.

An owl sounded from somewhere nearby, and its call echoed faintly across the water. "And why, specifically, were you listening to the Divine Image Group?"

Morgan stared at his untouched can of beer. "I was listening to everybody."

There had to be more. I waited.

"When my fiancée showed up with her old boss," he said, "I put them at the GT because I *wanted* to listen in. I had to know what was going on. When I heard them talking, I knew in an instant that they were sleeping together. It felt like somebody ripped my gut out with one of those fillet knives they use in the kitchen. But I kept listening. I learned that they were together the whole time she was with me." Morgan looked straight into my eyes. "I'm glad I found out the truth. Now I know what a shallow, conniving, immature person she is. I'm glad she didn't marry me."

"And after that?"

His eyes left mine and found the water, a bright moon giving its surface ripples a reflective glow. "I just . . . I just put the earbud in one more time. To listen to another conversation. I didn't even know the people. I guess I wanted to listen to somebody—anybody—because everyone else's life is so much more interesting than mine."

"And tonight? Why were you listening to the Green Table tonight? The hostess said you weren't here, but I saw your car in the parking lot, Morgan. I even knocked on your office door. What do you care about the private business of a television series producer?"

"I don't care who sits at the GT. It doesn't matter. I listen to everyone, even the random groups of tourists who get seated there because they know somebody. It's . . . it's hard to explain. It's an escape from my real world." He dropped his head into his hands. "Oh, Lord, what have I become?"

He might have been crying, but I didn't want to know. I can't stand to see an adult cry. "Morgan, people can get addicted to anything. Drugs, gambling, looking at porn, whatever turns you on. I'm no shrink, but it sounds like you've become addicted to eavesdropping on people."

Head still in his hands, he nodded. "I suppose so. I can't wait to get to the office every evening, so I can put in my earbud and listen. Sometimes I'll watch them on the overhead monitor, so I can see who is saying what. Mostly, I listen. My life sucks, Jersey. But when I'm hearing about other people's issues and problems and plans, I feel . . . really . . . *alive*. Energized. You know?"

I didn't know. I couldn't quite grasp the appeal of eavesdropping on total strangers. The judge had warned me that her brother was an outsider, a shy introvert with no friends and no social life. Perhaps he got off on living vicariously through his dining customers, even if only in short snippets.

"You do realize that what you're doing is illegal?"

He sat up. Breathed deep, straightening his posture. Took his first drink from the can of beer and regained his composure, once again looking like an attractive young professional. "Yes. I'm sure it probably is."

"Were anyone to find out, there could be criminal charges. And civil lawsuits. Argo's would likely be forced out of business."

"Yes," he said. "I've thought about that."

But just like a junkie using the pharmaceutical drug network, Morgan allowed the pleasure he derived to override any fear of getting caught.

"Are you recording people's conversations, too?"

He shook his head no. "I wouldn't even have a clue how to do that," he said. "I just listen."

We stepped off *Incognito* and returned to the dining room. Spud was teaching Fran how to play blackjack. Their dessert plate had been cleared, and they were slurping coffees. Spud explained that Fran needed practice for the cruise ship's casino.

"I'll be a few more minutes," I told them, and dropped a credit card on the table to pay our tab.

"I'd comp you guys," Morgan said as we walked to his office in the back of the house, "but I've already given away a four-hundred-dollar tab tonight."

At least he'd kept a sense of humor about my little stunt.

Argo's kitchen brimmed with hurried staff, and I wondered how they managed to get through a shift without crashing into one another. Three chefs stood over burners and a fourth tended a grill, all of them communicating in a clipped language that I couldn't quite decipher. It was an entirely different world from the laid-back kitchen at the Block.

Morgan unlocked his office and we went in, shutting the door behind us. One more person in the little space and it would be uncomfortably crowded. He showed me the small blue box he'd talked about, along with the wired earbud coming out of it, and showed me how to adjust the volume with one of the dials. I held the bud to my ear and heard a woman talking about a Lexus they'd recently bought and how she hated to have a car payment again, but what a great financing rate they got. A man told her that she deserved a new car. A younger female, probably their daughter, asked if she would get the car in a few more years, when she left for college. All of the voices were intimately clear. I felt as though I were sitting at the GT with them, and when I looked at the security monitor overhead view, I suddenly understood how Morgan might get a rush by doing what he'd been doing. Especially since he didn't have a life outside of Argo's. And especially since people will talk about almost anything while they're having dinner: finances, travel, sex, work, gossip. Probably, though, Morgan's interest in the Green Table would quickly fade if he were to make some friends and take up a hobby and find a new girlfriend and get a life of his own.

I killed the volume, removed the earpiece, and examined the blue box. I hadn't seen the exact setup before, but it appeared to be a basic box with audio connectors. A single cable ran downward and connected with the back of the computer console. I asked Morgan how he switched to the hostess stand microphone.

"What hostess stand microphone?"

"The Green Table is the only hidden mike you're aware of?"

He nodded.

"What about the computer?" I said.

"What about it?"

"Any audio files on there?"

"You mean like a song that somebody would listen to on their iPod?" He shrugged. "I don't think so."

I called Soup and found him at home. He answered on the first ring.

"I'm still working on it, Jersey. I'll call you the nanosecond I have the full scoop on your divine doctors."

"I have another question."

"I couldn't be more surprised." Rapid keyboard clacking sounds. "Does my time *on this particular question* pay?"

"It's one question, Soup. Good grief."

He told me that lawyers charge for their time, even for single questions that come over the phone.

"Then get a law degree," I said. "Listen, I'm in front of a desktop PC at Argo's restaurant. I need to find out if there are audio files on here. What do I do?"

Soup wanted to know what type of audio files.

"There's more than one kind?"

"Next time I come to the Block," he said, "I'm bringing friends. And we're going to order lots of shrimp and whatever the fresh catch of the day is, and a boatload of bottled imports."

"Fine," I agreed.

He gave me detailed instructions as to what to do on the desktop, and we went back and forth for five or six minutes when I came across a drop-down list of files that ended with ".aif." The letters stood for audio interchange file format, Soup explained. Like I'd actually remember that in ten minutes.

"There are about twenty or twenty-five files with that same extension, and each one is titled by a date, I think," I said. I double-clicked on one to open it, but nothing happened.

Soup asked if I had Internet access. I asked Morgan. Morgan told me to click on the little Internet Explorer icon. I did. In a few seconds, the World Wide Web lay at my fingertips.

"Send me an e-mail with all the files." Soup gave me an e-mail account address to go to, along with the password to get in. "This account will handle large file sizes, so you can probably send them to me all at once."

I did as instructed, and after four attempts, Soup had received all the audio files I'd found on Morgan's computer.

"I'm headed to your place," I told my hacker friend.

"Bring me soup, then. Whatever their soup of the day is. And beer. I'm about out of beer."

Soup is an ex-fed who got tagged with the nickname because he always eats soup when he works. He's something of a soup aficionado. On the way out, I cautioned Morgan to keep up his normal routine but to stop listening to the Green Table. Unless the doctors came back. He agreed.

I collected my father and Fran, signed the tab, and left Argo's with a self-adhesive wireless microphone and three Styrofoam containers. The bug had come from the underside of the top panel of the wooden hostess stand. Whoever had placed it could only be listening from the road or the parking lot in front of the building. And since its battery remained good, it had to have been installed recently. The to-go containers held a catfish-and-mango-lime soup and a "midnight" snack for Spud and Fran. I forced myself not to think about why they might need a midnight snack.

We cruised back to the Cape Fear Marina, navigation lights cutting through the darkness, Spud and Fran debating the merits of their bananas Foster flambé, prepared tableside for dessert.

"If I want burnt food," Spud was saying, "I can light something on fire at home, for crying out loud."

Concentrating on the water, I tuned them out and wondered what Ox was doing and if he'd been thinking of me as much as I'd been thinking of him.

TWENTY-TWO

Still driving the bodymobile, I see," Soup said when he let me into his place.

"The price was right." I handed him the container of soup and a six-pack of Coors Light. "Besides, it grows on you. Great sound system."

Although it was well past eleven, Soup's place was brightly lit and buzzed with energy.

A mixture of genuine retro and modern tech, it held a U-shaped command center in the living room. Monitors, printers, computers, and a plethora of electronic stuff connected by a highway of wires and cables were placed strategically so he could wheel his desk chair to position himself in front of anything. Each time I visited Soup's place, the screens were flatter and larger, the computers smaller, and his collection of gadgetry bigger.

"Those files you e-mailed were taped conversations." He held up a stack of stapled papers. "I used a voice recognition program to translate them into text documents, so you'll see a few strange words and punctuation marks."

While Soup made food appreciation noises over the Styrofoam container of catfish-and-mango-lime soup, I sat down with my bounty. The top of each page was labeled with the audio file's date and total length. The conversations spanned a seven-month time period, and all took place before Morgan relocated to Wilmington. Before his father died. Which indicated that Garland had likely put the Green Table's bug in place for a specific purpose. He was the only person who had access to Argo's small office, and rumor had it that he always kept the door locked. Fanning through the conversations, I saw that they were all of the Divine Image Group doctors. Either Garland suspected them of something or he planned to blackmail them. Odd, since everyone said that they'd been family friends with Garland and Rosemary for years. On the other hand, people say that best friends make the worst enemies.

Flipping back to the first conversation, a brief one that didn't reveal anything other than a discussion over that day's plastic surgeries, I noted that it took place mere weeks after Rosemary died. Interesting.

Soup twisted the caps off two bottles of beer and gave me one. "Excellent soup. The spice is perfect. And whoever would have thought of pairing catfish with mango?"

"The chef at Argo's."

"I'd like to meet him," Soup said, meaning it. Skilled hackers and creators of appetizing chowders were his heroes.

I scanned each stapled stack of paper and was fast-forwarding through their headers when the doorbell sounded.

"You expecting anyone?" Soup asked. I told him I wasn't.

A video screen displayed a man standing outside his door. The doorbell sounded again. Soup did something to make the outdoor camera zoom in on the visitor's face. Brad stood there, hands stuck in his pockets.

"Crap," I said. "My DEA buddy. He must have followed me." Unless he'd put a tracking device on the hearse. Bastard.

"You want me to let him in?"

"If we don't, he'll sit out there and wait for me." I rubberbanded my stack of transcripts and put them on the floor with my handbag, facedown.

"Plenty of ways to get rid of your boy," Soup said, wicked grin stretched across his face. "Like, for example, I could hack into the local police dispatch, pop in a description of Brad and his vehicle, and code it with, oh . . . something like soliciting a minor. At a rest stop. Yeah, that'll work. Then we place a 911, using one of my voice modification programs. We'll make it a female caller, with a European accent, like a tourist. A frantic mama can say that a man just exposed himself to her daughter at this location. She stopped to get directions at the convenience store. She gives an exact description of Brad and his vehicle." Soup nodded to himself. "Then we sit back and watch the light show outside my window."

I sighed. "Soup, just let him in."

"My way would be much more entertaining." Soup opened the door. I introduced the two men. Brad scanned Soup's place, taking in all the electronics.

"What do you want, Brad?" I think my hands were on my hips.

He said something about driving by and seeing my hearse and stopping by to say hello. *Yeah, right.* I'd have known if he'd followed me. My government-conditioned brain has been trained to maintain a high level of awareness. Doing so is second nature. Which meant that Brad had probably attached a GPS device to the corpse caddy. It made perfect sense that someone in his position would do so. But the fact that he'd gotten away with it pissed me off.

I dug through my handbag, found the microphone I'd removed from Argo's hostess stand, and held it out. "This what you're looking for?"

He pocketed the quarter-size device without looking at it.

"I'll return the tracker you put on my car, too, soon as I locate it. Sometimes, though, I accidentally drop and smash those little GPS thingies. So you might want to go get it yourself and save me the trouble of removing such an expensive gadget."

Brad's arms moved without purpose for a few seconds before he folded them across his chest. "You do realize that you're interfering with an ongoing investigation?"

"I'd never do that." I made a show of imitating his stance. "As I told you before, I'm merely doing a favor for a friend."

We eyed each other, playing the who-will-blink-first game.

"Jeez, you two," Soup said. "Go get a room already."

I blinked first and threw my gaze on Soup. "What are you insinuating?"

He looked at the ceiling, as though everything were obvious. "Nothing. Never mind."

"A hotel room might be fun," Brad said.

"Sure, if I swept it for audio and video first."

"It's been real." Soup herded us to the door. "Not so fun, though." He claimed he had piles of work waiting, but I think he just wanted Brad out of his place. Even though Soup used to be a federal agent, he's leery of active uniforms and undercovers. They make him uncomfortable.

Seemingly not offended, Brad said that pancakes would be good, and I agreed to join him at a twenty-four-hour diner. Like I needed pancakes. Or live conversation from Brad at midnight.

Sitting across from each other in a corner booth at the Waffle House, Brad and I continued to eye each other like two wary tigers thrown together in a cage. Territorial. Stubborn. The same species, but not always hospitable to its own kind. Something about him got under my skin, like an unseen chigger that itched just enough to be irritating.

"Why have you been listening to the Argo's hostesses?" I asked. "And from where, just out of curiosity."

"Nearby house," he said. "Weekly rental. My team has been rotating shifts during restaurant hours. Main phone line is hot, too."

I should have known. "Learn anything interesting?" I asked. As if he'd tell me.

He chugged some coffee. "We know who is eating at Argo's and how many people are in their party every evening."

"Wow." I stirred cream into my coffee. "Your information-gathering skills are phenomenal. Do you keep a spreadsheet of the chef's nightly specials, too? Maybe a breakdown by entrées from land or sea?"

Our banter went on until the food arrived: his tower of pancakes and my egg sandwich. His looked better.

"Tell me, Jersey Barnes . . ." He poured syrup on the stack for a full ten seconds, until the little glass syrup pitcher was half-empty. "Are you this abrasive with everyone you encounter, or just me?"

I finished a bite of sandwich before answering and took my time to do so. "Nope, not everyone. Only con men."

"I'm a con man?"

"If I recall, you are the one who suggested that we work together on this Argo's thing. Said we could share information, help each other out. Yet all you've been doing is keeping tabs on me. You're

certainly not sharing." I drank my coffee. Ate a bite of egg sandwich. "You want to get something for nothing. Which makes you a
con man."

Brad burst out laughing. "My grade-school teachers always
noted on report cards that I didn't play well with others."

At least he didn't take himself too seriously. I gave in to a smile.
"I don't really have a good reason to stay mad, do I. You're just doing your job."

He stuffed a forkful of soppy pancake in his mouth and nodded.
"Right. And I don't really have a good reason to stay mad at you, either, do I."

"Nope," I said. "But there is *something* about us that rubs each
other the wrong way."

He wiped syrup from his lips, stared at mine. "Definitely something."

We finished our food and coffee, and Brad agreed to remove the
tracker he'd put on the corpse caddy. He put money on the table,
telling me he'd expense the meal. "Next time you want to expense
a meal with me," I said, "how about a lobster dinner?"

He asked what I'd learned at CC's Hair Boutique.

"Well, crap." I threw up my hands. "I start to like you a teensy
bit, and you go back to being a jerk."

The waitress returned with change, and we walked out to a
brightly lit parking lot. Brad retrieved a Swiss Army knife from his
Murano, got on his back, scooted beneath the front end of my hearse.
"Go easy on me, Jersey," he said through a grunt. "We both want the
same thing."

"What's that?" I asked.

He rolled from beneath the hearse, straightened up, brushed himself off. Held out the tracking device to prove he'd removed it. "We
both want to figure out who's the entrepreneur behind this prescription drug ring and put him out of business."

I showed him my cocky smile. "Nice pep talk, Brad. Translation: Your girl didn't get a thing from CC's hair place, did she."

He did the lopsided grin. "Nope. Except she got her roots done, whatever that means. Went back two days later for a haircut. Expense-reported both."

I found my keys and climbed into the wagon. "Let's meet tomorrow and I'll tell you everything I learned at CC's—where, by the way, Alex took care of my split ends. Forty-two dollars for a wash, cut, and blow-dry." I held out a hand, palm up. "Plus tip."

Mumbling like Spud often does, Brad found his wallet and passed me fifty bucks. Hey, I have to take perks where I can get them. Especially when I'm working for free.

He stuffed the wallet back in a pocket. "I'd also like copies of whatever you carried out of Soup's place."

"No can do," I said. "Besides, it's a memoir he's working on. Nothing you'd care to look at."

Brad leaned through the open car door and kissed me on the mouth. "Right," he said, and vanished before I could protest. Or decide to kiss him back.

I shut my door. "He really should stop kissing me," I said to nobody.

TWENTY-THREE

The next morning as I fixed breakfast, Cracker acted clingy, following me around and propping his big, wide body against my legs the second I stopped moving. With Ox being out of town and Spud spending so much time with Fran, the dog probably felt neglected.

I squatted on the floor at dog level. "Whazzup, stinky breath?" He went for my face, tongue lapping and tail wagging, and didn't stop until I'd fallen over laughing and rolled around on the floor with him. I pushed the animal off me and gave him a final pat on his backside. Appeased after some quality one-on-one time with a human, Cracker stretched out in a streak of sunlight that filtered through the kitchen balcony doors and promptly started to snore. If only my days were so easy.

I folded my limbs into a chair at the kitchen table and spread out the report Soup had just e-mailed to me. It would have taken me weeks—lots of legwork and time-consuming research—to amass the same intelligence. Thankfully, Soup is an expert at finding the right databases to hack. His way is much quicker.

Eating a cup of yogurt with fresh pineapple chunks, I learned that the Divine Image Group doctors—Leon William Haines, Jonathan O. Rosch, and Michael J. Pratt—had attended medical school together at Duke University in Durham. Not only were they in the same fraternity, they were also roomies. After completing internships at different hospitals and clinics, they had reconnected to open the Divine Image Group in Wilmington. Quite an impressive undertaking for thirty-year-olds. Since then, they'd moved locations twice, ultimately buying a patch of undeveloped dirt and erecting their own building. Collectively, the three looked like saints on paper. Successful. Altruistic. Positions on several boards of directors. An anthology of awards. Articles published in medical journals. Guest speakers at conventions. The group appeared *too* perfect. Until I reached the part about their personal lives. Leo was the only one still married to his original wife. The other two had three divorces and several kids between them. And Jonathan had a public intoxication arrest on his record.

Their financials piqued my interest, too. Soup found no evidence of scholarships or wealthy families. They started as three ordinary kids from middle-class America who wanted to be doctors when they grew up. All three paid off their student loans in full, immediately after graduation. They also opened a joint savings account that was later used to start their medical practice.

I leafed through the final pages of the printout: spreadsheets of prescriptions they'd written over the previous four years, broken down by the drug's prescribing physician and category, or schedule. There were no schedule 1 drugs, but there were plenty of schedule 2's such as amphetamines, morphine, and oxycodone.

I dialed Soup's home number, figuring that he'd be at one of his keyboards, venturing through cyberspace. He was.

"Can you get me any patient information?" I said when he answered. "A master list of Divine Image Group patient names would be great."

"Your outpouring of gratitude overwhelms me."

"*Thank you* for the info," I said. "Can you get me any patient names?"

The keyboard sounds stopped. "Here's the thing. Since cosmetic procedures are rarely covered by insurance, there's not a data dump to follow. And even though health insurance *will* cover psychiatric treatment, rich people don't want it noted in their medical files that they're seeing a shrink. All of a sudden, a bad mood turns into a preexisting condition. You follow? Medical privacy is bullshit. A diagnosis of mental problems, for example, could be used against a person in the future for all sorts of things. Child custody hearings. A new job position. A weapons permit. You name it."

"So . . ."

"So the only way you're going to get a patient list is to burgle the Divine Image Group offices. They're probably computerized, but they're using a self-contained PC with no Internet access."

I asked Soup if he could go through all the local pharmacy databases and pull patient names by the three prescribing doctors.

"And you're paying me how much?"

"Never mind," I said, but I think he'd already hung up.

I don't mind a little breaking and entering now and then. I could always ask Trish to help. Or take the direct approach and boldly confront the three medicos. I had enough to make them squirm. At the least, I'd stir the pot and possibly dredge up a few morsels from the bottom.

Spud and Fran clomped up the stairs from the Block and beeped their way into my kitchen. They wore matching T-shirts. In block letters, hers said, HOKEY. His said, POKEY.

"We need to get an elevator in this building, for crying out loud," Spud said.

Fran pinched his butt. "Walking the stairs will keep you in shape for more *strenuous* things," she said, winking at me.

He didn't catch the innuendo. "I get any more strenuous, my heart's gonna blow a valve."

I cringed and waited for another Fran comment. Spud had teed it up—a big fat white ball—and she would be compelled to swing at it.

"It's *a different* valve I'm thinking about, baby."

If only a person could shut their ears like they shut their eyes. It was way too early in the morning to visualize Spud and Fran having sex.

Still not clueing in, Spud told her that he didn't want *any* of his valves to blow and, thankfully, changed the topic.

"Thanks for leaving these papers out for us," he said, pointing at the stack of Green Table transcripts with the tip of his walking cane. "Frannie and I read them last night."

I hadn't left them out on purpose. "You read them all?"

The cane went back to the floor and Spud used it to settle himself into a kitchen chair. "Yeah, and we've got some theories for you about the doctors."

Fran nodded. "We figure somebody is blackmailing them."

I did, too.

Spud's mustache twitched from side to side. "Question is, why would three successful doctors start doling out drugs like a Shriners clown tossing candy at a parade?"

I didn't know.

"According to Soup, they have plenty of money," Fran said. "Their finances look good."

"You talked to Soup?"

Carrying a basket of mini blueberry muffins, she dropped down next to my father. "Sure did, sweetie. He called last night around ten-thirty to let you know that he e-mailed a detailed background report on the Divine Group." She pointed at my report. "Looks like you've already printed it. Anyhow, Soup and I chatted awhile."

"You chatted?" Soup doesn't normally "chat." Not with me.

Eyebrows arched high, Fran nodded. "Such a nice man, and so smart, too. I'm going to cook him a pot of homemade red curried lentil soup. It's a shame that Jennifer isn't around anymore to do for him. He really misses that girl."

I think my jaw fell open. "Who's Jennifer?"

"She was his girlfriend."

"Soup had a girlfriend?"

"Why, they've been dating on and off for months. He took her to Amsterdam." Fran breathed out a falsetto sigh. "Unfortunately, that's where Jennifer met the famous photographer and dumped Soup."

I really needed to work on my friendship skills, I decided.

"I didn't climb those stairs to listen to girl-talk, for crying out loud," Spud said. "We're investigating a peccadillo."

It had to be a calendar word.

"A peccadillo is actually a *petty* misdoing," Fran said. "This thing is much more serious than a peccadillo."

Spud muttered something about spending ten minutes learning how to pronounce the word, and what good is the stupid calendar anyhow if the words of the day don't work into his sentences?

The two of them just might be helpful, I figured, if I could keep them focused on the topic at hand. Especially since I couldn't conjecture with Ox. "You guys said you had several theories. Blackmail—we all agree on that. What else?"

"They ain't only writing bogus prescriptions," Spud said. "They're paying out money to somebody. Probably the same person, the one they keep talking about when they're eating at Argo's. They never say his name. They might not know his name."

"Right." Fran fed my father a bit of muffin. "Which makes your daddy think the doctors had a set dollar amount to pay."

Spud washed down the muffin with a swallow of Yoo-hoo. "The way I figure, they couldn't come up with all the money at once without causing questions from their wives. So they gave what they could from personal accounts. They set up a schedule to pay each month out of their office account. But that still didn't satisfy the debt, 'least not soon enough for the blackmailer. So he got them to agree to start supplying the drugs, too. Sounds like he's got 'em by the cojones."

My father stated the obvious, which I hadn't quite put together yet. And it made perfect sense. "At which point," I said, "Morgan's mother and father somehow got involved in the drug side of things and were basically dealing at Argo's."

"Not necessarily, kid." Spud's mustache did a miniature version of the electric slide. "The mother, Rosemary, for sure. Maybe she did it to help out the shrink, since they were supposedly tight. Chat chums. He was her sexless squeeze."

Sexless squeeze? *That* wasn't a calendar word.

"Or maybe she was hooked on dope," he continued. "The mother could have got caught up in the mess for any number of reasons. Not so sure about Garland, though. Put it all together, especially the fact that he's the one who bugged that table, it makes me think he *wasn't* in on it. I don't think he knew what the doctors and his wife were up to."

I wasn't used to my father making sense. He caught me appraising him.

"What, for crying out loud?"

I snatched a muffin. "Nothing, just thinking. Maybe Garland was doing exactly what I'm doing: trying to figure out what his wife had gotten involved in and how the doctors fit into the picture."

Fran fluffed her hair. "Your daddy used to be an acclaimed detective, don't you know."

"A detective?" I knew he'd spent his career in Lexington, Kentucky—home of the University of Kentucky. Since suddenly coming back into my life a few years ago, my father hadn't wanted to talk about the past. We never discussed my mother, my childhood, or why he'd walked out on us. And we never discussed his working days. I'd always assumed his shifts as a cop were relatively mundane, dealing with petty crimes and domestic disturbances.

Fran fed him another half of a mini muffin. "Why, they did a big story about him solving the flip-flop killer case. Man raped girls all over the country. He'd always take their shoes and leave a pair of flip-flops at the scene. What magazine was that article in, sweetie?"

"*Police and Security News.*" Spud's smile returned. "Was no big deal, for crying out loud."

Fran gazed at my father as though he were royalty. "You tracked him and found him and arrested him."

I stared at Spud. "You did?" My father—the Spud I knew—leaned more toward troublemaking, poker-playing, alligator-shooting, often illogical, bumbling and grumbling, sometimes crotchety old man. Not only did I need to work on my friendship skills, apparently I needed to work on my family communication skills, too.

Spud waved a hand. "Was no big deal, for crying out loud."

"Huh," I said.

Spud threw back his head to get to the bottom of the chocolate Yoo-hoo bottle. "Frannie, how's about you make us a pot of coffee and maybe dish up some of that fruit salad with the little marshmallows?"

She jumped up to do so.

He looked at me. "Kid, get your notes straightened out and let's go over everything. And we need a big board to draw on. Or a pad of paper will do."

I found a legal pad and returned to the smell of coffee brewing.

Spud waved his cane like an orchestra conductor. "First off, how did each of this Morgan kid's parents kick the bucket?"

Rosemary died of a drug overdose, I said, but Garland had told everyone—including his two kids—that she'd died of a heart attack. The police report stated that Garland had come home late after closing the restaurant and found his wife dead in their outdoor hot tub. The real reason she'd drowned, though, was that she'd passed out and fallen facedown into the bubbling water. The autopsy turned up an obscene amount of drugs in her system, and after a brief investigation, the death was ruled accidental.

Garland's body, on the other hand, wasn't autopsied. His death circumstances were simple and straightforward: injuries sustained during a fall. He'd been on a ladder, adjusting a floodlight attached to the side of Argo's, when the ladder slipped. A witness saw it happen and called an ambulance. Garland never regained consciousness and was pronounced dead upon arrival at the hospital.

"Who was the witness?" Spud said.

I looked at my notes and gave him a name.

"You follow up on that witness?"

I shook my head no. I hadn't. I should have. "I will."

"Where are they buried?" Fran wanted to know.

Another good question. I tried Morgan's number but got his voice mail. I hung up and tried the judge's cell phone number. Out of court, she answered on the second ring. I learned that both Rosemary and Garland had been cremated. Their ashes rested at Wilmington's Maplewood Memorial Cemetery, in a prayer bench.

"Inside a bench?" I said.

"It's a marble bench that you engrave, like a headstone. The base of the bench is hollow, so the front panel can be removed. The urns with the ashes are inside."

"I didn't know you could put ashes inside a bench," I said.

"You'd be surprised at all the options for grieving family members," my judge friend said. "Mom always wanted to be cremated. Dad decided to do the prayer bench because you can put them anywhere. Some people put them in a backyard or private park. At the cemetery, it's a way you can go visit the grave, so to speak. Even though there is no actual grave."

I thanked her for the information and tried to disconnect, but she wasn't going to let me off that easy. She wanted information and didn't quite believe me when I told her that I didn't yet have anything solid to report. We hung up, me promising to have something for her soon and her threatening to get in her car and drive to Wilmington.

Cracker circled the table, nose working. Spud fed him a muffin, which he chewed exactly once before swallowing. We went over the rest of my notes, from Morgan's car being searched to the encounter with Earless at Argo's to Brad and his ongoing DEA investigation of a drug ring, possibly called the network.

"Let's get to the cemetery, for crying out loud," Spud said.

Cracker sat against my legs and begged for another muffin. He got one. "Why?" I asked.

"Just got a feeling," my father said, "that we ought to go take a look."

We finished breakfast, piled in the hearse, and pointed it toward Maplewood Memorial Cemetery. At least it would be one place where people wouldn't stare at my unusual vehicle.

TWENTY-FOUR

Think of all these people," Fran said as we trudged through a shaded, grassy area of the cemetery, looking for the prayer bench. "All the family histories and wonderful stories that rest here."

And all the dead bodies. "I'd rather not think about them," I said. For me, strolling through a cemetery is six short feet shy of a full-fledged necrophobia panic attack. My chest began to constrict and I couldn't get enough air.

"Pretend you're walking through a park, for crying out loud," Spud said. "You'll be fine."

"What's wrong with her?" Fran said, as though I weren't standing right there.

"She's got this thing about being around a dead body," Spud explained.

Fran launched into a speech about the cycle of life.

I kept walking. "Can we please just go find the bench?"

We trekked to the area near a pond and, on the third prayer bench we checked, found one with the correct names on it. It was made from solid marble coral-tone slabs and positioned beneath a giant hardwood. The top was about four feet wide and maybe twenty inches deep. The rectangular base that supported the top of the bench was slightly smaller, and its front panels were engraved with two names, two dates of birth, and two dates of death.

"Now what?" I said.

Spud's mustache moved from side to side. I'd never noticed him moving his mouth before when deep in thought, so it must have been a newly developed habit since the addition of the facial hair. Either that or I'd never before witnessed him deep in thought.

"Wait here." Spud made his way to where two men were digging a grave with a small tractor. He spoke to them, his walking cane animated. The one driving the tractor jumped off, and the three men headed to where we waited at the bench.

"Never heard of kinfolk polishing the urns," one said as they took positions on either side of the marble top. "Most people put a permanent seal around the panels so you don't have to worry about them getting dirty. Might want to consider it."

My father said something about keeping that in mind. With a three count, the workers lifted the heavy bench seat and set it on the ground. Inside the base were two identical brass urns. The men stood back to wait.

Spud acted like he was wiping tears from his eyes, and not wanting to be left out, Fran let out a wail and dropped to her knees.

"Uh, we'll go finish up what we were doing," a worker said, retreating. "Let us know when you're ready for us to put the top back on."

Sniffling, Spud nodded at them.

I rolled my eyes. "Maybe you two ought to join a community theater group."

Spud found a handkerchief in his pocket, waved it around in the air just for show, and handed it to Fran. He removed the urns. They, too, were engraved with names. Inside the first urn was a plastic liner of ashes, secured with a ribbon at the top. Spud told Fran to untie it.

"What are you doing?" I asked.

He dismissed my question with the wave of a hand. "You were impatient coming out the womb, and you're still impatient today, for crying out loud."

He'd been there when Mom gave birth, but not while I was growing up? Something to think about later.

When Fran got the plastic bag untied, Spud dipped three fingers into the ashes, studied them, smelled them, shrugged.

"Oh, gross." I nearly turned away, but I didn't want to make a scene. A lone black man wandered among the graves and stopped at one nearby. I didn't see a vehicle, and I wondered if he'd walked in. He caught me looking. Seemingly unconcerned, he stooped to clean off the headstone.

Fran retied the liner and opened the second one. Spud repeated his finger-dipping process and made a face. "Smell this," he said, and stuck his fingers in front of Fran's nose.

She sniffed and made a similar face. "Smells like a dirty ashtray."

Spud dug further into the plastic liner and brought up a handful of sand. "Don't know where your Garland fellow is, but I'm pretty sure this ain't him."

Driving back, I asked my father how he'd known.

"Timing was too ironic. Death report too clean. And the whole part about dead upon arrival at the hospital?"

"Yeah?"

"It's all pretty perspicuous, really," my father said.

I knew it to be a calendar word and waited for the definition.

"That means clear-cut," Fran said from the backseat.

Spud slid on a pair of mirrored aviation-style sunglasses. "First off, all the ground surrounding Argo's is loaded with grass and shrubbery. If a man took a fall off a ladder anywhere around that building, he might have hurt himself something bad. But a lethal fall? Only if he broke his neck or had a head injury."

His mustache worked. "Second of all, let's say he *was* hurt that bad. The medics never would've moved him. They would have radioed for a chopper to carry him to the nearest trauma center."

Fran reached through the hearse's dividing window to pat Spud's shoulder. "That's right, sweetie. Wilmington's trauma center is a level two. He'd need a level one center for a cracked-open head."

I eyed her in the rearview.

She withdrew her arm to shrug. "Seniors know these things."

"And third off," Spud continued, "the report said Garland was fixing a floodlight on the side of the building. There ain't no floodlights on the side of the building. When we were coming up from the marina, the place was all lit up. All the floodlights on the building were attached to the corners."

I chewed on that for the remainder of the drive to the Block. Spud was right. Somebody wanted to make it look like Garland was dead. And the most likely suspect was Uncle Sam himself. Who else could pull off a fake death in Wilmington, North Carolina—including medical examiner collaboration and a signed death certificate? Had it been the DEA? Was Brad in on it? And if Garland was alive, where was he?

TWENTY-FIVE

The next best thing to burglarizing the Divine Image Group's office, I figured, would be to schedule an appointment and mosey around. Since I've got all the fake body parts I want, Fran volunteered to be the patient. She was supposed to say that she wanted noninvasive options to look younger and complain about a pulled back muscle to see if they'd write her a scrip for pain pills, just for the asking.

I played the role of Fran's daughter and chauffeur. And Spud decided to tag along, because his poker pals were volunteering at an NAB fund-raising car wash.

"Ain't no way I'm gonna spend my day washing cars when I'm not even allowed to drive one, for crying out loud," he said for the third or fourth time as my hearse traversed Wilmington's streets. After the state of North Carolina deemed Spud too visually impaired to drive, he became obsessed with getting rid of his car. When he couldn't sell it, he tried to collect on the insurance money by sinking it, burning it, and paying someone to steal it. When all his plans failed, he had an epiphany: Keep the Chrysler so other people could tote him around in it. That's when a stolen garbage truck driven by a crazy woman plowed into it while the car was parked outside the Block.

We arrived ten minutes early for Fran's appointment and stepped into an uncluttered, inviting reception area. It was the kind of waiting room that opened directly to the front-desk gal, with a basic floor-to-waist counter separating us. No tiny sliding window to shut out the offending patients. There was also a single-cup brew coffee machine and a beverage cooler with bottled water and fruit juices. Two flat-screen televisions on the walls. And current magazines.

"You want me to work up a diversion once Frannie gets back there?" Spud asked. "Then you can slip behind the counter and take a look-see."

"Let's hold off on that for now, Spud. This is a passive recon effort."

He grumbled something about being bored. "All the magazines are foo-foo. I should've brought the *Star-News*."

Five minutes and he'd gotten bored. I wondered how he ever managed a stakeout back in the day. Like a kid spotting a new toy, Spud found the coffeemaker and brewed three cups before a beaming nurse with perfect skin called Fran's name.

"I'm off for a walk," my father said. "See what's around here."

"It's mostly all medical buildings, Spud."

He waved his cane. "Well, then, maybe I'll find a urologist. At least they have decent magazines in their waiting rooms."

He ambled out the door with one of his cups of coffee, leaving me alone in the reception area, except for one woman and a pharmaceutical sales rep. I studied the area behind the counter. Two telephones, a single desktop computer, bins of samples, a brochure rack, a green plant, and not much else. No sliding file drawers with patient records and no cluttering signage. The phone chimed and the receptionist smiled when she answered, just like in the television commercials. She changed computer screens to key in an appointment, and when she hung up, she flipped through an appointment book and wrote something down. Apparently, they kept a manual backup of the doctors' schedules.

The reception counter was built in an L shape, and the left side was a glass retail display stocked with skin products. Overall, a pleasing environment. Even the air smelled good, tinged with aromas of peach and citrus.

I asked the nurse if I could join "my mother."

"Sure," she said. "Patient room three. The door is open. Dr. Haines will be in to see her in just a minute."

The building was larger than I'd expected, with several treatment rooms, two consultation rooms, and an outpatient surgery area that appeared to be shared with an adjacent medical building. Another single computer sat inside an open workstation, but I still didn't see anything that resembled hard copies of patient files.

I went back to the main reception area, found a *Coastal Living* magazine, and read about the in-vogue vacation spots. Places I, too, could visit if I were retired as planned. There were also recipes I could try and home-decorating ideas I could incorporate, if I had the time. With a sigh, I closed the magazine and checked my watch. It had been almost an hour, and like Spud, I'd grown bored. I also wondered what could possibly be taking Fran so long to ask for pain pills. I was about to check on her when she emerged, escorted out by a nurse. She had huge lips—Fran, that is. And a wide-eyed expression.

"Hi, sweetie," she said, her "s" sounding thick. "I'm all set. Where's Spud?"

I couldn't stop staring at her lips. "He, uh, he went for a walk."

The nurse gave Fran a stack of patient brochures and an ice pack. "This will help keep the swelling down, Miss Cutter. Five minutes on and five off, for the next hour. You look beautiful!"

Fran said good-bye with a hug and promised to bring one of her famous lemon pies to her follow-up appointment. We left to search for my father, Fran gripping her ice pack and me carrying her purse and patient brochures. The weather was mild and I'd parked in shade, so Fran decided to stretch out in the bodymobile while I looked for Spud. His brand-new cell phone, Fran told me, was in her purse. He didn't like to carry it, she said. Too clunky in his pocket.

I scanned the immediate area, thinking that Spud's arthritis would have prevented him from walking too far. No restaurants or sports bars were in sight. He had to be sitting in one of the doctor's waiting rooms. I went from building to building. The fourth was a cosmetic dentistry clinic. I asked someone in a pink smock if she'd seen an elderly man walking with a cane.

"Big white mustache, yellow shirt with parrots all over it?" she asked. That described Spud, sporting another of his new cruisewear shirts.

"When did you see him?"

"Oh, he's almost finished," she said. "He should be right out."

Before I could inquire as to what he was almost finished with, Spud emerged.

"Hey, kid," he said. And showed me a row of teeth that were the color of white paint. The glossy, bright white kind that goes on interior crown molding and window frames. "You like 'em?"

I looked at Pink Smock, eyebrows as high as I could manage.

"That's the great thing about laser whitening—immediate results," she said. "Doesn't he look ten years younger?"

"Twenty," Spud said. And remembered to smile.

When we got back to the hearse, a woman stood next to it, peering in the backseat, cell phone out. She wore a pair of boxy, jet black wraparound sunglasses that fit over her regular glasses.

I asked if I could help her.

"I'm trying to call the police, but I can't see a darned thing! My eyes are dilated." She shoved the phone at me. "Here. Dial 911."

"May I ask why you need the police?"

She pointed at Fran, stretched out in the rear of the hearse. "I don't think that woman is breathing! And it looks like she's hurt. Like maybe somebody has hit her in the mouth!"

Keep in mind that the back of my hearse is similar to a limo. Leather seats. Sound system. Compartments for ice and drinks—and weapons. Normally, people can't see through the windows, but Fran had rolled down all the tinted glass before she fell asleep. Head back and huge mouth hanging open, she did look sort of, well, dead. I handed the woman's cell phone back to her.

"Fran, wake up." I reached through the window and shook her. "I found Spud. We're ready to go."

Fran stirred and her eyes popped open.

The woman gasped. "Wh-why is she in a hearse?"

"Why not, for crying out loud," Spud said. After a beat, he thought to show off his newly lasered teeth and aimed them at the Good Samaritan.

Fran sat up and stuck her puffy lips out the window. "Give me a kiss, baby!"

The woman hustled away, much faster than a senior citizen with dilated eyes should be walking through a busy parking lot.

"Did Dr. Haines give you any drugs?" I asked Fran once we were on the road, cruising back to the Block. She and my father had chosen to ride in the back. They wanted to be chauffeured.

"No, nothing," Fran said. "I tried my best to get him to pull out that prescription pad, but he said that ibuprofen would work fine."

I eyed her in my rearview. "You were supposed to be getting a *consultation*."

"We consulted," Fran said. "Then I got my wrinkles Botoxed."

She fluffed her hair. "And he filled in my marionette lines and plumped up my lips. He's such a nice man. And I look fabulous!"

"Me too," Spud said. And smiled. "We both look fabulous, for crying out loud."

Jersey Barnes and crew, supersleuths in action. We hadn't gleaned much intel about the Divine Image Group. But Fran and Spud had shaved years off their appearances. And I'd managed to grab the Divine Group's appointment book. It wasn't a completely wasted trip.

TWENTY-SIX

Morgan was waiting when we pulled open the Block's over-size warehouse-style garage doors, and he came in with the sunlight. I was helping to fill ice bins, open the registers, and prep the bar—and hadn't been expecting him.

"Morgan," I said. "Good to see that you're getting out and about in Wilmington! You here for an early lunch?"

He positioned himself on a bar stool. "Just coffee, please. I don't usually eat anything until midday."

I poured his coffee, and he explained that he was trying to cut back on the amount of time he spent at work. I could "listen" between the lines. Translation: He knew eavesdropping to be wrong in so many different ways, but the craving to do so remained strong. Cutting back on his work hours was Morgan's way of staying away from the temptation as much as possible.

"So anyway," he went on, "I got a visitor's guide and I've been checking out all the attractions around here. I feel like a tourist."

"Smart move on your part," I said. "Get out there. Meet people. Have fun."

Morgan sipped from his coffee cup, frowned, smelled the brew, frowned again.

I sat beside him. "Something wrong?"

He asked what type of coffee we were using. I told him.

He took another sip. "The coffee has a bitter, almost metallic aftertaste. When's the last time you cleaned your brewer?"

"Huh?" I didn't know you were supposed to clean a coffee machine, other than the pot. Ox normally made sure that type of thing got done.

Morgan laughed. "It's very simple. After you close tonight, run a cycle of half white vinegar and half water through the brewer. Then flush it out with two cycles of plain water. Need to do that once a month to keep the flavor of the coffee from getting spoiled by mineral deposits."

I gave him a light punch on the shoulder. "You're a natural at this restaurant stuff!"

"I'm told I have a *perceptive* palate." He grinned. "The chef asks me to taste his new creations."

"That's excellent, Morgan. When the DEA finishes their investigation and all that mess is behind you, you might love your new life as restaurateur."

"You could be right." He forced down some coffee. "Speaking of the dope police, any new developments?"

I gave Morgan a vague update. "You need to be careful until this is all over. Stay aware of what's going on around you. I don't think you're in any danger, but you still need to be on alert. Call me the instant you sense anything fishy."

"Ready to implement the 'free lunch' plan?" he asked.

I nodded. It was a good idea. It could work. Determined to help, Morgan had come up with the idea to open Argo's for an invitation-only lunch. All of his regulars were invited. It would be Morgan's way of saying thanks for the patronage and continued support after his father's passing. He'd purposely scheduled it when the doctors could attend, and we'd be recording them to have something for leverage if needed.

"When's the big day?" I asked.

Two days from now."

Perfect. That gave me time to have a chat with the Divine Image Group in advance of their free lunch. Further stir the pot. That's me: Stir, stir, stir, and be ready to duck.

Morgan finished the coffee and declined a refill. "You really should clean your brewer."

I agreed I would. He left to catch a matinee movie and, on his way out, passed Dirk coming in. I cleared Morgan's coffee cup, and Dirk slid onto the just vacated bar stool.

"Any good lunch specials today?" he asked. I had no idea. Fortunately, Ruby did.

"Trout sandwich or fried trout bites. Comes with sweet-potato fries and cranberry slaw," she said.

Dirk said he'd take a sandwich. I asked Ruby to make it two. We moved to a table to eat, and Dirk filled me in on everything the department had on Garland's alleged accidental death. Which wasn't much. No police report. And an investigation hadn't been implemented, since foul play was not an issue. Nothing on record at all, in fact, except a 911 call made from Argo's main phone line. Dirk pulled out a pocket-size digital recorder and pressed a button.

[Excited male voice.] *Caller: A man just fell off a ladder and I think he's really hurt.*

Operator: What is your location, sir?

Caller: Argo's restaurant on Bradley Creek. I don't know the exact address.

Operator: We have the address, sir. Is the victim still breathing?

*Caller: Yes, I think so. He was up there replacing floodlights, you know,
the bulbs, I guess. And the ladder slipped and I saw him fall.*

Operator: An ambulance is on the way. . . .

And it went on from there.

"Seems to me like the caller was intent on explaining what happened, even though the operator didn't ask," I said.

Dirk agreed. "Other than the 911, there's an M.E. report, signed death certificate, and newspaper obit."

I'd already seen all that, but the 911 call confirmed that Spud's instincts had been on target. Not to mention an urn full of sand inside the prayer bench.

Dirk asked about Lindsey and Ox, and I inquired about his family. He was going on duty soon, he said, and had to scoot. I took care of his tab. I'd just finished helping Ruby clear the table when Brad swaggered in.

Hands on her wide hips, Ruby followed his progress like a buyer at a fashion show. "Why, I do declare!" she said, pouring on the southern accent. "You've got a regular string of hunky male callers today."

I made a face at her. "Good thing I'm not on the clock."

"Hah!" she blurted, going toward the kitchen. "You couldn't find the employee time clock if it was framed in flashing neon."

"A string of hunky men, huh?" One corner of Brad's mouth went up. "Does that mean she thinks I'm hot?"

"What do you want, Brad?"

He wanted to sit on the outside patio, he said, to take in the ideal weather. Mostly sunny and a steady breeze moving off the water. What he really came for, he added, was the information I'd promised him on CC's Hair Boutique. Two days ago.

"I've been busy." We propped open a big canvas umbrella and secured the latch on its wood post before stretching out in chairs.

Ruby followed us out. "Are you eating again?"

I made a face at her. "Just a beer, please."

She looked at Brad. "Hungry?"

"I'm always hungry, darlin'."

Ruby's posture warmed up a good ten degrees when Brad turned his hazel greens on her. "How about you bring me whatever your lunch special is. And I'll take a beer, too."

"You got it." There was a little extra "shay" in her sashay as she headed inside. He could charm the bark off a tree. I did a mental eye roll.

A smattering of birds chirped along the paver bricks, scavenging for dropped crumbs. The patio held a decent crowd, and the lunchgoers piled in. To be helpful, I fetched our beers, and when I returned, Brad's head rested back, his face soaking up bright rays that fell beyond the umbrella's circle of shade. If he didn't irritate me so much, I might have found the pose alluring. Before I had too much more time to think about it, Ruby delivered Brad's food.

While he ate, I gave him the lowdown on what I'd learned at CC's Hair Boutique: that a woman named Theresa had told the housewife Karen about the network. That's how Karen came to be on the list I'd found at Argo's—because she picked up her drugs there. Theresa left the salon one day with her boyfriend to eat lunch and they never saw her again, I explained to Brad.

"Anything on the boyfriend?" he asked.

I told him about Earless and the first time I'd encountered the tattooed thug at Argo's. "A clock face with no hands on it," I said. "A prison tattoo, I think. Anyway, he seemed to be searching for something, and he commented on how Rosemary could sell the rich bitch crowd. He knew about the drug dealing. Then he tried to lock us in the cooler and he ran off. That's pretty much it."

Brad's plate wasn't empty, but he'd stopped eating. He glared at me through narrowed eyes. "You didn't think to tell me about Earless before now?"

"Not much to tell," I said. "Besides, Morgan filed a police report. The gun I took away from Earless went through ballistics and came up empty. Cheap revolver, no serial number, probably stolen."

Brad picked up a sweet-potato fry, pointed it at me, started to say something, tossed the fry back on the plate. "Anything else you've been withholding from me?"

"Not a thing," I lied.

A woman at a nearby table got Ruby's attention and asked for a glass of Merlot to go with her hamburger.

"Sorry, ma'am, we're out of Merlot. The only red I have right now is house Zinfandel. I can whip you up a red wine cooler," Ruby offered.

The woman's forehead crinkled up. "You only have one single type of red wine available?"

I saw a notepad lying on the chair beside the customer's purse, pen tucked into the spiral binding. She wore a casual outfit and slip-on leather flats. No wedding ring. Her companion looked like a college coed and might have been her daughter.

"Normally, we have a right many wines to choose from," Ruby said, eyeing me, "but *somebody* made a mistake and didn't get the wine order in on time."

"No big deal," the younger girl said. "Mom just likes a glass of wine when she's work—I mean, uh, well, you know. Never mind."

The woman had to be a restaurant reviewer, probably one accustomed to more upscale places. Wilmington is loaded with great restaurants, foodies, and, of course, critics. Maybe she had let her daughter pick their lunch spot.

"You advertise"—she consulted the menu—"five different red wines and six whites. Not an extensive selection by any means, but still, I'd think you'd at least have something besides *Zinfandel*." She said the word as though the wine were tainted with dog poop.

Ruby looked at me to see which way we wanted to go. Sometimes snooty customers just aren't worth the trouble, and I don't mind a bit if a server recommends they eat elsewhere. On the other hand, this woman reeked of column inches. I can ignore a stench and brownnose when necessary.

I got up and introduced myself. "I have a bottle of Merlot upstairs. Very nice wine from a private collection. I'd be delighted to open it for you, and your glass of wine will be on the house."

Ruby bit her tongue and fake-smiled at the woman. "I'll have that right out to you, ma'am."

I returned to our table and told Brad I'd be right back.

"You're a wine aficionado?" he asked.

I shook my head. "I don't even like wine. Morgan insisted I take a few bottles from the wine cellar when I searched Garland's place. I figured Spud and Fran would drink them."

"Want me to go up and get the Merlot for you?"

"No."

"At least let me go with you."

"You're dying to see my place, aren't you."

"Yes."

We cut through the Block and climbed the stairs, Cracker on our heels. I beeped us through the security system. "Don't even think about planting any bugs in here," I told him. "I swear, you go near a telephone or a lamp, you get a roundhouse kick to the back of the head. In fact, don't touch anything. Don't even *breathe* on anything."

"No problem," Brad said. "I'd love to take a tour, though."

"Fine. Spin in a three sixty. Entryway, kitchen, living room, bedroom, bath. Through those French doors is another kitchen, which leads to my father's apartment. Satisfied?"

"Sure," he said. "Great tour. Real homey feel to it."

I pointed at him. "Stay."

Both Brad and Cracker stood still, side by side, and watched me rummage in the liquor cabinet. I found the bottle of Merlot. I dug through a drawer and retrieved a corkscrew.

"Want me to open that for you?"

"Okay."

"Am I allowed to move now?"

I waved him over. "And recork it, please, so I don't spill any wine carrying it down to Ruby."

"Hey, I'll personally deliver it to your surly customer."

"Ruby would get a kick out of that." And a bigger tip, if Brad turned on his charm.

The cork made a sucking pop as Brad pulled it out. "I never order expensive wine. Mind if I try a sip to see what I'm missing?"

"Sure." I found a wineglass. When he poured, an odd-colored liquid came out, something with the transparency of grape Kool-Aid. He smelled it and passed the glass beneath my nose. It smelled like stale water to me. Brad poured more until the liquid slowed to a dribble and stopped. He held up the dark green bottle to my ceiling light, but we couldn't quite see through it. Whatever the bottle contained, it wasn't wine. He wrapped a dish towel around the bottle and smashed it against the inside of my kitchen sink. We found three stuffed Baggies in the soggy mess.

Cracker nosed his way up to the kitchen counter to beg.

"I don't think you want any of whatever this is," I told the dog, and gave him a Greenies instead.

Brad tore open one of the Baggies, to find another sealed bag inside. When he cut it open, crystalline, fine white powder poured out.

He dipped in a fingertip and dabbed it on his gums. "Man, oh, man. We'll have to test it, but I'm guessing this stuff is pharmaceutical-grade cocaine. I can't feel my teeth."

"There's a medical use for blow?" I didn't know pharmaceutical-grade cocaine existed.

"It's an analgesic. Rarely used in the U.S. because there are other, better, safer substitutes. But some countries manufacture pure cocaine for medical use."

"I'm guessing these three Baggies are worth a bunch of Ben Franklins?"

"Something this pure? Oh, yeah. You have more bottles of wine?"

I found the other two, and Brad did the smash routine with them. One held nothing but wine—real white wine. Inside the last one, we found more Baggies of pure coke. We needed to get to Garland's wine cellar.

"I'll drive," Brad said. "Let's go!"

Forgetting about the waiting food critic, we hustled back downstairs, jogged through the Block, and jumped in Brad's Murano. "I'll bet that's what your earless fellow is looking for. Rosemary was in deeper than we thought." He peeled away from the curb at the first opening in traffic.

"Or maybe," I suggested, "she was storing the stuff for him. And then she died. And he's been trying to figure out where she hid it ever since."

"*That's* why we saw recorking equipment in the wine cellar," Brad said. "Rosemary must have been hiding the stuff in wine bottles."

"Hiding it from who?"

"Her husband, for starters," Brad said. "And maybe this earless dude you had a run-in with."

I thought back to when Earless tried to lock me and Morgan in the cooler at Argo's. He'd been there to look for *something*. And he'd seemed genuinely surprised that Morgan didn't know anything about his mother's second job as a dope dealer.

Who *was* this guy?

TWENTY-SEVEN

Brad handled the SUV like a professional driver, and we made it to Garland's estate in twenty minutes and got flipped off only once. Circling the estate, we saw no signs of activity. Brad found a box on the exterior of the home that housed cable and telephone wires and started to bust into it. I asked why.

"They have a digital phone, which operates via the cable television system. If I cut the main coaxial cable feed and we trip the security system, it won't be able to send out a distress call."

"I have the security system code." After all, I *was* working for the family, even though I'd never see a paycheck. I'd gotten the code from Morgan.

"Oh," Brad said.

He pulled out a small set of lock-pick tools and headed for a side door. I asked why he needed it.

"Uh, to get us inside?"

I held up a key. He stood back to let me have the lead. I let us in and deactivated the alarm.

We did a walk-through. Everything appeared just as it had the last time I'd been inside the house: fashionably decorated, clean, undisturbed. We went to the wine cellar, which was really a converted room. It's rare to find a home with a basement in Wilmington—the underground water table is simply too high, and the land is too flat. That, and the fact that most builders in the area wouldn't have a clue as to how to build one.

We went into the wine room through two wooden hand-carved doors. Each had a large half-moon pane of stained glass. I heard a faint electronic hum from the room's climate control system. About the size of a large bedroom, the area was lined along each wall with crisscrosses of wooden wine racks. A tasting table in the center of the room held a fancy mounted corkscrew and, in cabinets below, a variety of wineglasses.

Starting on opposite walls, we examined the wines, searching for the same label affixed to the bottle that we had opened at the Block. We found seven such bottles. They looked and felt like real wine, and we couldn't tell if they were bogus or not.

"Guess there's nothing to do but open them," Brad said.

Arms loaded with the suspect bottles, we headed to the kitchen sink. The first bottle Brad busted open held only wine. Same for the second. Bottles three, four, and five contained Baggies of white powder. He pulled a phone from his pocket and made a call. Soon, Garland's house would be swarming with agents. I didn't like it, but I understood. After all, how could he waltz in and dump hundreds of thousands of dollars of illicit product in the evidence lockup without ever having a thorough search of the grounds?

"You're not planning to do the same for the Block, I hope."

Brad said no. "No reason to mention that the original bottles came from your place. I'll spare you the hassle."

"My goodness," I said. "You actually seem human sometimes."

We returned to the wine room for another, more thorough search, examining every bottle carefully.

"It would be a shame," Brad said, "but we may end up having to open up every bottle in here just to be sure. Too bad you don't like wine."

"We could always gather up some friends for a wine-and-cheese shindig—"

I heard a sound outside the double doors and, drawing my weapon, spun to see Earless standing in the wine room entryway with a gun of his own.

"You!" His face showed a split second of recognition before he started firing. Brad and I dove for cover behind the tasting table, took blind aim for the double doors, and let loose. A firestorm echoed in the enclosed room as bottles exploded and wood splintered in every direction.

"New mag," Brad said, and stopped firing long enough to eject the magazine and shove in a full one. The instant I heard it click into place, I did the same with my gun, timing it so we wouldn't both be dry at the same time. The incoming shots had stopped, and we stayed stock-still to listen for movement in the echoing silence. Earless had trapped us in a confined room with only one way out. It was a huge tactical disadvantage.

"I'm going to take a look," Brad whispered. "Now!"

I peppered the doorway with bullets to cover him while Brad exposed his head enough to see out of the wine room. He dropped back down and squatted next to me. "Nothing."

Muzzles leading the way, we crept to opposite sides of the tasting table and surveyed what we could see. Without warning, a chunk of

Sheetrock burst inward. Bottles exploded behind us and we scrambled back behind the tasting table.

"He's shooting through the wall!" Brad said. "Do you remember what's on the other side of this room?"

I visualized the layout. "Open area, pool table, card table. Like a game room."

"We've got to get out of here."

"I'll second that." We moved out of Garland's wine cellar, me crouching low and Brad going high. Once out of the room, we stood back to back, guns quiet, moving in a slow circle to look for the shooter. Nothing.

"I've only got two shots left," I told Brad. "Maybe one." Back as a SWEET agent, I would have known exactly how many rounds remained during any firing exercise, regardless of the handgun I used. Right now, that seemed like ages ago. And this wasn't an exercise.

Brad glanced at me. "You don't carry a backup piece?"

"I'm retired."

We continued through the house, went outside the same way we'd come in, through a side door, and headed to the long, shaded drive. I saw movement near the Murano.

"Somebody's by your car!"

We got close enough to see Earless. He spotted us, took aim over the hood of the Murano, and started shooting.

We scrambled behind a tree. "Pick your shots," Brad said, meaning that he didn't want his car trashed. I took aim just when a figure with a shovel came up behind Earless and hit him over the head. Earless staggered to his knees and crawled a few paces before he scrambled up and ran off. The other man dropped the shovel and took off in the opposite direction, disappearing into a section of thick trees that separated the estate homes.

"I've got Earless," Brad shouted, and took off running.

I went after the benevolent gardener, who looked more like an elderly bum than someone who should be digging holes. An elderly *African American* bum. I had a pretty good idea who he was.

Even running in strappy flats, I caught up with him four houses away, on somebody's pool deck. I threw my weight—all 130 pounds of me—against his back, sending us both tumbling into a padded lounge chair.

"You hit like a damn linebacker, for Pete's sake," he grumbled, rolling out from under me. "What are you—one of those girly body-builders or something?"

When we were both standing and had brushed ourselves off, I got a close-up look at his face. It was bearded and scraggly—not the same clean-shaven, smiling one I'd seen in the picture on Morgan's wall. But it held the same features and the same bushy eyebrows. Just thinner. And tired.

"Garland?" I stuck out my hand. "I'm Jersey Barnes. And I wouldn't have had to tackle you if you hadn't run."

He didn't shake my hand. "I've seen you hanging around my son. Who are you?"

I told him that his daughter, the judge, had enlisted my help.

"Does she know I'm alive?"

"Nope," I said. "Where have you been living?"

He decided to shake my hand. "Nowhere. Everywhere."

"Why aren't you in protective custody?"

He showed me a grin that, despite the circumstances, was full of mischief and rebellion. "I sprung myself, for Pete's sake."

I stared at the man who could have been my father's brother, except for his skin color. "I think you and Spud are going to get along fabulously."

I told Garland about the private stairwell that ran from the street directly to Spud's apartment above the Block. Back when the old building had been a brothel, the stairwell was a necessity. It was no longer used, but it was still there, the worn wooden steps solid.

"There's a sign that says, NO ENTRY. I'll see that the door is unlocked. And I'll tell my father to be expecting you," I said. "Now get out of here before the DEA agent sees you. We'll talk when you get to the Block."

Grumbling about a bruised shoulder, Morgan's dead father loped through a patch of pink oleanders and disappeared. Watching him go, I suspected that Brad was behind the faked death. What I didn't yet know was why. Once again, it occurred to me that my new DEA friend wanted every ounce of information I had to offer regarding Argo's. Yet he sure wasn't sharing his intel with me, including the fact that Garland was still among the living.

When I got back to Garland's estate, Brad had a phone to his ear, his expression livid. He gave a description of Earless and slammed the phone shut.

"I lost him," he told me.

Fresh grass stains dotted the knees of Brad's jeans. He caught me looking.

"I tripped over a Big Wheel, dammit."

I almost kept a straight face. "I lost my guy, too. He vanished. Maybe he lives around here and disappeared into a house."

Brad eyed me.

I shrugged. Until I knew more, I wasn't sharing anything else with Brad.

"What was Earless doing here?" Brad rubbed his knee and bent it a few times, checking for damage. "He recognized you, right before he started firing. But he was surprised. He didn't expect to find anyone in the house."

"He was here for the same reason we were," I reasoned. "To look for the cocaine. He suspected it was here, but he didn't know where. And he probably assumed that enough time had passed—that everyone who was going to had finished trudging through the house for the time being."

We went back inside Garland's home to survey the damage. DEA agents would arrive shortly. I felt sure that a neighbor had reported gunshots, so the local PD was probably on their way to the party, too. I called Dirk, just to give him a heads-up. Neighborhood shootings in Wilmington are not common. There would be a lot of hoopla, even though there wasn't a body.

"I just saw you a few hours ago at the Block," Dirk's voice came through the phone. "How do you manage to stir up so much trouble in so little time?"

"Long-handled spoon," I told him, and hung up.

Brad came out of the wine room, where reds and whites mingled into potent-smelling puddles on the tiled floor. "We've got a bloody print," he said. "Looks like a clean print, too. And a few drops of blood."

I didn't think either one of us had grazed Earless. I knew we hadn't made a direct hit. "He must've gotten cut by flying glass."

"Thank goodness for that, because if he's in the system, now we'll have a name."

TWENTY-EIGHT

I surveyed Argo's. A nice crowd had come. Most important, the Divine Image Group—all three of them—were in place at their customary table. Morgan had hired a courier to deliver the invitations for Argo's customer appreciation luncheon. Between the "valued patrons" and their guests, more than one hundred hungry people had shown up to claim their free lunch. The plan would cost Morgan some money, but in his words, he'd pay anything to get a normal life back. The servers were happy to work an extra shift, too, since they knew that free food usually equated with generous tips.

I walked through the back of the house to find Morgan in his office, fiddling with the earbud. Soup had thoroughly swept Morgan's computer to eliminate all traces of the saved audio files. He'd also set it up so that Morgan could record a GT conversation directly to a memory stick.

"You still listening for recreational purposes?" I asked.

He met my look. "Not much."

"Once we get the doctors' conversation today, you need to dismantle the hidden microphone."

"I know."

"By the way," I said, "you should know that your main phone line is hot."

"Pardon?"

"There's a wiretap on Argo's main phone line."

His dark skin paled. "DEA?"

"Of course DEA."

"Can they do that?"

"Morgan, they *have* done it."

He asked if I thought his home phone line was tapped, too. I told him that it likely was.

The vertigo hit him and he swayed.

"Is there something you're not telling me?" I asked.

"No," he said. His reaction indicated otherwise.

"Look. I'm putting my ass on the line—not even getting paid to do so—and you're holding out on me. Who have you been talking to?"

"Penelope."

"Who's Penelope?"

"She's at a 900 number. Sort of a mix between a physic hotline and a sex line."

"Good grief, Morgan. You need to get a life."

His fists balled up. "I can't believe the bastards are listening to my phone conversations!"

I glared at him until something clicked inside his socially screwed-up head. He shut his eyes. Now he knew what it felt like to be on the receiving end.

An acoustic jazz duo had set up in one corner and was strumming out background music when I returned to the front of the house.

Happy chatter filled the dining room. Servers delivered plates of cold lobster salad and baskets of hot rolls. I glanced at the small overhead bubble cam, knowing that Morgan watched, earbud in place, memory stick already capturing the doctors' conversation.

"Hello, gentlemen." I stepped up to the Green Table alcove and saw that the Divine Group had already been served. "Enjoying your lunch?"

"Sure are. We haven't seen you before, darling," said the doctor named Leo. "You must be new. Would you mind bringing a few extra lemon wedges when you get a chance?"

"I always get extra lemon for seafood, too." I slid into a seat next to him. "Or sometimes an orange slice. Really, any type of citrus works well."

"Do we know you?" Michael asked.

I helped myself to a piece of bread and dipped it in their herb-infused oil. "No, you don't know me, although I know you and what you've been up to lately. The three of you have been very, very *bad* boys."

Leo dropped his fork to speak with his hands. "What the hell are you talking about?"

A waiter stopped by with a plate of lobster salad for me. I asked for a beer. Jonathan pointed at his empty lowball glass. With a nod, the server left.

"I'm talking about prescribing drugs for patients who don't exist. For starters." I pulled their office appointment book from my handbag and slid it to Leo. I'd checked the names, and they'd all turned out to be real people with real Wilmington-area addresses. I hadn't seen anything suspicious. Which meant they were writing bogus scrips only for names Denny gave them. Not actual patients. "By the way, I believe this belongs to you. Found it on the sidewalk the other day."

Michael's voice went flat. "Who are you?"

"A person who could destroy everything you've worked for." I threw out interesting factoids about their financials, just for show. My beer and Jonathan's drink arrived. His looked like pure liquor, on the rocks. The waiter started to replenish our bread basket, but Leo waved him away.

"Fortunately for you"—I took a miniature bite of lobster, chewed leisurely, and swallowed—"we want the bigger fish, so to speak. If you tell us who the ringleader is, you'll probably come out of this without seeing jail time. I'm not so sure about keeping your medical licenses active, but we'll see."

Jonathan withered. "I knew it. I knew we were headed for trouble. And it's all my fault. All of it."

"Shut up!" Leo snapped under his breath. "We don't even know who she is. Or if she's wired, or whatever."

"My name is Jersey Barnes, and I own a specialized security agency. I'm not a cop, but I have lots of cop friends. I've been retained by Morgan's family to get to the bottom of the illegal activity that has been taking place in his restaurant." I unbuttoned my blouse all the way down to my navel and held it open to reveal a black, lace-trimmed Camille plunge bra. I aimed my size D's at Leo. "And as you can clearly see, I am not wired."

Accustomed to examining breasts, Leo showed little reaction. A couple across the restaurant, however, caught my act and were staring openly. I rebuttoned my blouse and smiled at them until they went back to minding their own business.

"Your options are these, Drs. Haines, Pratt, and Rosch. You can cooperate by leading me to the top dog. If you do that, your collective reputations may remain intact and you'll stay out of jail." I held up my other hand. "Or, you can tell me to get lost. I make a phone call. Drug enforcement agents will be waiting outside the restaurant to arrest you. Probably a few local cops, too. In broad daylight, in the parking lot, in front of everyone else who happens to be a valued Argo's patron." I ate more lobster. "Your choice."

The doctors had stopped eating, but the lobster salad was scrumptious and I thoroughly enjoyed mine. That, and the imported Moretti Italian beer, which the waiter had recommended. It was a good recommendation.

"How do we know you're legit?" Michael watched me eat for a time. "I mean, *he* could have sent you. Like this is a test or something."

Shrugging, I flipped open my cell phone and started dialing.

Leo reached over to shut it. "What do you want to know?"

A smile warmed my insides, exactly like it used to when I worked undercover. They'd bought my act and my story. I always got a rush when that happened. "Start by telling me why three prominent medical professionals would suddenly forget their code of ethics and hook up with the network."

Jonathan shrunk into himself and seemed to tune everything out by staring at Bradley Creek. Michael looked at Leo. Leo nodded his consent. Michael started talking.

"We found some money back when we were in med school," he said. "We made a pact to be smart about it. We kept quiet, finished school, paid off our loans, and put the rest in an investment account. We scrounged like all the other young doctors—no new cars or parties or expensive clothes—and left the money alone to grow. Then we opened our own practice. Everything went according to plan. The more established we became, the more we did for charity, you know, to give back. To pass along some of our good fortune. Life was good."

"Until *he* showed up, out of the blue. Said we took something that belonged to him when we were students at Duke. He wanted it back. With interest," Leo said. "We told him to go to hell. That he couldn't prove anything."

Michael ran a hand through his hair. "That's when he killed my dog. Slit her throat. *Inside* my house. At nighttime, no less, while I slept. The alarm system on."

Leo loosened his tie. "He said that our families would be next."

"So you agreed to give him the money?"

Leo joined Jonathan in staring out the windows. Michael nodded. "Problem was, we didn't have that kind of dough lying around. Our money is in our medical equipment and our building and homes and such. We sold investments and scraped together almost half a million. Gave him that. And set up a payment plan of sorts, where we give him a cash payment out of our general fund each month. Bookkeeper enters it as a consulting fee."

"How much does he want?"

"One and a half million."

"And none of you thought to negotiate or get outside help?"

"He said he'd kill our families," Jonathan said. He was paying attention, but he was also getting drunk. His speech came out slurred.

"We agreed to keep paying him off," Michael said. "Then he wanted more. He wanted drugs. Told us if we'd supply prescriptions, the 'loan' would get paid off much quicker."

Appetite gone, I pushed back my plate. "And 'he' is . . . ?"

Leo sighed, short and sharp. "We don't know. We've never seen him. He goes by the name D-man. He runs the network. He's the one you want."

"How do the transfers take place?"

"Always in cash. He sends somebody."

He used a runner, then, like he'd been doing with the drugs. "Always the same person?" I asked.

"A woman," Michael said. "She wears hats and sunglasses, but I think it's always the same person. He makes us do the drops in a way that we can't ever get too close to her. And we never know where to go until the last minute."

"Was it his money that you stole?" I asked.

"I told you," Michael said, "we *found* the money. In a car. The men driving the car were both dead, and no, we didn't kill them."

People had begun finishing their free lunches, and I spotted Morgan going from table to table, shaking hands, nodding, smiling. I knew he continued to record every word at the GT, even though he'd left his office. He approached our table with a formal smile.

"Jersey, how nice to see you. I didn't realize that you were friends with the most popular drug dealers in the house."

Michael put his fingertips to his forehead, as though in prayer. Jonathan gulped his drink. And Leo remained speechless for a beat while his mind processed what he'd just heard.

"Yes, I know all about the network, too. I know a lot about all of you." Morgan stared directly at Jonathan. "After all, you were *such good friends* with my mother."

I took a swig of beer and shot Morgan a look over the tall glass. If he let his emotions take over, he might expose the Green Table's secret. As it was, the doctors had no idea how they'd been found out.

"Well, feel free to stay and talk to Jersey as long as you'd like," Morgan said pleasantly. "The wait staff will be resetting for dinner, but you won't be in anyone's way."

"Thanks, Morgan," I said. "I believe we'll take you up on that offer."

The four of us remained at the Green Table long after the restaurant had cleared out. The Divine Group told me how they'd stumbled upon the money to begin with. How they'd justified keeping it. How so many years had passed without any mention of their appropriated fortune. How Rosemary had inadvertently gotten involved. And how Garland never knew that she'd become close friends with Jonathan and was helping the Divine Group pay off the D-man by delivering drugs to restaurant patrons.

I was digesting the information when I spotted Brad strolling through the empty dining room. There was nothing to do except offer introductions.

I did, leaving out the part about him being a drug enforcement agent.

Brad's eyes shot invisible daggers at me, but he decided to play along. "Looks like I missed the party."

"You are late for lunch," I told him. "The good news is that Drs. Haines, Pratt, and Rosch have agreed to cooperate in helping us find their blackmailer. Fellow who goes by the name of D-man. Runs the network."

Brad had to be suitably impressed with my investigation skills, even though he wasn't happy about being left out. I raised an eyebrow at him. He almost smiled.

"We'll do what we need to do to help you find him," Leo said, sliding out of his seat, ready to go. The other doctors followed suit. "But if you involve the law, we're as good as dead. Even if he finds out that we've spoken to you, it won't be pretty. He is a scary man. And as I already said, we don't know who he is, where he lives, or what he looks like."

"Then I suppose we'll need to set up a meeting, won't we?" Brad crossed his arms. "Besides, I've got a pretty good idea who he is. Fingerprint from Garland's wine room came back as a match. Ray Donnell Castello. Did time in the state prison system."

The Divine Image Group exchanged looks.

"Anything else you'd like to tell us?" I asked them.

"We know that name. We saw it in the newspaper, back when we were students," Michael said. "They were going to arrest him for murder. Another article said that there were several charges pending against him for other crimes. And he'd escaped from a New Jersey jail. So he was definitely going to jail, with or without the murder charges."

"One of you needs to tell us the entire story of what happened in Durham that night," I said. "And you leave anything out this time, doctors, forget about our deal."

After a beat, they folded their bodies back into seats at the Green Table. Dr. Michael Pratt did the talking. Brad and I did the listening. And Morgan, I felt sure, still did the recording.

TWENTY-NINE

The weekly call came in just as the doctors were about to break for lunch. The receptionist buzzed Leo in his office. "Dr. Haines? You have a call from Mr. D. He's holding on line two."

Leo thanked her and beeped Michael and Jonathan on their office intercoms. They hustled to Leo's office and shut the door.

"We do this as planned, agreed?" Michael said. "Working with the Barnes Agency woman might be our only way out of this mess without jail time."

Leo nodded his agreement. He punched the flashing button for line two and turned on the speakerphone. "Dr. Haines here, with Drs. Pratt and Rosch. We're on speaker."

"Well, isn't this cozy," the caller drawled in a tone simultaneously lazy and cocky—a man whom the doctors now knew to be Ray Donnell Castello. "I've got you all at once. You have my prescriptions and consultation fee ready, boys?"

"Tell me something, *Denny*," Leo said from behind his desk, motioning the other doctors to sit down. This phone call might be longer than usual. "Did they give you the D-man nickname in prison, or is that something you came up with all by yourself?"

"My, my, my," came Denny's voice. "So you figured it out. Congratulations, I'm impressed. Do you have my prescriptions and consultation fee ready for pickup?"

Leo felt nervous but didn't want his partners to pick up on it. He leaned back in the desk chair, fingers laced behind his neck. "Here's the deal, Castello. We know who you are. So you have something on us, we have something on you. The good news is that we have the rest of your money. All of it. We give you the last payment and we're done. You go about your merry way and we get on with the business of running our practice."

The silence held thick as the doctors stared at the telephone base.

"That's a right interestin' proposition," the drawl finally came through the speaker. "How'd you come up with the cash? To hear you whine and complain before, you was all piss-poor broke."

Leo nodded at Michael. It was his turn to talk. They wanted to reinforce the fact that they were, after all, three against one. "We did some creative financing," Michael said. "The details aren't important, but basically, we took out a loan using our building as collateral. We've got the cash. Do you want it or not?"

Another long silence. "Okay. I accept your proposal. I'll call the cell phone later with a drop spot and instructions."

Jonathan grabbed the telephone handset, cutting off the speakerphone. "Listen, asshole. You want your money? We do it on *our* terms. Don't send your girl this time. You want your money, you come to get it. Right here, tonight, after the office closes. And bring my damn student ID card with you. I want it back."

Leo reached across the desk, took the handset away from Jonathan, and punched the speakerphone button. "Our last patient will be out of here by four-thirty and all the staff will be gone shortly after that. Come then."

"If this is a setup, I'll have friends standing by," Denny said. "You make a lot of good friends in prison. Anything happens to me, they'll have the list. Your home addresses, your kids' addresses, your mamas' addresses. They'll start at the top and keep going."

"It's not a setup, Denny," Michael said. "We don't want to lose our medical licenses any more than you want to go back to jail. This deal is between you and us. Just come get your money and then leave us alone. That's all we want."

Leo disconnected before any further conversation could take place. Pumped with adrenaline and nauseated, Michael held his stomach. Jonathan's entire body vibrated with rage. Maybe he should kill the bastard.

Leo made a call. "Jersey, it's Leo. He called us. We went with the plan. Told him to pick up his final payment tonight, here at the office."

He listened, nodded, hung up, and pulled a medical supply bag from beneath his desk. It held about fifteen thousand dollars in cash—nowhere near the half million that Denny would be expecting. At a glance, though, the twenty- and fifty-dollar bills on the top of the banded stacks concealed all the one-dollar bills beneath. And if everything went according to plan, they'd be able to deposit all fifteen thousand back into their general office fund, where it belonged.

THIRTY

I hung up from talking with Leo at the Divine Image Group and immediately called the Barnes Agency. Andy the masseur answered.

"Tell JJ to get her ass off your massage table," I said. "She has a doctor's appointment."

"No massages around here for a few days," Andy said. "I hurt my wrist playing basketball."

"Good, then maybe my partners will actually get some work done."

JJ came on the line and I gave her the rundown on the time frame. Her toy bag—as she called it—was already loaded with weapons and ready to go.

"Great," I said. "See you in an hour."

We met in the public library parking lot, at the back of the building, and took JJ's car to the Divine Image Group. Looking completely unlike a sniper, she wore a pair of oversize glam shades, heeled sandals, and a chic, above-the-knee dress.

"Nice hair color on you," she said, cruising through traffic. "A little lopsided, though."

I flipped down my visor and, using the vanity mirror, adjusted my dark brown wig.

"And I love the nose bandage," she said. "Nice touch."

My face was wrapped in one of those funny-looking splint things that rhinoplasty patients wear while they heal. "It's uncomfortable as hell, but at least I'll blend in with the other patients."

We parked in a convenience store lot a block away, bought junk food, and walked to the Divine Image Group's building. All of the people in the waiting room looked like patients or loved ones, but then you never know. I looked like a patient, too. After an appropriate amount of waiting, JJ and I were escorted to the conference room, where we settled in to wait. Meanwhile, Brad and his team were taking undercover positions around the area. Somebody had installed a tracking device in the handle of the money bag, and another person had attached hidden cameras above the main entrance and back exit doors. Two agents turned themselves into a mobile car detailing team. One was a stocker at the convenience store. One roved on foot, walking a dog. Another, dressed as a nurse, roamed the halls at Divine Image Group.

Staff members were told only that there had been a threat from one of Dr. Rosch's patients, so security measures were being implemented.

At four-thirty, a woman walked in and announced to the receptionist that she was the niece of Dr. Haines. After I hid in an exam room and JJ stuffed herself beneath Leo's desk, Leo personally escorted the woman into his office. I stepped into the hall and stood just outside the door of the office, my back against the wall.

"Funny, I don't recognize you," Leo said.

"I'm here for the delivery," she said, and shut the office door behind her.

I strained to hear through the closed door.

"Where's Denny?" Leo asked. "He was supposed to come in person. After the office closes."

"He couldn't make it," she answered.

I burst through the door, holding a hand to my bandaged face. "Dr. Haines! My nose just went numb! Totally numb. I can't feel a thing. What if there's no blood circulation and it falls off?"

"He'll be with you in a minute. Get out of here." The woman gave me a one-handed shove back through the door. Her other hand went inside a leather purse that was slung across her body with a long strap.

"You don't have to be so rude." I punched her in the stomach, a straight jab, and twisted enough to put my body weight behind it. She doubled over with a grunt. JJ Tasered her in the back. Yelping, the woman crumpled to the ground. Unlike a stun gun, a Taser delivers electrical pulses by shooting out two tiny metal probes that are attached by wires, and it keeps doing its thing for thirty seconds. While the woman was incapacitated, I stomped down hard on her wrist—the one concealed inside her handbag—and removed a .45 Taurus revolver. Big gun for a little woman. I ejected the ammo—tactical rounds designed to mushroom upon impact—and pocketed them. The woman began to move. She rolled over and threw a string of choice words at JJ. The Taser probes were still attached, and JJ hit the button to deploy another thirty seconds of agony. Another yelp. I cuffed the woman's hands with a zip-tie restraint.

The DEA agent dressed as a nurse appeared, gun drawn.

"All secure in here," I said. "She came in alone, but he might be outside."

The nurse spoke into a hidden shoulder microphone and sprinted off.

Denny's runner sat up and moaned. She didn't have the presence of mind to yank out the Taser probes when she regained control of her muscles.

"What's your name?" I asked.

She used the F-word in a combination run-on sentence I'd never heard before.

JJ delivered another thirty seconds of electrical impulses. "Aren't Tasers great? The battery pack in this one is brand new. It could probably go for days."

"What's your name?" I asked again.

"Theresa."

"Is Denny with you?"

She felt her back, reaching for the tiny metal probes that stuck in her like fishhooks. "I came alone."

JJ pulled out the probes before Theresa had a chance, ejected her spent Taser cartridge, and popped in a new one.

Leo sat quietly in his desk chair, like a spectator observing an interesting stage play. A crowd had gathered in the hall, and I toed the door shut for privacy. Under threat of being Tasered again, Theresa stopped with the foul language and confirmed that she was Denny's girlfriend. She was also the person who recruited his drug runners— usually cash-starved college kids—whom Denny would use for a month or two before dropping them for fresh runners. Denny had a rental house, Theresa said, but swore that she didn't know where he lived. She'd originally met him while he was incarcerated. After his release, he had always come to her house. Never the other way around.

"Don't you get it?" I said. "You are as disposable to Denny as all the runners you've recruited. He's just using you, and at some point, you'll no longer be valuable to him."

Hands secured behind her back, she awkwardly got off the floor. JJ helped her to one of Leo's guest chairs. "We love each other," Theresa said.

Brad came through the door and told Theresa that we could help her only if she was willing to help herself.

"The deal was for Denny to pick up the final payment," Leo said. "He needs to honor our agreement."

"He'll kill you, you know. You should just give me the money."

I found a cell phone in Theresa's purse and flipped through the stored numbers until I came across one labeled only "D." I dialed and held the phone to her face. "Nobody in this room is a cop, Theresa," I lied. "You tell Denny that we've got the money. If he wants it, he comes in person."

Leo unzipped the medical bag, slung it atop his desk, and held it open so Theresa could see the cash.

"Denny? I'm at the doctors' office. They have our money. I'm looking at it right now. Cash. But they'll only give it to you in person, like y'all agreed."

Theresa's eyes teared up at the response we couldn't hear. She nodded toward Leo. I passed her cell phone to him.

Leo spoke briefly, listened, hung up. "He says the deal is off. That we can take our money and, well, shove it you-know-where. And that he doesn't give a you-know-what about Theresa or what we do with her. He said we can turn her over to the cops for all he cares. And then he said that he's *very much* looking forward to meeting Lilly," Leo said. "That's my wife."

"We'll get immediate coverage on your house and the other doctors' houses, too," Brad said. "You need to warn all your kids and other family. They need to be on alert."

Leo returned the phone to me. "We've already done that. Hired private guards for all of our kids—even my daughter, who is overseas right now. Costing us a shiny dime, I'll tell you that much."

"Keep them in place until this is over," Brad said. "And you'll need to cancel your patients. Shut down the office."

"Who are you people?" Leo asked. "You sure as hell aren't average private citizens."

Brad produced a badge. "I'm DEA. Jersey and her friend are associates from a private security firm."

"We're going to lose everything, aren't we," Leo said. "Our licenses. Our practice. Everything."

"The main priority right now is to stop this drug ring," Brad said. "We'll figure the rest out later."

"And my main priority," I added, "is to straighten out the situation at Argo's and eliminate all danger to Morgan so he can get on with his life."

"We're working together," Brad said with just a touch of sarcasm. "Jersey and I."

Leo closed the office and sent staff members home with lists of patients to notify about the temporary shutdown. Jonathan's patients would be referred to another psychiatrist. Leo's and Michael's patients would be asked to reschedule their cosmetic procedures, even though the Divine Image Group doctors weren't sure whether or not they'd ever practice medicine again. One thing was certain: Life, as all three doctors knew it, had changed forever.

Once the office had mostly cleared out, there was the issue of what to do with Theresa. Brad could turn her loose and hope she'd lead him to Denny. Problem was, Denny could kill her first. The other option, and the one that made the most sense, was to retain her for questioning. JJ escorted her to the Divine Group's employee break room and kept a loose eye on the woman.

"Let me have a go at Theresa before you arrest her," Jonathan said.

Everyone agreed: Not a good idea.

"I might be a damn drunk," Jonathan said, "but at one time I was the best psychiatrist in North Carolina. I got referrals from stumped peers. I was called on to testify in high-profile court cases. I won awards." He paused to make eye contact with each of us. "I think I can handle interviewing a woman with abandonment issues and a thrill complex."

Brad shrugged. "I'm in no hurry. Why not?"

"I'll take her in my office. Alone. Just the two of us. I need to gain her trust. The sooner we get information out of her, the sooner you can track down Ray Donnell Castello."

THIRTY-ONE

Surprisingly, they agreed to let him have an hour with Theresa. But then, he did have a knack for sincerity. People trusted him. People opened up to him. People told him things.

Except this screwed-up woman. Theresa was a tough case. She had convinced herself that Denny loved her. She refused to betray him. Denny would love her even more, she said, once he realized that they'd tried to get information out of her but she'd held strong. She didn't care if she ended up in the can, Theresa told him. She'd be comfortable in a prison environment. After all, she'd originally met Denny through a penpal correspondence program, and the first time she'd visited him in person, she'd known they'd end up together. She went as often as they'd allow—once a week—and had the drill down pat. For years and years and years. Until, finally, he got out. And they could be together every single day, forever. As much as Jonathan tried asking the same question in different ways, Theresa kept swearing that she didn't know where her boyfriend lived.

Jonathan tried to think of her as a patient. He knew he had to remain professional and keep his frustration in check. "You are a beautiful and smart woman, Theresa. Your future is a wide-open book with blank pages, and you have the power to fill those pages however you wish. But, see, Denny isn't the right person to help you write your future."

"Why not?"

"If he accepted you as an equal, Theresa, he would have let you come to his rental house. He would have *wanted* you there."

Theresa's eyes flicked briefly to the wall behind him and landed back on the desktop. So she *had* been to Denny's rental house. She was lying to protect him. "He's just being cautious," she told Jonathan. "He doesn't want me to know where it is for my own protection. Besides, once he finishes business in Wilmington, he's going clean. We're going to take the money and start a new life somewhere."

"You sure he's taking you with him?"

"Of course he's going to take me with him, you head-shrinking idiot! Denny is a good man. All he wants is the money that rightfully belonged to him. I mean, if college punks stole your money, wouldn't you want it back?"

With a loud sigh, Jonathan scooted back his desk chair and opened a bottom drawer. There was no way he would get anything out of her in an hour. Not without chemical help, anyway.

"What are you doing?" she asked.

"Getting my flask. I need a drink."

Jonathan found what he looked for and slipped it into his pocket. He found the flask, too, and took a swig of lemon-flavored vodka. Stretching, he stood and walked around his desk. He locked the office door before moving to stand in front of Theresa. Her hands were still restrained, and Jersey had zip-tied each ankle to a chair leg to keep the woman from bolting. She looked up at him, and Jonathan noticed that her nose ran. He pulled a tissue from a nearby box—shrinks helped to keep Kleenex in business, he thought—and wiped beneath her nostrils.

"You look like you could use a drink, too," he said. "You want some? I'll hold it to your mouth."

Theresa nodded her acceptance. Jonathan put the flask to her lips with one hand and shoved the hypodermic needle into her neck with the other. She squealed in shock and coughed up the vodka. The office had been acoustically designed for privacy and was nearly soundproof, at least when it came to the human voice.

Jonathan returned to his desk chair, put his elbows on the desk, and rested his chin on top of laced fingers while he waited for the drug to take effect. It happened quickly. Theresa's lids closed slightly, and the muscles in her face sagged.

"Are you ready to be truthful with me, Theresa?"

She nodded. A bit of spittle ran from her mouth. She tried to wipe it away with her shoulder but didn't have the coordination to turn her head that far.

"Good. Now, let's start from the beginning. I'm going to ask you some questions, and you're going to answer. Everything you tell me will help you and your boyfriend. Help you. So you can get married and be together. I'm here to help. All right?"

She nodded again.

"Answer aloud, please."

"Yes."

In the employee break room, Drs. Haines and Pratt discussed the logistics of shutting their doors and made a list of other plastic surgeons they'd feel comfortable referring patients to. JJ and the DEA agent dressed as a nurse played cards. Two male agents were stationed outside the building on watch duty. Jersey Barnes sat quietly, waiting for the shrink to finish interrogating Theresa. And Brad paced.

"What's taking so long?" he said.

Jersey consulted her watch. "It's only been thirty minutes, Brad. Give it a rest. You're making me tired just watching you."

He yanked out a chair and sat down to face her. "You do realize that because of you, everything going on is completely against protocol."

"Yeah, well, because of me you actually have a number of solid *leads*," Jersey said. "You know, those little pieces of crucial information that help you put away the bad guys?"

Brad stood. "If you were a guy, I swear I'd kick your ass right now."

"I'd like to see you try."

JJ flicked a playing card at them. "Chill out, you two."

Jonathan smiled. The injection had worked as he'd hoped it would. He had only one final question to ask before he needed to sober her up and turn her over to the DEA agent.

"Where is Denny right now, Theresa? Is he at the beach house, or is he waiting for you somewhere else?"

She watched Jonathan with bloodshot eyes before focusing on the window behind him.

"You're doing fine, Theresa. Look at me. I want you to be a good girl and tell me where Denny is. Where is Denny right now?"

"Denny is . . . Denny is . . ."

"Yes?"

"Denny is . . ." She tried to point, but her hands were still restrained.

A blast sounded and glass flew inward. Theresa slumped in her chair. A patch of glistening bright red spread across the front of her shirt and pooled in the creases of her lap.

Jonathan scrambled off the floor in time to see the dead woman slump farther forward. Somebody pounded on the door. Realizing what he had to do, Jonathan busted out the remaining jagged glass and hurled himself outside. The time for atonement had come.

THIRTY-TWO

The Divine Image Group was closed for the safety of the doctors and patients. Argo's was closed for the safety of Morgan and the patrons. A generic reason was given for both establishments, but anyone driving by the physical locations would likely see the security guards on duty. Shocked people speculated and gossiped, I guessed, but something else would soon come along to snag their attention. It always did.

We'd gathered at the Block—the whole lot of us—to brainstorm. Brad, Leo, Michael, Spud, Fran, and me. Morgan was at the restaurant, making calls to those who had dinner reservations. And Dr. Jonathan Rosch was MIA. His neighbors hadn't seen him, his ex-wives hadn't heard from him, and his house revealed nothing except an open gun safe. Which nixed the theory that Denny, the shooter, had kidnapped him. Besides, the doctor's car was gone. Presumably, Jonathan had driven home to grab one of his long guns and was now on the hunt for Denny. Based on the boxes of shotgun shells in the safe, the doctor used only 12-gauge shotguns to shoot trap and skeet. But a 12-gauge can blow a hole through somebody's midsection at close range much easier than it can bust a clay pigeon at thirty yards. If Jonathan managed to find Denny, we figured, he planned to kill the man.

After an hour of spinning our mental wheels on where Jonathan might be and how to locate him, his partners decided to head home and make phone calls. At least that way, they reasoned, they'd be doing something.

As soon as they left, Brad ran a hand over tired eyes. "You do realize that my ass is on the line here, right? Our one solid lead is dead. Obviously, Denny was the shooter. I don't know how he got past my people without being seen." He drank some water. "If we don't find the bastard before he kills somebody else, I can say good-bye to my career with the DEA."

We were in the shoulder hours of the day—the slack time between lunch and evening cocktail hour—when a steady trickle of customers kept Ruby and the bartender occupied but not too busy to chat it up. They laughed and greeted and served and seemed to be having a good time doing it. Brad's mood wasn't quite as light.

"How so?" I asked. "You can't always control the outcome of a grab."

Brad stuck out his chin while he formulated a response. "Ever since you entered my life, Jersey, I haven't controlled anything about this investigation. After months and months, I finally get close, and then *bam!* There you are. Screwing things up." He searched the air, struggling to find words, as though his thoughts had floated away on a parachute. "Everything has been so ass backwards, unplanned, on the fly. If I tried to go back and do things by the book now . . . well, that would be impossible anyway. There is no going back."

"Hey, I'm just doing a fav—"

"Do *not* pull that line on me again," Brad said. "I'm sick of hearing about your favor."

"Okay. Although you did agree that we would help each other out."

"Some help you've been."

"Don't blame me for your shortcomings," I said. "At least I've tracked down solid leads."

Spud held up a hand. "You'd think the two of you was married, for crying out loud. Stop it already." He smiled as an afterthought so everyone could appreciate his white teeth.

"He's right, sweeties," Fran said, her "s" still sounding thick from big lips. "Arguing won't help anything."

"Truce?" I smiled. Brad's job really might be in trouble if we didn't find Denny and shut him down before the body count went up. I could play nice.

"Truce."

Spud's mustache danced, and he took charge. "Assuming our boy is still in town, what's he after? Denny knows we're on to him. His girl is dead. His cocaine has been confiscated and is locked in an evidence room."

"And with Theresa gone and the doctors no longer writing bogus prescriptions," I added, "his Wilmington drug delivery service is probably out of business."

"Right," my father said. "I were him, I'd cut my losses and skip town. Take whatever money I'd stashed away so far and set up shop somewhere else."

Brad rubbed his eyes again. The heavy lids gave him a rebellious, pouty sort of look that would be considered provocative in a magazine spread. "He's not gone, not yet. I agree that his plan is to start a new prescription drug ring somewhere else. He's got the niche marketing and the delivery system down pat. That kind of operation he can set up in any city, anywhere, 'long as he doesn't upset the cart by treading on somebody else's turf. That's why Wilmington was a perfect setup for him. No organized crime."

"But?" I asked.

"But he's not going anywhere yet. Something tells me that he wants something first."

Spud nodded his approval. And smiled. "Good instincts will bring you across the finish line. Back in the day, I acted more on gut feelings than anything else. Got me in trouble sometimes, but I sure helped scrape a lot of scum off the streets."

There was much more to my father, I realized, than the bumbling, grumbling, frail-looking man who'd appeared on my doorstep five years ago. I suddenly wanted to delve into his past. And I wanted to know why he'd walked out on my mother and me, back when I still drew smiling depictions of him in Crayola. Back when he had normal-colored teeth.

"Hello?" Spud snapped two knobby fingers in front of me. "You still on planet Earth? We got investigating to do, for crying out loud. Quit daydreaming."

I ate a sweet-potato fry. Even cold, it tasted good. "I'm here, Spud. I was just thinking about, uh, the doctors. How one mistake, way back when they were kids, changed the course of their lives."

Before anyone could focus too much personal meaning on that, Brad spoke up. "Speaking of the doctors, Jersey, tell me. How did you figure out the Divine Image Group was a key player in this drug ring?"

"Basic legwork," I lied.

"Bull. Those doctors have been eating at Argo's for years, always at the same table. Deanna told me that. It dawned on me last night that the doctors and the Green Table was the one constant here." Brad checked his wristwatch. "There must be a bug in place. Legalities and criminal charges against you and Morgan aside, I need to listen to everything you've got. All of it. We have experts that can probably pick up on something you missed."

"Interesting theory, Brad." I produced a smirk for his benefit. "If you're so certain of that, why haven't you already barged in to check it out?"

"As we speak, I've got four agents on their way to Argo's with a warrant."

"You son of a bitch." My whole purpose was to keep Morgan safe and keep the judge happy. If Morgan ended up in jail on felony charges, he wouldn't be safe and his sister definitely wouldn't be happy. Last time I checked, recording a private conversation—when nobody involved consents—was illegal in North Carolina.

Brad read my face. "What's the matter, Jersey? Worried?"

I found my car keys and stood to leave. Spud said that he and Fran would stay put and to call him on his new mobile phone if I needed to be bailed out. "Whatever you do," he added, "don't use that text-messaging garbage."

I headed to the hearse, and Brad hustled after me. "I've got a job to do, babe, and nobody—not even you—is going to stop me."

I turned. *"Babe?"*

Brad leaned back on his heels. "You prefer to do things on your own terms. Well, so do I. *Babe.*"

I slugged him and made solid contact with the bridge of his nose and left eye. In a loose fighting stance, I waited for retaliation. It didn't come.

Brad shook his head, like Cracker does after eating a scrap of dropped hot wing off the Block's floor. "Damn, you've got a mean right hook."

I slid behind the wheel of the bodymobile. Brad got in the passenger's side. "There's an instant cold pack in the first-aid kit," I said. "Compartment beneath your seat."

He found the cold pack, activated it, and held it to his face. "Nice wheels," he said. "I mean, for a casket cruiser."

Wow. A term for the hearse I hadn't yet heard. "It was custom designed for a drug dealer. All sorts of nifty compartments. Leather. Great speakers."

Bobbing my head to the beat of a classic rock CD, I cranked the volume and pointed the casket cruiser to Argo's. Brad shut his eyes and kept the cold pack pressed to his nose. When we arrived at Argo's, we practically stumbled over each other getting through the front doors.

Drug enforcement agents were already there, doing their thing with electronic sweeping equipment. Uniforms were posted at all the exit doors. Brad looked smug. My stomach twisted into one giant knot.

I spotted Morgan in the dining room, watching the agents move from table to table, inching in the direction of the GT. My mind already fast-forwarding to a list of lawyers I knew, I joined him. Morgan smiled. And winked at me.

Thank goodness. He'd removed the hidden microphone and receiver, as promised. The knot in my gut disappeared. I could enjoy the moment. An agent shadowing us, Morgan and I went into the empty kitchen and he prepared sandwiches of sliced prime rib with red onion and black truffle mozzarella cheese. We ate in one of the booths and discussed movies while Brad's people scoured Argo's.

THIRTY-THREE

As I figured he would, Garland decided to take me up on my offer of accommodations. He'd finally shown up—three days after I'd tackled him—complaining to Spud about the fact that his shoulder still hurt. After he'd had a long shower and more than twelve hours in a comfy bed, Garland's next order of business was food. I found him and Spud downstairs, in the Block's kitchen, tending to a row of gas burners loaded with sizzling pans. The aroma of roasting garlic and unfamiliar spices brought my taste buds to attention.

"What are the two of you doing?" I asked.

"Garland is teaching me how to make booey-base." Spud's tall white chef's hat sat cockeyed on his head. "That's a fancy name for fish stew, but if I can learn to make it from scratch, Frannie will be totally impressed."

I'd never heard my father use the word *totally* in such a fashion.

Garland moved among the pans, turning and flipping and adding ingredients. "Your daily specials menu is rubbish. I'm making bouillabaisse and chipotle-lime bacon-wrapped jumbo shrimp," he informed me.

"Alrighty, then." I eyed the Block's cook, who stood back, observing.

"Hey," he said. "Opportunity knocked. Who am I to turn him away?"

I moved between Garland and my father. "First of all, Garland, you do realize that you are a fugitive of sorts? You're supposed to be a pile of ashes inside a prayer bench, not out here whipping up gourmet meals! Second of all, Spud almost burned down the Block trying to cook Spam-and-cheese sandwiches. We promised the fire chief that he wouldn't use any heat-generating appliances. And third of all, the Block's customers—"

Garland shoved a spoonful of something in my mouth. "Taste this."

Flavors of shallots and garlic and sweet red pepper exploded on my tongue. I closed my eyes to fully savor the moment of ecstasy. "My gosh, that is *good*."

"You were saying something about me being dead?" Garland asked.

I found a tasting spoon and ate another sample. Even better than the first mouthful. "Just stay out of the dining area, would you? Brad—your DEA friend—has a tendency to pop in without warning. Obviously his people are still looking for you, since you bailed on their attempt at witness protection. Everyone else still thinks you're dead. And I'm not in the mood to be accused of the accomplice thing."

"Yes, ma'am." Garland did a half salute and went back to his food. "I've really missed playing around in a kitchen. That's been the worst thing about being dead. That and not being able to talk to my kids."

Ruby bustled through. "What's going on back here? Our

customers are salivating like dogs out there, from the smells. Did we get a new cook or what?"

"Or what," I answered. "And the specials today are bouillabaisse and chipotle-lime bacon-wrapped shrimp."

"Huh." Ruby stared at Garland. "What's a bouillabaisse?"

"Fish stew with several kinds of fresh fish, for crying out loud. And spices," Spud said. "What planet have you been living on?"

Ruby pointed at Garland as though he were a foreigner and didn't understand English. "Who's that?"

"A friend," I told her. "He's helping out in the kitchen today."

"Huh." She plucked a shrimp from a big pan, took a bite, and let out a moan of pleasure. "How many orders of this shrimp can he make?"

The Block's regular cook grinned. "Fresh batch of shrimp just came in today. I'd planned to batter and fry it, but we'll give 'em something different tonight. We've got enough for thirty-five, maybe forty orders."

"Fifty," Garland said.

"Huh." Ruby grabbed another bacon-wrapped shrimp and ate it on her way back to her customers.

"That's if the help would quit eating it," Garland muttered.

Spud adjusted his tall hat. "How much longer do I have to keep stirring the pots of booey-base? My arm is about to fall off, for crying out loud."

An excited buzz spread fast among the Block's regulars. Garland ran out of bouillabaisse by nine. The last order of shrimp went out at nine-thirty. Spud said he'd had enough cooking lessons for one night and clomped upstairs to bed, but Garland put the Block's cook to work and whipped up single-egg crabmeat omelets for the late night partying crowd. I closed the kitchen at eleven, told the bartender to put out bowls of pretzels if anyone was starving, and hauled Garland—and a plate of mini omelets—upstairs to my kitchen table.

Cracker met us at the door, his nose working. I served Garland a glass of Pinot Gris, poured myself a beer, made a stack of toast, and we plopped down to eat our feast.

"I know you have lots of questions for me," I said, "but I'd like to go first."

Swirling his wine, he nodded approval. I took it to mean a yes for me going first.

"I'm assuming it was the DEA who faked your death. Possibly Brad Logan's idea. What I need to know is, why?"

Garland sipped from his wineglass, looking much more like the famous chef than a street bum. The rest and a shave had done him wonders. "How much time do you have?"

I made a hand motion: *All the time you need.*

"I knew that something was eating away at Rosemary. She never did tell me what was going on." He played with the wedding band on his ring finger, turning it in circles absentmindedly. "When I found drugs in her bathroom, I realized she had a problem. And here's the thing that really got me: The prescriptions were written by one of my best friends."

"Jonathan."

"Right. He'd written her a scrip for an antidepressant, sleeping pills, and something that was supposed to be for weight loss. Rosemary didn't need to lose weight. And I never suspected her to be depressed." Garland ate a few bites of omelet. "I confronted John about it, and he got defensive. Spouted the rules about patient confidentiality and all that garbage. That's when I realized that John was drinking much more than usual. And Leo and Michael weren't exactly themselves, either."

"When was this?" I wanted to keep the time frame straight.

"Right before Rosemary died. Of an overdose, dammit! Rosemary had never taken anything more than an Excedrin in all her life, and all of a sudden she's dead from a drug overdose? I knew she had to have gotten the drugs from John or one of our other doctor friends." Garland's face went sour. "*Friends*. You think you know somebody . . ."

"You think they were supplying her with drugs and she became addicted?"

"I know she was using something. I'd get home from work to find Rosemary relaxed, like zoned out. Never out of control, but spacey. I begged her to talk to me, to tell me what was going on. She never did. And she'd always be bright and happy the next day, kiss me, act like her old self. But I knew she had to be on something. And the only place she could have gotten the pills was from one of the doctors. Our *good friends*."

"And then she died," I said.

"She left Argo's earlier than usual, said she had a splitting headache. When I got home, she was slumped over in the hot tub, not breathing. EMS got there in minutes, but they couldn't revive her." Garland's eyes grew wet. "I didn't want the kids to know, so I told everyone it was a heart attack."

Understandable. "Is that when you bugged the Green Table?"

"Yes. I had to know why Rosemary died. I knew the doctors were involved, even though they acted like they were still my best friends in the world. Came to the funeral, sent flowers, called every day. Kept coming to the restaurant to eat on Fridays, like usual. So I set up the microphone and started recording everything I could when they were at the table. I had to learn the truth."

I nodded. "Morgan, of course, found the microphone. I have all the transcripts from the computer—the conversations you recorded. Argo's is now clean, by the way. Morgan disassembled and destroyed the electronics."

"Before they raided the place?" he asked.

"Fortunately, yes."

Garland made the sign of a cross before continuing. "Listening to the doctors, I learned that they were part of a prescription drug ring. They owed somebody, the ringleader, a bunch of money. And I figured that Rosemary was involved in the whole mess."

"If it's any consolation, drugs make people do things they would otherwise not do. Your wife had a drug problem, I'd guess." I gave Cracker a crumble of omelet remains. "Anyway, you've explained the hidden microphone. But you didn't tell me why the DEA wanted everyone to think you were dead."

Realizing no more gourmet crumbs were forthcoming, Cracker found Garland and laid his wide head across the man's knee. Garland rubbed Cracker's neck. "I went ballistic. I overheard the current phone number for the network—one of the docs read it from a piece of notepaper while the other dialed. I called later that day, set up a meeting, pretended to be a buyer. My plan was to go after them and deal with the doctors later."

"What happened?"

"I met the runner at a deli. I had him by the throat, trying to get some information out of him, when I realized he was just a kid. Maybe eighteen, nineteen years old. I let go and he ran off. That's when Brad and another agent appeared. They'd been tracking the drug ring and keeping tabs on me, too. Of course, they wanted to know how I knew about the network and why I'd been arguing with the kid."

My beer bottle was empty. It might be a long evening. I got another from the fridge and refilled Garland's wineglass. "What did you tell them?"

"That I didn't think my wife's death was an accident." Cracker puffed out a sigh of contentment and shut his eyes. Garland kept stroking the dog's fur. "And that I was trying to find out what had been going on in front of my own nose."

"And they decided to fake your death because . . ."

It was to keep him safe, Garland said. Before the kid ran off, when Garland had him by the throat, Garland was screaming at him. Told the kid who he was and that his wife, Rosemary, was dead because of the network. Brad figured the information would filter back to the ringleader and that Garland might end up dead, too. So he came up with the fixing-a-light-on-the-ladder plan to speed up the process. They hid Garland away and put him on twenty-four-hour protection for the duration of the investigation.

"I hated to put my daughter and son through that, but Brad swore that it was the only way to ensure my safety. And *their* safety. He promised me that the DEA was close to busting the case wide open, after which everything could go back to normal." Garland rubbed his eyes. "As though living life without Rosemary would be normal."

So then, basically, Garland had been in protective custody. Probably holed up in an out-of-town hotel. He must have ditched the program. I asked why.

"They put me in a dingy hotel near Camp Lejeune. I was going stir-crazy. Your dog could protect me better than those numnuts they had watching me. Besides, I wanted to keep an eye on my son. I had to make sure he was okay."

"It was *you* following him, then!" I felt a smile come on, despite the bittersweet circumstances. "The DEA was watching Morgan, but you were, too. He said he kept getting the sense that he was being followed. And he kept imagining that he saw you at different places."

"Guess I don't make a believable bum." Garland returned my smile. "They froze my accounts. I tried to use a credit card and the clerk said it had been reported stolen. My house was being watched. I've been sleeping and showering at the homeless shelter."

I raised my beer bottle. He raised his wineglass. "Welcome to the Block," I said. "Make yourself at home, Garland. Really, though, I'm not so sure that teaching my father how to cook is a good idea. He has a knack for getting in trouble. Something in his DNA, I think. He can't help himself."

Garland replied that Spud made a fine sous chef and said I shouldn't worry so much. And it was his turn to ask questions. We talked long into the night, even after the Block downstairs went quiet and I heard the staff pulling down the big industrial garage doors to lock up. I told Garland what I knew, leaving out the unnecessary parts. Such as the part about Jonathan being in love with his wife. And the part about his son eavesdropping on folks just for kicks.

When you're flying at the right altitude and staring at the big picture, certain facts cease to serve a purpose, other than to cause hurt and confusion. Garland was a good man. He didn't need all the details.

THIRTY-FOUR

The next morning, Fran arrived bearing edible gifts: home-made banana-nut bread, mini sausage biscuits, and fruit salad. We gathered around the feast for brunch. Spud and Garland were talking about an upcoming coastal fare cook-off, which raised one of my mental red flags, but I didn't have too much time to think about it. The phone rang and, making herself at home, Fran answered.

"It's for you, sweetie! Sounds like the cute drug man, Brad."

I took the handset. "Hello?"

"The cute drug man?" he said.

"It is descriptive."

"You *do* think I'm cute, then."

"I think bulldogs and donkeys are cute, too."

"Mind if I come over?" he said.

"Yes." I certainly wasn't going to let him come sniffing around my house again. Garland was not the type of man to hide in a closet. "I'm about to take Cracker for a walk."

"I need to be walked, too," he said. "I'll be there in a few."

$Cracker$ isn't fond of being hooked to a leash, but he puts up with it as long as he can be in the lead. I let him forge ahead, nose to the ground, energized by whatever scents he picked up from the paved Riverwalk.

"Theresa had a drug in her system when she got shot through the window," Brad told me. "A long-sounding name I can't pronounce, but it's one of those psychoactive drugs used for interrogation. People call them truth serums. There's not an accepted medical use, except some psychiatrists may use such drugs in conjunction with hypnosis, with the patient's consent."

"You think Jonathan injected her to make her talk about Denny?"

"The woman seemed perfectly sober when she showed up looking for the money." Brad frowned. "This is a drug that's relatively fast-acting, I'm told. So, yeah, I think the doctor injected her. And I have a hunch that he got something pertinent out of her before the shooting."

"Jonathan is still MIA?"

"Nobody has seen or heard from him since we decided to let him have a go at Theresa in his office. He's not using his credit cards or cell phone. Driving a vintage Chevy Corvette. Fully restored. A '69, I think. Anyway, there's no GPS tracking on that baby."

We stopped to let Cracker sniff the base of a tree. He seemed to enjoy it. "If Jonathan did get anything out of Theresa, why didn't he share it with us? Why did he take off?" I pulled on Cracker's leash. If I didn't, he'd hang out at the tree all day. "Unless he's out there, toting a shotgun, playing vigilante."

"He was sober and sincere when he convinced us to let him have a private talk with Theresa," Brad said. "It seemed like a good idea at the time."

I agreed. "But not in hindsight, I guess. We shouldn't have left him alone with her, especially since he blames himself for the doctors' predicament with Denny."

"We've got to find Ray Donnell Castello and do it soon."

We stopped at The George, a popular dock-and-dine restaurant on the Riverwalk. I tied Cracker to a shaded bench, and we found an outside table where we could keep an eye on the dog. Brad pulled stapled papers out of his hip pocket. "This is a list of everything found on Theresa's person and in her purse. The other pages are copies of wallet contents."

Still full from my late breakfast, I didn't want more food. Brad ordered a soft-shell crab po-boy. We both opted for sweet iced tea. "You have an address on her yet?"

He shook his head. "Turns out that she gave us a bogus last name. The old Chrysler van she drove isn't registered. Stolen tag."

I went over the list of Theresa's belongings: makeup, cigarettes, loose change, prepaid cell phone, hairbrush, tampons, key chain with a car key and two unidentified house keys. Nothing unusual, except for an aspirin bottle that contained a variety of yet-to-be-identified pills. Brad took a bowl of water to Cracker. I turned my attention to the photocopied stuff. No driver's license or other ID. No credit cards, insurance cards, or even preferred customer discount cards for the grocery or drugstore. Sixteen dollars and change in cash. And several receipts. Brad returned to find me studying the receipts.

I pointed to one. "You notice anything odd about this one?"

"No. Pay-at-the-pump, date and time stamped. It's a mom-and-pop convenience store. They don't have any exterior security video. And the employee working at the time didn't recognize Theresa's photo. Which means that it's a useless gas receipt."

"She bought premium," I said. "Why would she put premium gasoline in an old Chrysler van?"

"She wouldn't," Brad said. "Which means that either she has another car or she was putting gas in Denny's car. Good catch."

"Maybe he's trying to enjoy all the finer things in life that he couldn't get in prison. A sports car. And fresh seafood." I pointed to a generic cash register receipt with a printed message at the bottom: "We like to get fresh!" "There's not a business name on here, but I recognize this receipt. I've been there. It's from Akel's Seafood Market, near Carolina Beach."

"So she eats seafood."

Brad's sandwich arrived and he dug in.

"*They* eat seafood," I said. "This receipt is for three items, and at twenty-four dollars, I'm guessing it was food for more than one person."

"And?" Brad said.

"The area around Carolina Beach is low-key, right? Lots of cottages and beach rentals. Relatively quiet. It's a perfect place for Denny to hide." I snagged one of his French fries. "Your people have been showing his photo at extended-stay hotels and businesses in Wilmington. What if he's living somewhere else?"

Brad ate, drank, wiped. "We don't have the manpower to encompass a larger radius."

I found a second Akel's receipt. Both were dated within the past week. "Why would she drive all the way to this market, unless it's near Denny's nest? Wilmington has plenty of fresh seafood everywhere. Why not buy it around here, closer to where the network has been doing business?" I answered my own question. "Because she wanted to wait until she got closer to his house, so the fish wouldn't spoil in a hot car."

"I guess we're taking a trip to Akel's, then," Brad said.

He finished his lunch, and we walked Cracker back to the Block.

A big A-frame menu board had been set up at the hostess stand to peddle a lunch special: "Grilled salmon on a couscous salad with a zesty orange glaze and sautéed asparagus."

"Crap," I griped, scanning the restaurant to see a bigger than usual lunch crowd. Garland was at it again.

Chef's hat towering over his head, Spud hustled over to us and waved his walking cane at the people. "We've got a lot of the same regulars who ate the booey-base last night, for crying out loud. This cooking thing is fun!"

Brad's gaze wandered toward the kitchen.

"Spud is taking a cooking course," I said, and led Brad outside. "Let's get on over to the seafood market, shall we?" I threw Spud a warning glance over my shoulder on our way out. I didn't want my customers getting too used to Garland's creations.

THIRTY-FIVE

Rubbing the scab behind his ear, Jonathan drove steadily toward the beach, doing the speed limit. The cut from flying glass probably should have been stitched up, but as long as it didn't get infected, he'd be fine.

Theresa didn't know the actual house address where Denny lived, but she had described the general area and given Jonathan a detailed description of the beach cottage, including the fully fenced backyard and the single dead palmetto tree in the front yard. It was a third-row rental in need of repairs, she'd said, but it was quaint. Perfect for another month, until they left North Carolina and headed south.

The drug Jonathan injected had performed beautifully. He'd pilfered helpful details about Denny, such as the fact that the ex-con loved fresh seafood, which Theresa prepared on a charcoal grill. He liked to take early morning swims in the ocean, just as the sun came up. He often hung out at the docks, talking to the fishermen, and would sometimes help unload and sort their day's catch.

Jonathan learned that Denny had several prison contacts who would be joining him in the network once they moved to a new location. And Denny owned three or four handguns, Theresa had said, right before she was shot through the window. Jonathan wasn't too worried about the guns. He planned to incapacitate Denny before the man had a chance to go for a gun. With an injection. He'd hold Denny at bay with his shotgun if he had to, while he waited for the drugs to take effect and the police to come. With Jonathan's eyewitness testimony of Theresa's murder and whatever the DEA had on Denny, the man would end up in prison. Hopefully for life this time.

Dressed in shorts and boat shoes, windows down on his vintage Corvette, Jonathan cruised the streets for half an hour, stopping periodically to snap digital photos with his cell phone. He paid special attention to the cottages on the third row back from the beach, looking for a fenced backyard and a dead palm. People injected with "truth serum" drugs sometimes confused fantasy with reality, so he didn't place too much emphasis on the fenced yard. Perhaps Theresa's dream house had a fenced backyard and Denny's rental didn't. The dead palmetto tree, on the other hand, had to be an accurate detail. He took photos of one in particular that looked promising, as the dead tree with dried-up brown palms was just in front of the front door, as Theresa had described. Unfortunately, though, he spotted dead palms in the front yards of several beach rentals, and he couldn't go barging into every one of them.

Taking a break, Jonathan found an oceanfront snack bar and ate a hand-dipped ice-cream cone while he studied scattered clumps of people spread out on the beach. He watched a father help his two young daughters build a sand castle while their mom took pictures. A woman jogged by with a beautiful Dalmatian. An elderly couple napped beneath a flapping umbrella. Jonathan took more pictures using his cell phone, capturing the shoreline and the rows of beach houses beyond. Finishing the last bites of his crunchy waffle cone,

Jonathan decided right then and there—standing on a patch of Atlantic near Carolina Beach—that it was time for a change. He used to believe that his work made a difference in his patients' lives. Now he'd become weary of listening to people yak on and on about their problems. He'd begun to loathe going to the office. *Everybody* had problems. Hell, he had his own problems. More precisely, one main problem. As soon as he cleared up the mess with Denny, he would notify his partners of his departure from the Divine Image Group. Leo and Michael would understand. They'd probably be glad for him.

Jonathan climbed back in the 'vette and explored until he found boat docks that accommodated big fishing boats and shrimp boats. He parked in a dirt lot and saw exactly what Theresa had described. With the cell phone, he took more photos, figuring that he could always pass them along to Jersey Barnes if he failed to locate Denny today. As he unfolded himself from the driver's seat, a sense of déjà vu pricked at the main nerve running along Jonathan's spine, as though he'd already experienced what was about to happen. The marina *was* Denny's hangout. It had to be.

Jonathan didn't smoke, but he bummed a cigarette from a dockworker. Lighting up to blend in, he spotted a shrimp boat moored to the dock, its crew laboring to secure the boat and unload their haul.

"Hey, how's it going?" he said to a kid who was tying a rope to a giant cleat. "I'm trying to find a friend of mine. I think he helps you guys out sometimes when you dock."

The kid carried another thick rope to a different cleat on the dock. "What's his name?"

Jonathan pulled a small square photo out of his pocket. Denny and Theresa were the subjects, the picture taken in an arcade photo booth. Theresa always carried it in her cigarette case, she'd said, and shown it off proudly. Stoned from the injection, she hadn't noticed when Jonathan kept it. "Depends on what nickname he's using at the time," Jonathan said through a chuckle, and held up the photograph. "When we were kids, everybody called him Denny."

The kid scanned the parking area and pointed to a white Mazda MX-5. "That's his car. He's around here somewhere. Probably on the boat, shootin' the shit with the guys."

"Okay if I go aboard? I've got a big surprise for him."

The kid checked out Jonathan's boat shoes. "No difference to me," he said. "Probably mess up your new treads, though."

"They need to be broken in." Jonathan finished his cigarette and thanked the kid, thinking he should break in the new shoes on Denny. Heading to the ramp, he captured a cell phone picture of both the shrimp boat and Denny's Mazda. He paused to save all the recent photos in a single file, which he attached to an empty text message. He wasn't sure if he'd have to send the photographs, much less what to write, but he'd figure that out later.

Nobody paid much attention to Jonathan as he made his way along the finger dock and stepped aboard the boat, trying not to grimace at the overwhelming stench of fish. He came across a group of wiry men gathered around a cooler, and one instantly caught his attention. Jonathan couldn't see the man's face, but he knew instinctively it was Denny. The criminal who'd thrown his life into a tailspin. The man who had crushed his heart.

"Why did you have to kill her, Denny?" Jonathan said to the man's back. "Rosemary was *working* for you, trying to help me out. She didn't deserve to die."

Denny pivoted, a beer can halfway to his mouth. He was probably nearing fifty, maybe more, but there wasn't an ounce of fat on him. His pores reeked of meanness, Jonathan thought.

"Well, looky who we've got here," Denny drawled, his voice rough like a smoker's. "Dr. John, our very own headshrinker. You look a lot older than your photo in the medical journal. Not to mention that pimply-faced runt on your college ID."

The blood left his extremities and Jonathan wanted to strangle the asshole. He forced himself to remain detached, like he did when talking to patients. "Honestly, Denny. I'd like to know why you felt it necessary to kill her."

Denny's friends sensed a disturbance and got cocky with their body language. Denny waved them off and finished his beer with one tilt of the can. "Just an old acquaintance," he told them.

The men finished their beers with long chugs and went to work to unload their haul, damp shirts clinging to their backs, cigarettes dangling from their mouths. Seagulls circled overhead, foraging for discarded scraps. Denny retrieved a smoldering cigarette from atop a rusty ice chest, took a long drag, and flicked it overboard. So he littered, too, Jonathan thought. A murderer, a dope pusher, and a litterbug. The scum that somehow managed to float to the surface of humanity's pond.

"Rosemary snorted some nose candy—you know, to experience the product she'd been storing for me," Denny said. "She did line after line. Of course, I had a knife to her throat at the time. Although I probably didn't need the blade. Hell, she was already half-wasted."

Jonathan suddenly wished he had a gun. He wanted to kill Denny, regardless of the consequences, but the shotgun in his car wasn't doing him a bit of good. He probably couldn't have gotten on the commercial boat with it anyway. He should have stopped somewhere to buy a pistol. He gripped the cell phone in his pocket. Whatever happened between him and this monster, he decided, the photos needed to be sent. "Why? Why did you overdose her? You had to know it was too much!"

Fishermen and deckhands continued to work, minding their own business, making it a point to stay out of hearing distance.

Denny let out a cackle and, bending over, reached into a cooler for another beer. Jonathan seized the moment to open his phone and push the menu button. He palmed it by his side when Denny stood back up.

"She threatened me, and I don't take well to threats, you know?" Denny continued. "She wanted out. She didn't want people picking up their meds at the restaurant anymore. And she wanted me to leave you and the other doctors alone. Ain't that sweet? Her trying to look out for you and all."

Jonathan turned his face up to the squawking gulls so he wouldn't have to look at Denny's mocking smirk. Both hands behind his back, he felt the phone's large navigation button and pressed it from memory.

"So I tell her that's not going to happen, and she agreed to keep working. But I could see it in her eyes, that she'd made up her mind. She turned on me. Became a liability to the network instead of an asset. Nothing to do at that point but get rid of her."

Jonathan thought of his best friend's last moments and prayed that she'd been too high to realize she was about to die. If there was such a thing as mercy, she'd have passed out first.

"I hated to drop Argo's from the network, but I couldn't chance her talking to the wrong people. I couldn't chance going back to prison." Denny seemed to be thinking out loud now, as though he were no longer talking to another person. "Prison gives you a lot of time to think. Month after month and year after year of rotting away . . . missing out on the life I was supposed to have. All because some punk kids stole my money right out from under me."

"Just out of curiosity, how did you get caught?" Suddenly calmed by a sense of purpose, Jonathan really wanted to know. He *needed* to know. He wanted an answer while he figured out how to get close enough to plunge the needle into Denny's neck.

"A deal went sour and a couple of idiots tried to run with my money." Denny's mind traveled back in time to a night that remained as fresh in his memory as when it first happened. "I know where they're headed, right? So I go after them. I'm driving, it's raining, it's dark. Then I see that they've run off the road. The engine's still smoking, so I know they just wrecked. I find them both dead, slumped in the front seat. Blood everywhere. Don't know how it happened and I don't care. I just want my money, but it's gone. And I see a car disappearing in the distance and get this real bad feeling, like I've been had. I search all around the wreckage, you know? Thinking maybe my bag of money flew out when they crashed against that big oak tree." Denny lit a cigarette, inhaled, and blew the smoke out his nostrils. "Never found no money. Did find a plastic picture card, though. Covered in vomit."

Jonathan's voice caught in his throat. "My student ID."

"So I take the gun out of the driver's lap. He didn't have a need for it anymore, right? And I get back in my car to track you down. I'm pulling out to the road, and *bam!* I'm freakin' surrounded by pigs."

You shouldn't have taken the gun, Jonathan thought. Greed had put Denny away.

"They eventually proved that the gun on me was the same gun that shot the two in the car. My lawyer said I'd go in for life, especially after all the charges from my past record added up. I did go in for life. But then, surprise, surprise! He pays me a visit in the clink and tells me that the pigs are willing to make a deal if I rat out some of my old business associates. They'll drop all charges except the current one, the one where I got accused of poppin' the two idiots who stole my money. But, it's not a bad offer, I think. Better than dying behind bars, right? So I gave the badges what they wanted in return for a lighter sentence. Damned if I still didn't get twenty years. *Twenty lousy years* for a crime I didn't do."

"The newspaper said you were a career criminal."

"That's the good thing about such a *career*." Denny took a drag from the cigarette and flicked it overboard, like the other one. "You meet a bunch of others in the same line of work and you can rat them out when the time comes. I talked my freakin' heart out and still got the twenty. It was a whole lot of time with nothing to think about except coming after you. Lot of time to decide exactly how I'd do it. How someday I'd have *you* working for *me*."

"We didn't kill them," Jonathan said. "Those men in the car."

"I don't give a rat's ass who killed them. All I want is my money. All of it. You think that just because I was in the clink I was out of touch? Oh, I followed your career, believe me. You and your friends. I watched you spend my money, opening your fancy medical practice and flying around the country to conferences. Everybody thinking the three of you is heroes when all you really are is petty thieves." Denny spat on the deck.

Jonathan wondered how things might be different if he and his friends had gone to the police way back then and told them what really happened. And given back the money. He wondered how life would be if they'd never been driving on that rainy road to begin with. If only they'd never gone to the stupid fraternity party. Or if they'd left at midnight, like they'd originally planned.

"Getting out of the clink and coming after you was the high point of my life," Denny drawled. "And after she threatened me, helping the bitch get high enough to kill herself was icing on the brownie, you know?"

Forgetting about the hypodermic needle in his pocket and the cell phone in his hands, Jonathan scanned the deck for something that would serve as a weapon. He no longer wanted to incapacitate Denny and call the police. He didn't even care about sending the pictures any longer. He just wanted the man dead. "Rosemary never did anything to you. You should have let her out, let her have her life back."

"Aren't you the one who recruited her, Doc?" Another smirk.

"Besides, she dug her grave when she agreed to store the powder for me but then wouldn't tell me where she hid it. She tried to use that as bargaining power, to make me leave the Divine Group doctors alone. But I don't take well to threats. Besides, I knew the stuff had to be somewhere at the restaurant or in the house. She won't tell me where she put it, there are other ways to find it." He spat again. "I never did find it, though. Had a buyer waiting on that blow, too. Put me in a big jam."

"I thought you only deal in prescription drugs." Jonathan inched closer, telling himself to stay calm. Go with the original plan. Drug Denny and let the law deal with him. He could do it if he stayed focused. He needed to go ahead and send the pictures stored on the cell phone, too, but he couldn't chance looking at the screen. Not yet. "You've expanded into street drugs now?"

"The stuff Rosemary stored for me *was* prescription." Denny displayed a row of tobacco-stained, crooked teeth. "It's amazing the contacts you can make when you're incarcerated. Even overseas pharmacists."

Jonathan felt himself float out of his physical body and hover above the shrimp boat, as though he were a moviegoer watching a scene unfold. Stacks of buckets were everywhere. He saw a wadded-up fast-food wrapper scuttle across the deck, fueled by a surprise gust of cool wind. He took in all the weathered wood and riggings and railings. A family cruised by on a pleasure boat at idling speed, and Jonathan watched brackish water from their small wake lap against the shrimp boat's hull. "You know what?" he heard himself say. "I'm glad Rosemary managed to screw you out of some money before she passed on. And just so you know, Theresa screwed you over, too. Before you killed her."

Denny's fingers worked. "Wanna elaborate on that, Doc?"

"Let's just say that your brief stint of freedom is coming to a screeching halt."

Denny charged at the same moment Jonathan focused on his cell phone's backlit display. Sweat blurring his vision, he quickly tabbed, finding the file he wanted, recalling from memory that the next feature he needed was two pushes away. Denny's fist connected with his jaw. Jonathan staggered against a grab rail that surrounded the wheelhouse. He flung himself against a line that ran up the main mast and, using the rope to hold himself upright, hit the green send button on his phone. Another blow knocked him to the deck, and it occurred to him that he had no idea how to fight back. He'd never been in a real fistfight in his life. He'd never even kicked somebody, he realized, thinking that his new shoes weren't doing him a bit of good.

A semicircle of men watched the altercation, but nobody stepped in to break it up. Still clutching his phone, Jonathan covered his head with his arms and took more blows without fighting back.

The phone was yanked from his hand.

"What do we have here?" Denny threw the phone into the water without expecting a reply. Jonathan heard the splash. An instinct to survive told him to throw himself overboard—anything to get away from Denny. But first he needed to accomplish what he'd come to do. With shaking hands, Jonathan managed to get the hypodermic needle out of his pocket and press his thumb against the plunger. He held it back like a knife, poised to stab, waiting for the right moment. But before he could jab it into Denny's neck, he felt something tighten around his own neck, and his body rose up the mast in jerks, toward the sky.

"Don't kill the man!" somebody shouted.

"I need everybody to get out of here." Denny lowered the body, saw the dropped needle, and threw it overboard just like the phone. Jonathan coughed between moans. "Don't worry, guys. I'm not going to kill the bastard. I'm just going to scare him, and I don't want any witnesses, if you know what I mean."

The deck cleared in a matter of seconds. With a grunt that turned to laughter, Denny used his full weight to hoist the flailing body back toward the sky.

The last thoughts that filtered through Jonathan's oxygen-starved brain were of his partners. Leo and Michael. He hoped they had received the photos he'd sent from his cell phone, right before Denny threw it overboard. He hoped they'd know what to do with them. He hoped they'd forgive him.

THIRTY-SIX

I was happy to let Brad drive the inconspicuous Murano, which currently sported a Virginia tag. We found Akel's Seafood Market without incident and were welcomed as soon as we walked in. Friendly place. We browsed the refrigerated glass counters of fish and shrimp and homemade containers of tuna salad and crab dips. When the other people in the store, a nicely dressed fiftyish couple, made their purchase and left, we made our way to the register.

"Finding everything you need?" the woman asked.

"Browsing," I said. "I bought grouper fillets here before and they were delicious."

"Thanks," she said.

Brad produced a badge and a photo of Theresa. She'd been dead when it was taken, but the shot was tight on her face, and from the angle of the camera, you couldn't tell that her eyes were vacant. Any blood splatters were concealed by the black-and-white print. "This woman is missing, and we're hoping you can help. A lot of people are worried about her. Do you recognize her?"

The woman studied the photo. "Sure, this is Theresa. Nice lady. She buys seafood here."

"You know her last name?"

The woman shook her head no. "Just Theresa. She always pays in cash. I think her and her boyfriend bought a vacation house around here. Or maybe they're renting. Anyway, she's been coming in for several months. What happened to her?"

"We're not sure." Brad showed his boy-next-door smile. "It may be nothing at all. In any event, we're looking for Theresa and her boyfriend. Did they ever come in together?"

The woman scrunched up her mouth to think. "Don't recall ever seeing her in here with anybody else. Though she always talked like she was married or something. You know, '*We're* going to grill and hang out around the house tonight.' That sort of thing."

The front of the market consisted of glass windows, only partially obstructed by sales posters and signage. Whoever worked the cash register could clearly see the coquina-shell parking lot. "Do you know what Theresa drives?" I asked.

"She used to come in an old van. Last few months, though, she's been in a little white sports car. Convertible."

"You know the make?" Brad said.

The woman shrugged. "A two-seater, I think. Maybe brown seats? Looked brand new."

A couple of teenagers in shorts and bathing suit tops drifted in and handed the woman a piece of notepaper. "Our mom wants to know if you have this kind of fish in. She wants the whole fish, if you do."

"But without the head," the other girl said, and giggled. "That would be totally gross."

Brad and I waited while the woman prepared and wrapped a

fish. The girls pulled cans of Red Bull from a drink cooler. One of them found a small display of snack foods and added a bag of Fritos to their purchase. Giggling about the fish-head thing, they paid for their purchases and pedaled off on bicycles.

We found out that the woman owned the market, and we quizzed her further. She didn't reveal much—not even gossipy tidbits about the residents that most small towns breed. On the flip side, she didn't appear to be hiding anything. We thanked her and bought a couple of bottled waters on the way out.

It was a bright, clear day, and the sun's rays burned hot despite the mild eighty-degree temperature. "A white sporty convertible describes a quarter of the cars around here," Brad said when we were back on the street.

"I'll bet it's one that takes premium fuel," I said.

Brad drummed his fingers on the steering wheel. "If we set up roadblocks along the main feeder roads, it will scare Denny off and we may never find him. Not to mention that there are too many ways in and out of here by water. And multiple stakeouts won't work. We don't know exactly what to stake out."

"You don't want to let Denny know we're on to his home location," I said.

"Exactly. We know he'll be on the move soon, if he's not gone already." Brad's fingers tapped the wheel. "My guess is that he's still here, wrapping things up. I don't want to spook him before we have a chance to snag him."

We drove the streets surrounding the market but didn't spot Denny, a sporty white car, or anything resembling a clue. We were deciding what to do next when my cell rang. A frantic Leo breathed fast on the other end.

"We just got a text message from John." His words rushed together. "Me and Mike. Well, not really a message. A batch of photos."

"Of what?"

"The beach. Some houses. A shrimp boat. A car."

"What kind of car?"

"A white Mazda convertible," Leo said. "We don't recognize any of it. They're random photos, but John wouldn't have sent them if they didn't mean something."

"Forward them to my phone right now, okay? I'll get back to you."

We found a spot of shade and pulled off the road to wait for the digital pictures. About two minutes later, my phone beeped. Heads together, Brad and I studied the small screen while we tabbed through the photos.

"It looks like they might have been taken around here," Brad said.

I agreed but played devil's advocate. "Or they could have been taken at most any small beach town on the lower North Carolina coast."

"We can keep driving until we recognize something."

I shook my head. "We don't have time. We need an exact location."

"It could take a day or more for my people to identify an exact location from the fuzzy cell phone photos," Brad said.

"Remember Soup?" I asked, dialing the number. "It won't take him that long."

After going through the favor-for-no-pay thing with Soup, I forwarded the photos to him. Brad pointed the Murano toward Soup's place. When we arrived, Soup had already downloaded the photo files to a computer and enhanced the images.

"I've got an exact make on the car for you. Mazda MX-5 Miata. A 2008, I think. Can't see the tag number, but"—he pressed keys, and an image appeared on one of his flat-screen monitors—"check this out. There's an air freshener hanging from the rearview mirror. It's the shape of a pine tree. How tacky is that?"

"Got anything else yet?" Brad said, leaning over to look at Soup's computer screen.

"Nope, and quit breathing down my neck. I've used a 3-D program to transform the rows of houses into an aerial view. Then I'll compare them to everything along the coast from Wilmington to Little River, South Carolina, using a satellite imaging program and a GPS coordinates grid. Once that's done, I'll try to identify the single house. He took three pictures of the same house."

I recited the street address of Akel's Seafood Market. "We think they were taken near there. Probably within ten or fifteen miles. Maybe closer."

Soup let out an exasperated sigh. "Well, why didn't you say so to begin with?" His fingers tapped out keyboard music. "That narrows the search area and saves a lot of time."

"What about the boat?" Brad rested his hands on the back of Soup's chair.

Bad idea.

Soup whipped around. "Back off, would you? I hate people looking over my shoulder."

Brad moved to a sofa and obediently sat. "What about the boat?" he repeated.

"From the angle of the picture, I don't have a good baseline of the marina layout. I might be able to enhance the boat's hull. Shrimp boats have to be registered. If I can get a number or the name of the boat—even a partial—I can find out who owns her and where she's moored when she's not at sea." Soup spun back around, and his fingers automatically found their place at a keyboard. "On the other hand, if we identify the area around your seafood market by the houses, we may not need to worry about an ID on the boat."

Brad paced. "How long before—"

"Get out of here," Soup cut him off. "The two of you are distracting me. I'll call you when I have something solid."

Brad started to try to pin him down on a time frame, but I held up a hand. Soup worked much faster when people left him alone. We let ourselves out, and I drove while Brad made important-sounding phone calls from the passenger seat. Not knowing where else to go, I figured the Block would be as good a place to wait as any. I'd just have to make sure that Brad didn't go wandering through the kitchen. Or that Garland didn't come wandering through the dining area.

THIRTY-SEVEN

After leaving Soup's place, we drove straight to the Block to wait for some news on the whereabouts of the unidentified house in the photograph. Knowing Soup, I figured it wouldn't be too long a wait. Which was what I told Brad when he asked to used my bathroom. My personal residence guest bath. The same guest bath that connected to the guest bedroom that Garland happened to be occupying. Since Brad wouldn't think it to be mere southern hospitality if he learned that I'd opened my doors to a DEA fugitive, I knew it would be in my best interest to keep hiding the man. I suggested that Brad use the downstairs public restroom, the one for the Block's customers.

"But I could really use a hot shower," he argued.

"Seriously?"

He nodded. "Helps me think. And calm down when I'm stressed. Believe it or not, I'm stressing. More than a year of investigation is now riding on finding Ray Castello, which is riding on Soup's ability to identify a generic beach house photo."

"Uh, it's broken," I said.

"Your shower is broken?"

"My guest shower is broken. Feel free to go jump in the river. That's what Cracker does when he needs to cool off."

Brad eyed the stairs that led to my residence. "Whatever."

"You want some food?" I said, to change the subject. It always worked with the dog.

"I guess. Sure. I'll be on the patio."

I put in an order for a couple of Swiss-cheese burgers and headed upstairs to check on Spud and Garland. My cell phone rang, and caller ID told me it was Dirk.

"Think we've found your doctor friend," he said. "Body just washed up in the surf below Topsail Beach. Wallet intact, which is why they notified us, because it has a Wilmington address. North Carolina driver's license identifies him as Jonathan Rosch."

"Positive ID yet?"

"No, but the photo and description appear to be a match. Looks like he got beat up and dumped somewhere offshore."

"Crap." Jonathan had gone after Denny on his own. And somebody—most likely Ray Donnell Castello—had killed him. The only good news about the tragedy was that Jonathan had found Denny. It reinforced our theory about the photos sent from his cell phone. "Where do you think the body was dumped?"

"No way to be sure, but probably somewhere below where he came ashore. With the Gulf Stream currents and the layout of the coastline, I'd guess he got tossed from a boat offshore," Dirk said. "South of Wilmington."

Which fit perfectly into our target search zone. "Thanks for the call, Dirk."

"No problem," he said. "You really should think about going back to work. Your retirement is wearing me out."

I asked Ruby to serve the cheeseburgers to the patio if the order came up before I got back, climbed the stairs, and beeped my way in. A tall black woman with big hair and a floppy hat stood in my kitchen. Huge lips pursed in concentration, Fran was tying an apron around the woman. Spud busied himself reviewing a printed list.

"The rules say all the cooking has to be done at the cook-off. You can bring stuff already peeled and cut up, but nothing that's already cooked. That's a dumb rule, for crying out loud," my father said. "It would be a lot easier to make a big pot of the fish stew here and carry it over to the site."

"That's okay, sweetie." Fran shoved a pair of sunglasses on the woman. "I've already got the cooler packed. And Bobby's on his way with the van. And Hal and Trip, too. So, you've got a team of five cooks, the maximum allowed. And I'll be there to cheer you on."

"Where is this cook-off? Where is Garland? And who are you?" I asked the woman.

When she laughed, a man's voice came out.

I took a closer look. "Garland? What have they done to you?" His boobs were lumpy beneath a baggy granny dress, and his feet were stuffed into white socks and a pair of Keds. Makeup coated his face. Lots of makeup that didn't quite mesh with his skin tone.

"We had to disguise him." Spud's mustache went from side to side. "We need him to win the cook-off."

I snatched the sheet of paper from Spud. It was a set of rules for the annual Downtown Chowder & Stew Cook-Off at Riverfront Park. The contest was open to all area restaurants. Chefs could make any type of soup, chowder, or stew that utilized locally caught seafood. The shindig began in five minutes.

"You registered under the Block?"

Fran squeezed and pushed on Garland's boobs, trying to shape them. "Of course, sweetie. With Garland cooking we can't lose! The grand prize is five hundred dollars. Plus, it will be fantastic PR for your pub."

"Then you'd better go," I said, too preoccupied to scold them. "You're about to be late."

Spud pointed outside with his walking cane. "Soon as Bobby shows up with the van, we're out of here."

"What are you making?" I asked the drag queen.

"Bouillabaisse."

"The Block doesn't serve bouillabaisse," I said.

Garland smiled through cherry red, glossy lips. "We did the other night."

Somebody banged on the kitchen door. The small security monitor displayed Spud's poker buddies. They wore aprons and tall white paper chef's hats.

"Good grief," I said, and went out at the same time I let them in.

Downstairs, my cheeseburger order came up. I grabbed a bottle of ketchup and carried two plates to the Block's patio. Brad talked on the phone, his free hand waving in the air. Cracker stretched out at his feet, tail wagging at the sight of food. I dropped the plates and went back for two Cokes. Brad was off the phone when I came back, looking miserable. And stressed. Maybe he really did need a shower.

"Jonathan is dead." I fed Cracker a French fry. "His body washed up on the shore, north of Wilmington."

"Son of a bitch. He did go after Denny." Brad put down his cheeseburger without taking a bite. "How do you find out about this stuff before I do? You're a private citizen! And you're retired at that!"

Over Brad's shoulder, I saw the four stooges and their drag queen load up Bobby's van with coolers and equipment. I bit into my burger. Perfectly cooked, a hint of pink in the center. "My guest shower is fixed," I said.

"What?"

"You said that when you're stressed, a shower calms you down." I ate another bite. "My shower is fixed." Now that Garland was out of my place. "Feel free."

"I don't want a damn shower anymore. I'm hungry. And I want to find Denny. Have you heard from Soup?"

"Not yet," I said. "But while we're waiting, there's a cook-off going on. It's right down the road. We can walk. Might do you good to get your mind off things for a bit."

Brad's phone rang. He answered and listened, a grimace tightening his face. "I know they just found Rosch's body, dammit." He flipped the phone shut.

"Come on," I said. "Eat your burger. We'll take a walk. Soup will probably have that address for us before the night is out. You've got your team on standby, right?"

Brad nodded.

"So tell them to gear up and be ready to roll out. Meanwhile, let's finish eating and go check out the cook-off. The Block is one of the competitors."

He picked up his cheeseburger and took a quarter of it in two bites, as though eating for sustenance instead of pleasure. "Were you always this calm on *your* assignments?" he asked. "Even when a bust was about to go down?"

"It's one of the things my handler loved about me," I said. "I'll get excited over a great lingerie sale. But I have a tendency to go in the opposite direction when lives are on the line."

"Until you see a dead person."

I nodded. "Until then."

"Well, let's hope we don't encounter any dead people tonight."

" 'Long as Spud's not cooking, we should be fine at the Chowder and Stew Cook-Off," I said.

As we approached Riverfront Park, a cluster of aromas melded into one tantalizing breeze and my appetite revved up, even though I had a full belly. The cook-off drew a sizable crowd of spectators and about fifteen competing restaurants. Each eatery had a poster announcing the restaurant's name and the menu item being prepared. Whoever printed the posters had taken Spud's application at face value. The Block's poster read: "Spud's Booey-Base" and, below that, "(Fish Stew)."

Soon after Brad and I arrived, judges with clipboards were strolling from table to table, tasting samples and making notes. Resembling a cross-dressing prostitute with bad fashion taste and too much makeup, Garland stood back and let my father do all the talking to the judges.

"Who's she?" Brad asked, eyeing Garland.

"One of the regulars at the Block. She, uh, fills in as cook for us on occasion. Great lady."

After the judges got their tasting samples, the crowd stood in lines for samples of everyone's stew and chowder. All they had to do was show a wristband, which the organizers sold for five dollars apiece. As soon as the Channel 6 news team showed, television camera rolling, one of the organizers stood on a small stage to announce the winners. Third place went to a blue crab chowder. Second place went to an oyster stew. And first place went to . . . the Block for Spud's Booey-Base Fish Stew.

The assembled crowd and television camera crew followed as the head judge and her cohorts made their way to the Block's table, toting a blue ribbon and a giant cardboard check. In his element, my father preened, chef's hat standing straight up, a clean apron tied around his waist, and the verbal bullshit flowing.

Brad and I stood to the side of the flock, close enough to hear what Spud said to the television reporter.

"Our fish stew at the Block"—he rattled off the street address and aimed a blinding, lasered-white smile at the camera—"is an old, cherished family recipe. We use different types of fresh fish, of course, but our secret ammunition is the spices we use."

Adjusting his stuffed bra, Garland whispered something to Fran, who relayed the message to Spud. "And we always praise our fish before it goes into the pot."

Fran whispered something into Spud's other ear.

"*Braise,*" he clarified into the camera lens. "We braise the fish fillets on a grill before they go into the pot."

One of the judges beside Spud started jumping up and down, making wild gestures with his hands. The videographer kept the camera trained on Spud.

"Oh, I'm excited, too," Spud said, his walking cane up, pointed at the animated judge. "It's a big day for all of us at the Block."

Fran whispered into Spud's ear again.

"He's choking?" Spud said. "Oh, for crying out loud."

Before anyone else—including Brad and me—could get to the choking man, Spud turned, tripped on a tree root, and lurched forward. The rubberized foot of his cane hit the judge square in the solar plexus. A piece of hard candy shot out of the man's mouth, straight at the camera. The man coughed a few times and, with watery eyes, proceeded to thank my father for saving his life.

We didn't stick around to watch the rest because Soup called. He'd isolated the single home in the photo. He had a street address and a GPS location.

"You're a civilian," Brad reminded me as we jogged the short distance back to the Block. "You need to stay out of this."

I eyed him sideways. "Give me a break. I'm going."

"Fine," he said. "Then vest up."

His gear was in the Murano, and a few short minutes after we arrived back at my pub, I'd changed into what Ox always dubbed my combat duds: black hiking boots, stretch jeans with a bunch of pockets, including one that held my backup piece, and a custom-designed bullet-resistant vest that molded nicely around my size D's. I covered the vest with a plain T-shirt. A lightweight jacket concealed the Ruger attached to my waistband, slightly behind the hipbone. Beneath it all, I wore a black satiny Victoria's Secret sports bra and hipster panties with a wide lace trim. It's just something I do.

THIRTY-EIGHT

Brad punched the street address into his GPS and we pulled out at the same time he deployed his team. On the way, he made phone calls to notify the local cops of a possible apprehension in their jurisdiction.

We took his SUV, with him at the wheel, looking like his old calm and capable self.

"Did you manage to squeeze in a shower?" I teased. "You're calm again."

"Impending action always calms me," he said. "It's the waiting that makes me nuts."

"That's good to hear."

We passed Akel's Seafood Market. The small store was dark except for security lighting. The sun had disappeared into the horizon, and the autumn evening was coated with a postdusk bluish tint. Brad's navigation system said we were a mere four minutes from our destination, and we looked at each other across the console, realizing how nearby we'd been earlier in the day.

When we were within two blocks of the target home, Brad killed the lights and pulled into a vacant rental home drive. Fingers tapping the steering wheel, he spoke into a small radio, confirming that his team was in place. Fourteen minutes later, they were. We drove to the house, headlights off, and surveyed the property. Television flickering in the front room. White Miata parked in the drive beside the single-story home, pine tree cutout air freshener hanging from the rearview. Blinds closed in all the windows. We compared an enlarged photo sent by Jonathan with the actual home. The roofline, window placement, and a dead palm in the front yard confirmed that it was the same place. An agent with an infrared detection device came over the radio to inform Brad that, best they could determine, one individual was inside. No animals. No heat-generating appliances, such as an oven, in operation.

Once satisfied with the intel, Brad reconfirmed that his people were where they were supposed to be and gave a command. He and I headed in on foot, behind two hunky men in full antiballistic gear who were equipped with a door-busting ram.

The front door splintered into pieces with a cacophony of noise as it broke from its wooden frame.

"What the fu—" Denny rolled upright from a sofa to the right of the entrance, a revolver in hand.

"Freeze!" somebody yelled at the same time Denny took aim. "Get on the floor!"

Denny fired at the hole where his front door used to be. The men with the ram charged forward, the lead man shooting. Brad and I dove and rolled to opposite sides of the sandy front lawn. Explosive pops of expended rounds were rapid and brief and ended almost immediately.

"Clear!" a voice yelled. "Suspect down!"

"Clear in back!" yelled a different voice.

Ears ringing, gun drawn, I followed Brad into the beach cottage. Denny lay sprawled on the floor, bleeding, handcuffed, moaning. A paramedic in Kevlar hustled to Ray Donnell Castello, hauling a trauma kit, and went to work. Brad made a phone call to somebody—presumably his boss—and I heard another agent call to request an ambulance.

Everyone kept their weapons drawn while the rest of the house and grounds were searched, but as the infrared indicated, Denny had been the sole occupant. I hoped he would live long enough to make it into the ambulance. I didn't want to have a dead-body meltdown in front of Brad.

"Thank you, Jersey Barnes." He hugged me to his body, long and hard. It felt good. But not exactly right.

I nodded. *You're welcome.*

Brad went to work, barking orders as a collection of emergency lights lit up the asphalt street in a coda of red, white, and blue. Holstering the Ruger, I inhaled the scent of sea air and walked the two blocks to the ocean. I knew it would be at least an hour or more before Brad would be ready to leave the scene. And I wanted to make a few calls. The wind swirled in forceful gusts, and moonbeams illuminated a choppy ocean. I sat on a thick piece of driftwood near the dunes, stripped off my boots and socks, and burrowed my toes deep in the sand.

I called Spud first, to congratulate him on winning the cook-off. Grumbling, he explained that our team got disqualified because none of the chefs were actually employees of the Block. I reminded him that it was a loss of only five hundred dollars—which he would have had to share anyway—and congratulated him on saving the life of a choking victim. My next call went to the judge, to let her know that Morgan was safe; it was over. I thought about revealing that her father was alive but decided the news should be delivered in person, by him. I explained that her brother could use her help, and without hesitation, she agreed to travel to Wilmington the next day. And my last call was to Ox, to see when he was coming home.

THIRTY-NINE

There were the murder charges, of course, but Denny had also been slapped with possession, intent to distribute, and a bunch of other scary-sounding things—once he woke up in the hospital, coherent enough to be read his rights. Castello's future would be incarceration until he died. That much was certain. North Carolinians don't like to sentence their criminals to death, but about five or six are executed each year, and Denny could very well end up on that list. Regardless, he'd be off the streets and no longer able to mess with Argo's or my judge friend's family.

Brad's team had hit the mother lode in Denny's beach cottage: a handwritten grid with network distribution details, a box of prepaid cell phones, more than one hundred thousand dollars in cash, a stack of shoeboxes full of prescription drugs, names of physicians and pharmacists, and guns, including Jonathan's trap gun. The greedy idiot had swiped the shotgun from Jonathan's Corvette after he killed him and dumped the body offshore. Basically, Brad had everything he needed to tie up his investigation and come out looking good. There was already talk of the DEA changing Brad's status to educator, where he'd travel the country to train other agents on the ins and outs of prescription drug rings.

"It is so good to see you, Jersey." The judge gave me a body-crushing hug, and when she stepped back, she looked as great as she always did. Beautiful smooth skin, killer clothes, and a commanding presence that made people want to please her. "Thanks for everything you've done," she said. "Although I don't know all the details yet. You'll have to fill me in."

"Plenty of time for that later," I told her. "For now, let's forget business and give you and your brother a chance to catch up."

The Block had just opened, and a few people filtered in for lunch. But my crowd took up a whole section, right next to open garage doors, where we could see the river and wispy, low-slung clouds and all the people walking by. The celebration was in full swing, and everyone from the Barnes Agency made it a point to be there. Trish, the local P.I. who'd tailed Morgan for me, had come with her new boyfriend. Spud, his buddies, Fran, and a clump of their New Age Babes friends. Dirk and several others from the Wilmington PD. Brad and a slew of drug enforcement agents. Soup and a gang of his hacker buddies. Friends, such as financier Sam Chesterfield and his son, Jared. And, looking splendid in a sundress and heels, Deanna strutted in on Morgan's arm.

"Morgan brought a date!" I told Cracker, rubbing noses with the dog. His tail wagged like as though he understood.

I was throwing an impromptu party with a double purpose: a thank-you to everyone who'd helped shut down the network and a retirement party for me. Of course, it was probably the third or fourth retirement party I've had. But I always enjoy them.

A local reggae-and-steel-drum band played at one end of the bar, and their island music enhanced the festive atmosphere. The

Block buzzed with upbeat energy. I felt good. It was a beautiful day to be alive, enjoying the company of my friends and family. And it was going to get even better. I found Morgan and the judge sitting outside at a patio table talking, bittersweet smiles on their faces.

"Now that I've got the two of you together," I said, "I have a big surprise. Somebody you need to meet. I'll be right back."

Garland waited upstairs at my kitchen table, pretending to read the newspaper.

"You ready?"

He nodded and stood, hugged me tight for a beat. "I don't know how to thank you for—"

I put a finger to his lips. "Garland, seeing you with your son and daughter is going to be all the thanks I'll ever need. The judge is like a sister to me. And I've come to know Morgan as a good, strong, successful man. They both love you—and miss you—like crazy. Enough said."

Garland stood up, sucked in a deep breath. "I look okay?"

"You look fabulous, Chef Garland."

I've never heard the judge squeal with delight, but that's exactly what she did when I escorted Garland downstairs, through the Block, and to the outdoor patio. She squealed, and after a beat of stunned silence, she flew into her father's arms. Morgan looked from me to the two of them and back to me.

"Is it really . . ."

I smiled. "It's really him, Morgan. Garland is alive."

"Dad." Morgan joined the group hug, and the trio laughed and cried and looked one another over and hugged some more. I left before the judge had a chance to recover. Otherwise, she'd be on me

like green on a grasshopper, demanding to know why I hadn't told
her about Garland sooner.

When I went back inside, Brad leaned against a garage door
frame, his forearms and ankles crossed. Despite the closed body language, his face held a smile.

I stopped in front of him. "Hi."

"How long has he lived here?"

I played dumb. "Who?"

Brad uncrossed everything and pulled me into a hug. It seemed
to be a day for hugs. "He was the woman at the cook-off, right? The
one that looked like a senior drag queen with lopsided breasts?"

I nodded.

Brad burst out laughing. "When he finishes up with his kids,
I'll have to say hello. And let him know that the DEA is officially
out of his life."

"They would all appreciate that," I said.

I sensed Ox before I actually saw him and let out a squeal similar to the judge's. "Ox! I thought you weren't back for a few more
days."

His arms wrapped around me. "We were going to stay in Connecticut for a few days after Lindsey's internship ended, but we decided that it's time to get her back in school and get me back to work."

I made the introductions. Brad, Ox—co-owner of the Block.
Ox, Brad—the DEA agent I told you about. The men shook hands
and sized each other up.

"I'm off to see Garland," Brad said. "Before I go, I want to let you
know that you won't be hit with any charges . . . aiding a fugitive,
impersonating an officer, illegal wiretap . . . those sorts of things."

"Yeah?" I copped a stance. "I want to let you know that I won't be
updating your director on all the little details . . . using a civilian
as an undercover, illegal breaking and entering, losing a protected
witness . . . those sorts of things."

Laughing, Brad kissed me on the cheek before taking another look at Ox. "If he's your complication, Jersey Barnes, I believe you're in very good hands." He shook Ox's hand again. "Later, man."

Before Ox had a chance to quiz me about Brad, his daughter came running and we went into a spinning hug. "Hiya, Jerz! The ESPN thing was fantastic. I can't wait to tell you all about it!"

Lindsey was bubbly and bright and captivating as always. She seemed to have grown an inch in the short time since I'd seen her last and looked way older than a senior at New Hanover High. "Welcome home, girl."

"Thanks." She passed me an envelope. "FedEx just delivered this and I signed for it. I mean, like, I do still have a part-time job here, right?"

"Of course you do, as long—"

"As you keep your grades up," Ox finished.

The envelope was addressed to my father. I recognized the sender—a gourmet food distributor. Fully prepared and flash frozen meals, shipped by mail order.

I found Spud doing Jell-O shooters with Fran and some of the NABs. I wasn't aware that anybody at the Block even knew how to make a Jell-O shooter.

"Spud, why are you ordering gourmet food when you live above a restaurant?" I handed him the envelope.

He ripped into the FedEx mailer and smiled, displaying his blazing white teeth. "It's not a receipt, for crying out loud. It's my check!"

I looked at the numbers on the check and my mouth fell open. *Fifteen thousand dollars.* "What's this for?"

"Remember how I saved that man's life at the cook-off?" Spud talked with his cane.

"As I recall, you stumbled and your cane accidentally hit the man."

Spud shook his cane at me. "That's neither here nor there. The point is that I saved his life and they interviewed me on Channel Six."

Fran walked up, fluffing her hair. "Then the AP wire picked up the story, sweetie! How your daddy won this cook-off with his amazing recipe *and* saved a judge's life. And then got his prize money taken away because his daughter had never put him on the Block's payroll, and he's not an employee."

"What?" I eyed my father. "You told a reporter it's *my fault* the Block got disqualified from the cook-off?"

Fran patted my arm. "Oh, you know your daddy. He didn't say it exactly like that. Anyway, Spud's story went all over the place. Even got a mention on Jay Leno. So these gourmet food people, they called Spud and bought his recipe."

"Fifteen thousand smackaroos!" Spud held up his check and kissed it. "They bought the rights to use the recipe and my name. Might even put my picture on the label, but I told 'em that will cost extra."

"They're changing the name a teeny bit," Fran said. "It will be called Spud's Buoy Base. You know, like a buoy that floats in the ocean? And they'll put 'fish stew' below that in parentheses."

"He's done it again," I told Ox. "How does he manage it? I've been working my ass off for free, as a *favor,* and my father somehow ends up with fifteen grand because he accidentally poked somebody in the stomach with his cane?"

"Hey, kid, if it'll make you feel any better, I'll give you the rights to serve Spud's Buoy Base here at the Block."

"We already *are* serving the bouillabaisse, Spud. Garland gave me his recipe!"

"Yeah, but now you can call it Spud's Buoy Base."

Ox took my hand and pulled me into the core of the party. "Let's go get a beer and you can catch me up on everything I've missed."

"I helped bust up a drug ring, I'm officially retired again, and my father continues to completely flabbergast me." I looked up at Ox's familiar face and focused on the wide jaw and square chin, realizing how much I'd missed him. "That's pretty much it. You're caught up."

"In that case"—Ox grinned enough to make his dimple deepen—"let's go upstairs and catch up on *other* things."

EPILOGUE

It's been a wild ride," Leo said to his partner. "I'm happy to have been on the coaster."

"It has been a wild ride," Michael agreed. "But I'm happy to be *off* that coaster."

The two physicians watched reflections of a blue jay as the bird flew across a shallow lake. The sprawling cemetery was lush and secluded, with plenty of aged hardwoods and shade. Jonathan had loved the outdoors. He would have liked it here, they knew.

"Roller coaster or not, at least we're getting to keep our medical licenses," Leo said. "I really don't mind selling Divine Image Group. Might be good to get a group of youngsters in there. Somebody who wants to do medical dermatology. Skin cancers and such. We're getting more and more retirees in this area. Lots of sun-damaged skin."

"That would work well." Michael picked up a pecan that had dropped from a nearby tree and rolled it in his fingers, studying his hands. "We designed our building with enough space to accommodate five doctors. Maybe they'll do a combination of medical and cosmetic."

"Speaking of cosmetic, what's your first case?" Leo asked.

Michael tossed the pecan toward the lake, thinking of all the surgeries his hands had performed in the past, realizing that he really would make a difference in people's lives now. "I've got a six-year-old girl, car accident, no seat restraint. They stitched her up and saved her life, but the scarring on one side of her face is hideous. Drooping eyelid. Deformed bottom lip. Both parents work, but they don't have health insurance. And they make just enough money so that they don't qualify for Medicaid or other assistance."

"I suppose that describes all of our new patients," Leo said. "People in need who are falling through the cracks."

Michael nodded. "When I finish with this little girl, she's going to be beautiful. She'll look just like every other kid at her school, and there will be nothing to tease her about. In fact, she gets to dating age, her father had better watch out."

Leo chuckled. "Guess we won't be doing any more lipo procedures. My next surgery is a breast reconstruction. Double mastectomy patient."

"Ah, I never liked doing lipo anyway," Michael said. "Wears you out. And the patient always thinks that you can make them look like Angelina Jolie."

The doctors had struck a bargain with prosecutors, and both sides were happy. They had agreed to sell their medical practice, but they could keep the proceeds. More important, they could keep their medical accreditations as long as they followed the rules. For the next three years—a probationary period of sorts—they would be volunteer physicians for a nationwide organization that provided free services to low-income and uninsured families. They'd have to travel to various participating hospitals and outpatient clinics, but

there were enough people falling through the health insurance system cracks in the Carolinas and Virginia to keep the men close to
home.

Leo squatted to prop a Duke University student ID card against
the engraved headstone.

"We love you, John," Michael said.

Leo stood, put an arm around his partner's shoulder. "Let's go
make him proud."

READER'S GROUP GUIDE QUESTIONS

About the Book

Jersey Barnes keeps trying to leave home without a weapon strapped to her body. She'd love to get an eye-stopping tan and maybe take up golf or tennis. She wants to retire. Well, sort of. When her judge friend asks Jersey for a favor, the unconventional security specialist readily agrees. The judge's brother, an introvert from Dallas, Texas, has moved to Jersey's stomping ground because he inherited a restaurant. But Argos isn't just *any* eatery— it's the hippest place in town where Wilmington's elite dine. It's also the site of a mysterious and dangerous secret that could land the judge's brother in jail . . . or worse, a cemetery.

Reading Group Guide Questions

1. *Southern Peril* is the third Jersey Barnes mystery, and in this book the author has delved deeper into Jersey's upbringing as well as her conflicted thoughts about being raised without a father. Do you think that knowing more about Jersey's past adds depth to the current story?

2. Do you like the nontraditional relationship between Jersey and her father, Spud? Note that Spud is a retired cop and Jersey was a government field agent. Do you think that their past careers make the interaction between father and daughter believable?

3. In *Southern Peril*, Jersey has begun to realize that there is much more to Spud than a grumbling, troublemaking, poker-playing old man. At what point in the book did Spud begin to help Jersey solve the Argos dilemma? What actions did he take and what conclusions did he reach?

4. All of the Jersey Barnes mysteries combine action, drama, and humor. Were there any scenes in *Southern Peril* that you found particularly funny? In your opinion, does the author effectively mix suspense and humor?

5. At what point did you realize that Morgan, the judge's brother, was hooked on eavesdropping?

6. What are some of the topics of discussion that you've shared with a friend or lover over a dinner table at a restaurant? When dining out at a nice restaurant, do you normally feel as though you have a sense of privacy?

7. Have you ever (intentionally or unintentionally) overheard somebody's conversation in a restaurant or other public place? If it was interesting, did you keep listening?

8. Do you think that black market prescription drugs are as much of a danger to society as other illegal drugs such as cocaine or marijuana? Why or why not?

9. At any point in *Southern Peril*, did you suspect that Jersey and the DEA agent, Brad, might get romantically involved?

10. Do you have any predictions as to Jersey's future with Ox, her business partner and best friend?

Fun Facts About the Book
Did you know . . .

Wilmington, North Carolina, is more than 250 years old, sits between the Cape Fear River and the Atlantic Ocean, and is home to a large container shipping facility?

The University of North Carolina at Wilmington has a Center for Marine Science that ranks among the top in the country.

Wilmington is home to EUE Screen Gems Studios, a full-service motion picture facility.

While the author uses many actual locations, landmarks, and restaurants in the historic port town of Wilmington, Argos is a fictitious eatery. Bradley Creek and its lovely views, however, are real.